The Doctor and the Dinosaurs

Also Available by Mike Resnick

Ivory: A Legend of Past and Future

New Dreams for Old

Stalking the Dragon
Stalking the Unicorn
Stalking the Vampire

Starship: Mutiny
Book One

Starship: Pirate
Book Two

Starship: Mercenary
Book Three

Starship: Rebel
Book Four

Starship: Flagship
Book Five

The Buntline Special—A Weird West Tale
The Doctor and the Kid—A Weird West Tale
The Doctor and the Rough Rider—A Weird West Tale

MIKE RESNICK

THE DOCTOR AND THE DINOSAURS

A WEIRD WEST TALE

an Imprint of Prometheus Books
Amherst, NY

Published 2013 by Pyr®, an imprint of Prometheus Books

Cover illustration and interior illustrations © Andrew Bosley
Images of the Buntline Special pistol © J. Seamas Gallagher
Cover design by Nicole Sommer-Lecht

Inquiries should be addressed to

Pyr
59 John Glenn Drive
Amherst, New York 14228–2119
VOICE: 716–691–0133
FAX: 716–691–0137
WWW.PYRSF.COM

17 16 15 14 13   5 4 3 2 1

Library of Congress Cataloging-in-Publication Data

Resnick, Michael D.
    The doctor and the dinosaurs / Mike Resnick.
        pages cm. — (Weird West tale)
    ISBN 978-1-61614-861-4 (pbk.)
    ISBN 978-1-61614-862-1 (ebook)
    1. Holliday, John Henry, 1851–1887—Fiction. 2. West (U.S.)—Fiction.
3. Alternative histories (Fiction), American. 4. Steampunk fiction, American. 5. Adventure stories, American I. Title.
PS3568.E698D623 2013
813'.54—dc23

2013028117

Printed in the United States of America

To Carol, as always,

And to Doodle, Aqua, and Baldy,
Fine writers, finer friends.

PROLOGUE

From the pages of the September 17, 1885, issue of the Leadville Bullet:

Kate Elder has put up for auction all the dental instruments of John H. "Doc" Holliday, as well as one of his pistols. The famed shootist remains in the Leadville Sanitarium, a victim of consumption, and is not expected to last out the week.

From the pages of the September 17, 1885, issue of the Jackson, Wyoming, Chronicle:

Edward Drinker Cope's expedition has announced the discovery of two previously unknown species of animal near his headquarters in the Grand Teton area, south and west of the Yellowstone.

A scientific expedition headed by Othniel C. Marsh and sponsored by his uncle, George Peabody of the Peabody Museum, is due to arrive at their campsite some sixty miles east of the Cope camp within the next twenty-four hours.

From the pages of the September 19, 1885, issue of the Cheyenne Bugle*:*

Heavyweight champion John L. Sullivan has arrived from the East for his much-touted title defense against William Smiley. This may well be the last bare-knuckle championship fight, as gloves are becoming increasingly popular and indeed the great John L. has worn them in his last three title defenses. A celebrity referee from New York has come out on the same train as the champion.

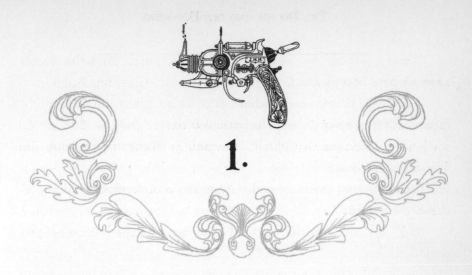

1.

THE EMACIATED MAN LAY ON HIS BED, his mouth open, gasping for air in the plain, austere room. A white-clad nurse mopped the sweat from his forehead with an increasingly damp towel as he stared out the window at the snow-capped mountains a few miles away.

"Is there anything I can get you, Doc?" she asked solicitously.

"Air would be nice," rasped the man, trying vainly to fill his lungs with the thin Colorado air.

"I could have a couple of the attendants move you to the patio downstairs," she offered.

"I've *seen* the patio downstairs," he whispered, wincing in discomfort. "I could use a drink, though."

"You know what the doctor said."

"I'm a doctor, too."

"He's a *real* doctor," said the nurse. "You're just a . . ." She searched for the word.

"Cold-blooded drunken killer?" he suggested wryly. "I'm not, you know. At least, not anymore. I haven't had a drink in a week."

"I was going to say dentist," replied the nurse. "And the doctor knows what's best for you."

"I don't see that knowing what's next for me gives him any insight into what's best for me," said the patient bitterly.

"No whiskey, and that's final!" she said. Then she smiled. "But I do have a treat for you."

"Let me guess," he muttered. "A church choir composed of apple-cheeked children?"

"No," she said, surprised. "But I could send for the minister if you want."

He shook his head and winced again at the effort. "He'll be reading over me soon enough."

"Why are you like this?" she demanded in exasperated tones, trying to clean some blood he'd coughed up off his chest with a damp towel.

"Dying of consumption?" he replied bitterly. "Beats the hell out of me."

"You make it very hard to be pleasant to you."

"I've been told that before," he said with a grim smile.

"Anyway, your treat," she continued, forcing a smile to her face with an obvious effort. "Your closest friend is coming here tomorrow."

The emaciated man frowned. "My closest friend?"

She nodded. "The famous Wyatt Earp!"

"I haven't seen him in three years. He's just coming to gloat."

"But the two of you are dear friends!" she said. "Everyone knows that! I've come out to Leadville all the way from Delaware, and even back there they've all heard about Wyatt Earp and Doc Holliday and the Gunfight at the O.K. Corral."

Another grimace. "They're never going to get that right," he growled hoarsely. "It took place in the alley *behind* the O.K. Corral."

"But it *did* take place, and you're famous for it."

"One bunch of shootists killed another bunch of shootists," replied Holliday. "Nothing to brag about." He tried to shrug, winced in pain, and lay back on his pillow, gasping for air. "More and more often these days I wish we'd lost. At least I wouldn't be gasping for less air than that damned bird puts in its lungs."

"What bird?" asked the nurse.

"That one perched on the windowsill," replied Holliday, pointing weakly.

The nurse turned, saw an owl sitting on the sill, and shooed it away, flapping the moist towel at it.

"Unclean things!" she complained, returning to bedside. "Carrion eaters."

"We all are, when we get hungry enough," said Holliday.

She stared at him. "John Henry Holliday, you are a most unpleasant man."

"I've been called worse," he said with a chuckle, then coughed again.

She walked to the door. "I have other patients to tend to. Call if you need me."

"And you'll hear me through the closed door?" he asked with a smile.

She glared at him, then walked out into the hall, considered leaving the door ajar, then let her anger get the better of her and slammed it shut.

Holliday looked ruefully at the door. "Yeah, John Henry," he said softly, "you're still a charmer." He turned his head, looked over to see that the owl had returned and was once again perching on the window. "I hope you've been enjoying yourself."

The owl stared at him.

"She's got a lot on her mind," he continued. "She didn't realize that you're not supposed to be out at mid-afternoon."

He was about to say something more, but he began coughing, reached for a handkerchief, couldn't find one, and soon coughed another mouthful of blood all over his chest.

"You'd better be who and what I think you are," he said weakly. "My gun's in a drawer of that night table, and I would take very unkindly to a real owl eating off my chest."

The owl stared unblinking at him for a long moment, then hopped lightly to the floor. Holliday simply stared at him, and as he did so, the owl began to change and grow. Its feathers vanished, its wings became arms, and a few seconds later the dying man was confronting Goyathlay, known to whites as Geronimo, the most powerful medicine man among the Apaches.

"You are dying, Holliday," said Geronimo.

"We're all dying from the minute we're born," replied Holliday. "I just do it a little more enthusiastically than most."

"There is every likelihood that you will be dead before your friend Earp arrives tomorrow."

"Just as well," said Holliday. "Saves me the trouble of apologizing for what I said about his wife. That's the reason he hasn't spoken to me for three years."

Geronimo stared at him for a long moment.

"Would you like to live?" he said at last.

"In *this* condition?" asked Holliday, trying to chuckle and coughing up more blood instead. "When did you develop a sense of humor?"

"I have come to offer you a bargain. If you accept it, you will need your health, and I will restore it."

"Who do you want killed?"

"Possibly no one."

Geronimo fell silent and Holliday stared at him. "Well? I'd at least like to hear the offer before I can't breathe anymore."

"Things are happening," said Geronimo. "Serious things." He stared at Holliday. "Things that must stop."

"I'm too sick and too weak to make a comment every time you stop talking, so just spit it out," rasped Holliday.

"We have not seen each other since I signed the treaty with Theodore Roosevelt, the treaty that allows the United States to cross the great river the white eyes call the Mississippi and go to the edge of the world, where the endless sea lies. The other medicine men opposed that treaty, but through your efforts and his, it was enacted. And until now it has been done peacefully."

"Let me guess," said Holliday, realizing he'd promised to be silent but unable to stop himself from offering opinions. "The army fired on your people. Nothing I can do about that."

"No, the army has kept its word," said Geronimo. "This particular problem was unforeseen, even by myself."

Lack a certain modesty, don't you? thought Holliday. Then: *What the hell. You've got every right to think that highly of yourself.*

"There are two men involved in this," continued Geronimo. "You are a learned man. Perhaps you have heard of them." Holliday made no answer, and Geronimo continued. "Cope and Marsh."

Holliday shook his head, then winced at the pain. "No, I never heard those names before."

"They are"—Geronimo searched for the right word but couldn't find it—"scientists."

"Like Tom Edison?" asked Holliday.

"No. They tear up the earth, searching for—"

"Gold?" interrupted Holliday.

"Bones," said Geronimo.

Holliday frowned. "Bones?" he repeated blankly.

"Yes."

"*Human* bones?"

It was Geronimo's turn to shake his head. "No, not human bones. But they are disturbing human bones as they dig for the bones they seek."

"Okay, they're disturbing human bones," said Holliday. "Where are they digging?"

"In the land the white eyes call Wyoming."

"That's out of your bailiwick."

"I do not know that word," said Geronimo.

"There are no Apaches buried in Wyoming, so why do you care?"

Geronimo smiled a humorless smile. "I knew you would understand."

"I don't understand a damned thing," growled Holliday, fighting back another coughing seizure.

"You know that we have burial grounds that are sacred to us. You helped me once before when the railroad was desecrating our burial ground."

"That was an Apache burial ground in Arizona," said Holliday irritably. "What the hell has it got to do with whoever's buried in Wyoming?" He fell back on his pillow, suddenly exhausted.

"The Comanche are buried there," said Geronimo.

Holliday used most of his remaining strength to utter two words: "So what?"

"The two men have many other white eyes working for them. If the Comanche kill them for desecrating their sacred burial grounds, they will have killed so many that the army will have to respond, and then we will be in a war of extermination. The white eyes have more men and more horses and more guns, so eventually it will be the People who are exterminated."

"All because someone is digging in the ground for bones?"

"Yes."

"And you think one skinny man riddled with consumption can make them stop?"

Geronimo stared at him expressionlessly. "If they are not stopped, there will be war."

"Then there'll be a war, with their arrows and stolen guns against the United States army. I wouldn't want to be on your side."

"The Comanche know that they cannot win with the weapons they have."

"Then they'd better let them dig," said Holliday.

"You do not understand after all, Holliday," said Geronimo. "This land is *sacred*. No one but the People may dig in it. If anyone else does so, it is desecration."

"Then the People are going to be on the wrong end of a war," said Holliday.

There was a momentary silence.

"Not necessarily," said Geronimo at last.

Here it comes, thought Holliday, but he remained quiet as he waited for the Apache to explain.

"There was a time before God made the People and other men that monsters walked the Earth, monsters such as you cannot even imagine."

"Spare me the fairy tales and get to the point," growled Holliday, and then suffered a coughing fit that lasted almost a full minute and drenched his hospital gown in blood.

"Many of those monsters lie beneath the sacred burial ground. I know the Comanche medicine men and their allies among the other tribes—they are the same ones who opposed my agreement with the man Roosevelt—and before they let a single warrior die they will bring forth those monsters to kill the white eyes. But," continued Geronimo, "they cannot control the monsters once they resurrect them, and the monsters might just as easily turn on the People. Do you understand what I am saying?"

Holliday didn't trust himself to answer without coughing again, so he settled for nodding his head.

"And once the monsters walk the earth, there is nothing to stop them from coming to the Apaches' homeland. I made the treaty with Roosevelt and against the wishes of the other medicine men because I did not wish to see our young warriors die in a battle against the white eyes. I do not intend to see them die now, fighting both the army and the monsters."

"I can't even walk to the door," said Holliday. "I don't know how you think I can kill these monsters." *If they really exist, which I doubt like all hell*, he added mentally.

"They do not exist *yet*," explained Geronimo. "You will go to the land called Wyoming and stop these two men from tearing up the sacred ground, and perhaps they will never exist again."

"Should be easy enough to scare them off," remarked Holliday. He stared at Geronimo. "Once I get my health back."

Geronimo shook his head. "It will not be easy, or I would not be speaking to you."

"Explain."

"It will become clear to you once you are there." He paused. "And you will find an ally there, if you can convince him to join your cause."

"It's *your* cause," wheezed Holliday. "*My* cause is to walk from here to the door without gasping for breath."

"Have we an agreement?"

Holliday nodded his head. "I'll agree to just about anything that will get me out of this goddamned bed."

"So be it," said Geronimo, and began chanting a prayer or perhaps a spell in his native tongue. When he was finished he turned to Holliday. "It is done."

Holliday lay motionless, afraid to find out that nothing had changed. Finally he sat up and swung his legs over the side of the bed.

"*Son of a bitch!*" he said, getting to his feet. "You actually did it!"

He spun around, grinning, then ran—not walked—to the bathroom door—

—and then grasped the edge of the door with one hand while his emaciated body was wracked by another coughing fit. When he was done he wiped his mouth with his sleeve. It came away soaked with blood.

"You lied!" he snapped.

"I did not," said Geronimo calmly.

"I'm still coughing, and I'm still gasping, and I'm still skinny as a rail!"

"You are breathless because you *ran* to the door," said Geronimo. "When is the last time you ran?"

"What difference does that make?" demanded Holliday. "You promised to restore my health."

"And I did," answered Geronimo, walking to the window and seating himself on the ledge.

"I've still got the consumption!" roared Holliday.

Geronimo smiled. "You see? You can run and you can yell. Could you do *that* this morning, or last week?"

"But I'm still—"

"What makes you Doc Holliday?" interrupted Geronimo.

Holliday stared at him, puzzled. "What the hell are you talking about?"

"I do not want a dentist," said Geronimo. "I want a cold resourceful killer who is not afraid to die because he welcomes the thought of death. And what has made you that?"

"You said you'd restore my health, damn it!"

"And I have," replied Geronimo. "To the day we first met, five years ago."

"I was dying five years ago."

"We are all dying. Do you want an extra year or not?"

Holliday frowned and sighed deeply.

"Get out of here," he said. He turned to close the bathroom door, and when he turned back, the room was empty. He walked to the window just in time to see a huge owl rising out of sight.

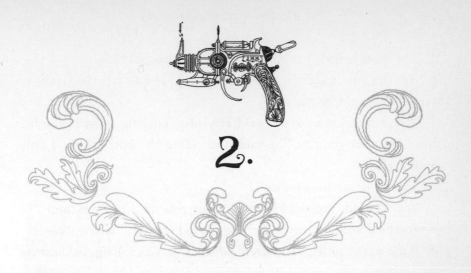

2.

THE TALL MAN WITH THE PROSTHETIC ARM took a last breath of the cool, fresh Colorado air, entered the crowded Monarch Saloon and Casino through its swinging doors, took a step inside, and then paused, looking around, past the long bar, the faro table, the half-dozen poker tables. Finally he saw a thin man dressed like a riverboat gambler, sitting alone at a table with a bottle and a glass in front of him, and walked over to him.

"What the hell are *you* doing here?" demanded Holliday, looking up from his drink.

"I'm glad to see you too," said Thomas Alva Edison, seating himself opposite the thin man.

"I thought you and Ned Buntline went back East once Geronimo lifted the curse and the country was able to expand past the Mississippi."

"We did," confirmed Edison.

"So what's the most famous inventor in the world doing in Leadville, Colorado?" said Holliday.

Edison smiled. "Believe it or not, Ned and I came to say good-bye to the most famous shootist in the world."

"The most famous left alive," Holliday corrected him.

"Anyway, we heard that you were dying, and to tell the truth we thought we might be too late."

"You damned near were," said Holliday, pouring himself another drink. "I'd offer you one," he said, indicating the bottle, "but I only have one glass."

"You could ask for another."

"Yes, I could," agreed Holliday. "But you might accept, and I've been too long without this stuff." He looked around. "Where's Ned?"

"Back at the hotel," answered Edison. "It was a long, exhausting trip, especially the last couple of hundred miles, and he didn't want to spend all night searching for you."

"Didn't seem to bother you," noted Holliday.

"I know your habits," replied Edison with a smile. "And how many places can you drink all night in a town as small as Leadville?"

Holliday chuckled. "Well, thanks for coming," he said. "I'm sorry it was a wasted trip."

"Nonsense. We're glad you're alive. I guess they misdiagnosed you."

"No, they had it right. At noon today any gambler would have given you even money that I wouldn't be around at noon tomorrow."

Suddenly Edison learned forward intently. "You want to tell me about it?"

"Not much to tell. We both know there's only one man with the power to let a dying man live."

"Goyathlay?"

Holliday nodded his head. "Geronimo."

"He had a reason, of course?"

"Of course," said Holliday. "The bastard."

Edison frowned. "I'm not following this. He brought you back from the precipice. Why is he a bastard?"

"He didn't restore my health, not that I ever had any by the time I was old enough to shave."

"But you were dying, and now you're not!" protested Edison.

"Oh, I'm dying, all right," replied Holliday as a gambler at a nearby table let out a triumphant yell. "Just not quite as fast as before." He took another drink. "He's made me the way I was when I met him. I've still got the consumption, but at least I can function."

Edison nodded. "He doesn't want to take that killing edge off you."

Holliday stared at him for a long moment. "You too?" he growled.

"I'm not saying I approve, Doc," answered Edison. "Just that I understand his reasoning. If he gave you perfect health, you'd be less inclined to risk it." There was a brief pause. "What does he need you for?"

"Some foolishness in Wyoming," said Holliday, frowning. "Hell, it doesn't even concern the Apaches." He grimaced. "Well, not unless it gets out of hand."

"What the hell is in Wyoming?" asked Edison, clearly puzzled. "There's no gold, no major rivers to be diverted, not much of anything valuable to be honest."

"There's a graveyard."

"I'm sure there are lots of them," said Edison. "So?"

"Let me re-word that," said Holliday. "There's a sacred burial ground."

"I'm still confused," said Edison. "There's no train tracks going through there yet, the way there were down near Lincoln City in Arizona when we got them to re-route it. In fact, to the best of my knowledge, there are no Apaches."

"You're right," said Holliday. "There's no Apaches, no railroad, no major rivers, and no gold."

"So what *is* there?"

Holliday stared at him for a moment. "Bones."

"I beg your pardon?"

"I knew you wouldn't believe it," said Holliday with an amused smile as a happy shout went up from the faro table and one of the gamblers, clutching a wad of cash, offered to buy drinks for the house, then amended it to drinks for the faro players when he saw how crowded the Monarch was.

"Someone's digging up bones from a Comanche burial ground?" repeated Edison, frowning.

"That's about it."

"But *why?*"

"To get at the bones that are beneath them."

Suddenly Edison's eyes widened. "Of course!" he exclaimed excitedly. "Cope and Marsh!"

"Has *every*one heard of them except me?"

"No reason why anyone out here should know the names. I'm surprised Geronimo did. I assume he's the one who told you about them?"

Holliday nodded. "Right."

"Damn! This is exciting!" enthused Edison. "Come back to the hotel with me! Ned'll want to hear about this!"

"They got any empty rooms?" asked Holliday. "I came right here from the sanitarium, and I'd been there maybe four or five months."

"We have a suite. If they don't have any more rooms, you can sleep on the couch in the parlor."

"What the hell," said Holliday, getting to his feet, putting the cork back in the bottle, and picking it up. "I can drink there as well as here."

He began walking to the door, followed by Edison. Once they were out in the street, the procedure was reversed and Holliday followed the inventor to the brand-new Delaware Hotel, which boasted the most luxurious wood-paneled rooms in town, each with its own indoor plumbing. They stopped at the front desk long enough for Holliday to rent a room, then climbed the stairs to the second floor and walked to the end of the long corridor, where Edison pulled out a key and unlocked the door. The parlor had Oriental rugs, dark furniture, and the windows were framed by tasseled drapes. Portraits of Victorian ladies and gentlemen, none of whom Holliday recognized, hung on the walls.

"Back already?" said a familiar voice.

"Yes," answered Edison. "And I've brought company."

Ned Buntline, portly and mustached, with thick, flowing sideburns, emerged from one of the two bedrooms, took one look at his visitor, and walked over to greet him with arms spread wide.

"Careful," warned Holliday. "I'm not *that* healthy."

"At least you're up and around," said Buntline, settling for shaking his hand. "I don't know if Tom has told you, but I've written some of our well, *your*—adventures up in a play."

"I hope you get Lillie Langtree to play me."

"Lillie Langtree?" repeated Buntline, surprised.

Holliday shrugged. "She's the only actor whose name I know."

Buntline chuckled. "Tell you what: if she's in New York when we're casting, I'll ask her—but don't hold your breath."

"It's been twenty years since I could hold my breath," said Holliday.

"Well, have a seat, Doc!" said Buntline, indicating a tufted leather chair.

"I'll take this one, if you don't mind," said Holliday, carrying an elegantly crafted wooden chair over from a large dining table. "I have a feeling I'd never get out of that leather one."

"Guess what this is all about, Ned?" said Edison enthusiastically.

"I don't believe in miracle cures," said Buntline. "I think our Apache friend probably had something to do with it."

Edison nodded. "It's his half of a *quid pro quo*."

"And Doc's half?"

"Ned, it's got to do with Cope and Marsh!"

"You mean they haven't killed each other yet?" asked Buntline with a smile.

"Who the hell *are* they?" demanded Holliday irritably.

"The two leading paleontologists in the United States!" said Edison.

Holliday stared at his two companions and frowned. "I've had both a classical and a scientific education—at least as pertains to medicine, dentistry, and literature—but I'll be damned if I ever heard that word before."

"No reason why you should," answered Edison. "I don't think the science had existed for more than ten or fifteen years before you graduated, and it truly wasn't worth the bother to learn about it until these two gentlemen came along."

"They're partners, are they?" asked Holliday, and Buntline laughed aloud.

"They're partners the way the Earps and the Clantons were partners," said Edison. "I doubt that there are two men anywhere in the world who hate each other more."

"Get back to paleo . . . paleowhatever."

"It's the study and science of dinosaurs."

"Okay," said Holliday. "What are dinosaurs?"

"Creatures, many of them huge beyond imagining, that walked the Earth long before Man arrived on the scene."

"Doesn't Mr. Darwin say that the fittest survive?" asked Holliday. "Seems to me something as big as this hotel is a lot fitter than a consumptive dentist."

"That's part of the science," said Buntline. "Learning everything we can about them, including why we're here and they're not."

"And there really *were* dinosaurs here?" asked Holliday dubiously.

"Yes."

"Why haven't we all heard about it before now? Hell, I not only never heard of the science, I never heard the word *dinosaur*."

"It's a very young field of study," answered Edison. "And it was going nowhere in this country until these two men met."

"Cope and Marsh?"

Edison nodded an affirmative. "Edward Drinker Cope and Othniel Charles Marsh."

"What about them?" asked Holliday.

"They were both interested in the infant science," said Edison. "I gather at one point, shortly after the War Between the States, they even went on a dig together."

"A dig?" said Holliday, frowning.

"You don't see dead dinosaurs—or dead men, for that matter—laying on the ground year after year, Doc," said Buntline. "The earth covers them up. So when you go prospecting for species instead of nuggets, you call it a dig."

"And on this dig," continued Edison, "Cope found a complete dinosaur, which he called a plesiosaur. Marsh said he had the wrong head on it, or on the wrong end of the vertebrae, something like that. Cope said he didn't. They argued, nobody won, and somehow they became mortal enemies. Now, I know that doesn't seem like much to be enemies about, but they were both brilliant, they were both egocentric, and they were both independently wealthy. Marsh was associated with Yale and its museum, Cope with a museum in Pennsylvania, and they each had their museum's clout and money behind them, as well as their own fortunes. And driven on by their mutual hatred, they have managed to discover and name more than a thousand dinosaur species in the last fifteen years, whereas all American paleontology could come up with before their feud was three species."

"They're *that* good?" asked Holliday.

Edison nodded. "Usually it takes months, often longer, to produce a scientific paper. Cope's already produced more than a thousand of them."

"So who's winning?"

Buntline smiled. "It'll be the last one standing, and *that'll* be the last one to go broke. They've sued each other, written scandalous and slanderous articles about each other, challenged almost every find the other has made, even tried to get the United States Congress to pass laws against each other."

"And now they're both digging up bones in Wyoming," said Holliday, amused.

"It's not as simple as that," said Edison.

"Oh?"

"They usually set up shop not too far from one another," continued Edison. "Do you know what the third most important job on one of their digs is?"

"Beats me," said Holliday.

Edison grinned. "Chief paleontologist."

Holliday frowned and poured himself a glass from a whiskey bottle on the table next to him. "And the second?"

"Riding shotgun to hold the Indians at bay. They do most of their digs in Indian country."

Holliday put the bottle back on the table, then leaned forward. "Okay, what's the most important job?"

"I was hoping you'd ask," said Edison, still grinning.

"Well?" demanded Holliday.

"Saboteur."

Holliday stared at Edison for a moment, then lifted his bottle and took another long swig without bothering to pour it into his glass. "I can tell I'm in for a fun time," he said at last.

28

"What's the downside of this?" asked Buntline.

"I get killed," said Holliday.

"I mean, Geronimo's downside," said Buntline.

"If I can't stop them from digging in sacred ground, the Comanche medicine men and their allies will bring the dinosaurs to life and kill the two teams . . . but according to Geronimo, they can't control them once they bring them back, and they're just as likely to wander to Apache land as anywhere else and kill anyone they come across along the way."

Buntline got to his feet and began pacing back and forth across the gaudy carpet. "That's a few hundred miles of mighty barren land. What would they live on?"

"Each other," answered Edison. "What if they resurrect a couple of thousand dinosaurs, including a few hundred carnivorous ones— and after they kill the paleontologists they head south and west? They might eat a thousand prey dinosaurs along the way, but sooner or later they'll run out, and then they'll kill and eat whatever's available."

"I agree," said Buntline, leaning against an empty bookcase. "I hadn't thought of that."

"What does one of these things actually look like?" asked Holliday.

"Ned, you're the artist," said Edison.

Buntline got a pen and a pad of paper and began sketching a carnosaur baring its teeth. When he was done he handed it to Holliday.

"Mean-looking critter," opined the dentist. "How big is he?"

"Oh, probably eight to ten times larger than a horse."

"Suddenly that sanitarium is looking a lot better to me," said Holliday.

3.

OLLIDAY WAS NOT HAPPY. The Bunt Line, the horseless coach created by Ned Buntline, terminated at Fort Collins, and he'd had to buy and ride a horse the rest of the way to Cheyenne. He was not fond of horses; he didn't like their smell, he didn't enjoy riding them, and he had a sneaking suspicion that most of them were just waiting for him to fall off so they could trample him.

He passed out of a sparse forest onto flat, almost barren land, and saw a sign posted that he was three miles from Cheyenne. At least then he could sell the horse and hunt up a horse-drawn stagecoach that would take him to the two paleontologists' camps. First, though, he planned to stop at a saloon and slake his seemingly endless thirst. He had a canteen, of course, but he figured that water was for bathing, whiskey was for drinking, and only a fool mixed the two up.

As he entered town he sought out the main street, rode up to the first saloon he could find, thankfully climbed down off his horse, and entered the place. The interior had the usual wooden tables and chairs, a faro game in the back that no one seemed interested in, and spittoons not just lining the bar but spread through the saloon. There was a huge picture of a shirtless man with his fists doubled up, hanging behind the bar, covering part of a long mirror, and Holliday studied it as he waited for the bartender to approach him.

"What do you think of him?" asked a man who was standing next to him.

"I prefer paintings of naked ladies," answered Holliday.

"That's our local champion, Bill Smiley," said the man proudly. "He's the one who's going to knock the great John L. down for the count this afternoon."

"Seems to me that people have been trying to do that for twelve or thirteen years now," replied Holliday, obviously unimpressed.

"Well, Smiley's the man who can do it," said the man adamantly. "And he's bringing the championship to Wyoming," he added, his chest swelling with pride.

"If you say so," responded Holliday, trying to cut off any further discussion.

"You think otherwise?"

"I'm a stranger here," said Holliday. "I have no idea."

"I've got fifty dollars says that Smiley wins," said the man pugnaciously, pulling out a fifty-dollar bill and waving it around.

"I'll take that bet," said Holliday, pulling out his own cash.

The expressions of the onlookers said he was throwing his money away, that no intruder was going to beat their local hero on his own turf.

"We'll let the bartender hold it," said the man.

"Fine by me," said Holliday.

"I just hope that damned ref isn't as blind as he looks," muttered the man. "Whoever heard of a referee with spectacles?"

"Spectacles?" repeated Holliday.

"Yeah."

Suddenly Holliday smiled. "Is he from New York?"

"That's what they say, though I hear he spent some time in the Dakota Badlands pretending to be a cowboy."

"Son of a bitch, I know him!" exclaimed Holliday. "I'll be damned!"

"If you're who I think you are, that's a given," said the man.

The saloon suddenly went completely silent, and every head turned toward Holliday. He stared at the man, then shrugged. "What the hell," he muttered. "When you're right, you're right. Now, when and where is this fight?"

"Maybe an hour from now, out there by Jake Gilmore's corral," said the man, walking him to the door and pointing to a large crowd perhaps half a mile away.

It took Holliday almost twenty minutes to traverse the distance on foot, and once there he walked up to the hastily constructed ticket booth and bought a standing-room ticket, well behind the seated area, since he was much less interested in watching the fight than meeting the referee.

There was a preliminary bout going on, and the crowd was cheering for its favorite, a short stocky man with a shock of blond hair. Holliday saw that the referee was a lean bearded man, and went off to find something to drink. The best he could do was a warm beer, so he took it, spent a few minutes polishing it off, and returned to where he could see the ring. A cheer went up from the crowd just as he reached it, and he saw that the stocky man's hand was being held above his head, while his opponent's corner men were trying to awaken the unconscious fighter.

There was another bout, which ended about ninety seconds after it began, and then the ring stood empty for almost fifteen minutes. Finally a band began playing. Holliday turned and saw the uniformed trumpeters and drummers marching down the aisle to the ring, leading a tall, broad-shouldered man who he recognized from photos and drawings in the few newspapers he had seen in the last couple of years as being John L. Sullivan. The crowd stood up and cheered, and Sullivan smiled and waved to them.

When they reached the ring the band stopped playing and Sullivan climbed the four stairs, stepped between the ropes, and stood calmly, awaiting his opponent.

A moment later William Smiley walked to the ring in solitary splendor. Again, the crowd began cheering when they saw him, and one woman even threw him a bouquet, which he caught, brought carefully to his lips, and then handed to a teenaged girl who was standing on the aisle.

Holliday studied Smiley as he gracefully made his way to the ring. He was a lean man except for his arms, which were heavily muscled. His face bore no marks of previous battles, and in a time of cauliflower ears and crooked noses that was remarkable in itself. He smiled and waved to the crowd as he entered the ring, then walked over to shake Sullivan's hand. Sullivan, straight-faced, said something that made Smiley laugh, and Smiley's reply elicited nothing more than a sneer from Sullivan.

But Holliday wasn't watching them. His attention was focused on a third man who was approaching the ring: medium height, broad of chest, wearing the mustache he'd grown during his last trip out West, and watching the world through a pair of rimless glasses.

A man dressed in his Sunday best entered the ring and held a bullhorn to his mouth.

"Ladies and gentlemen," he intoned, "welcome to the match for the heavyweight championship of the world. Cheyenne is proud to host this momentous event, and we are delighted to welcome the reigning champion, the great John L. Sullivan!"

Sullivan bowed from the waist as he received a huge ovation.

"Fighting against him will be our own undefeated native son, William Smiley!

The cheer was even louder this time, and Smiley waved to the crowd.

"And coming out from New York just to referee this momentous event is Theodore Roosevelt."

Roosevelt nodded his head briefly to the mild cheers, and then called the two fighters to the center of the ring to give them their instructions.

"Why the hell did they bring out a politician to ref the damned thing?" complained a man standing next to Holliday.

"He's a little more than a politician," said Holliday.

"Oh?"

Holliday nodded. "For one thing, he was a boxing champion at Harvard."

"Where's that?" asked the man.

Holliday smiled. "Little school back East." He was about to list Roosevelt's other accomplishments, including the treaty with Geronimo, but then the bell rang and the fight began.

Strategy wasn't Smiley's strong suit. He went right at Sullivan, and received a bloody nose for his trouble. Undeterred, he charged the champion like a bull, and like a matador Sullivan stepped aside and landed a powerful blow on his ear that knocked him halfway across the ring.

The entire first round went that way, and the crowd became increasingly silent, because the only mystery remaining was not who would win, but rather how much longer Smiley could stand up under Sullivan's sledgehammer blows.

The bell rang for the second round, and Smiley approached Sullivan more cautiously this time. It made no difference. Sullivan ducked under a left, and delivered a powerful blow to Smiley's solar plexus. Smiley went down to one knee, in obvious pain, and as Roosevelt began counting Sullivan stepped in for the kill.

Roosevelt pushed Sullivan back to give Smiley room, then resumed the count—but Sullivan's blood was up, and he took another swing at Smiley as the fallen boxer was attempting to rise.

Roosevelt pushed him back again, more firmly this time. Sullivan bellowed an obscenity and, to the surprise of the crowd, he took a swing at Roosevelt.

The Easterner ducked, threw a quick left that bloodied Sullivan's nose, and took his glasses off, folding them carefully and putting them in a breast pocket.

"Your friend's gonna get it now!" said Holliday's companion excitedly.

"Don't bet your last penny on it," replied Holliday.

Sullivan wiped the blood from his nose, roared with rage, and turned his full attention to Roosevelt. He yelled something at Roosevelt that Holliday couldn't hear, then swung a roundhouse right that would have almost beheaded him if it had landed, but Roosevelt ducked and landed a quick one-two punch to Sullivan's belly that doubled the champion over.

"We chose the wrong man to fight against Sullivan!" cried a man who was standing a few feet behind Holliday.

Roosevelt pointed to the timekeeper, who instantly realized what the referee wanted and rang the bell. That seemed to bring Sullivan to his senses, and he walked quickly to his corner, not even deigning to look at Roosevelt, who dropped to one knee beside Smiley and helped him to his corner. Then he approached Sullivan, said something to him, Sullivan nodded, and Roosevelt went back to the middle of the ring. The bell rang about forty seconds later, and the two fighters emerged from their corners. It was obvious that Smiley was still groggy, and it only took one punch—a right to the side of the head—for Sullivan to put him down for the count.

Roosevelt raised Sullivan's hand, they spoke to each other for a moment, and then shook hands and parted.

Sullivan collected a trophy and a check from one of the sponsors and strode off furiously to his dressing tent, while Roosevelt, noticing that Smiley was starting to awaken, helped him to his feet and led him out of the ring and down the stairs to ground level.

As the two of them began walking away from the ring, they passed where Holliday was standing.

"You should have beat the crap out of that pompous bastard, Theodore," said Holliday.

Roosevelt stopped and searched the faces until he found the one he sought.

"Doc!" he exclaimed. "What are *you* doing here?"

"Buy me a drink and I'll be happy to tell you," said Holliday.

"Sure," said Roosevelt. "But not here. I've got a horse and buggy waiting. Let's go back to my hotel."

"Where are you staying?"

"The Plains Hotel. And you?"

"I haven't checked in yet," said Holliday.

"Where's your luggage?" asked Roosevelt.

"Right here," said Holliday, touching his gun and his flask in turn.

"Well, we'll get you a room there," said Roosevelt. "How long will you be in town?"

"Just passing through."

"Where are you heading?"

Holliday smiled. "That's what we're going to talk about."

They reached Roosevelt's horse and buggy, which also had a driver, and were sitting in the Plains Hotel's elegant bar ten minutes later.

"Nice place," noted Holliday, looking at the polished walls and crystal chandelier. "How are the rooms?"

"You won't be disappointed," answered Roosevelt. "Now," he said as the waiter brought Holliday a glass of whiskey and Roosevelt some sarsaparilla, "suppose you tell me what this is all about."

Holliday took a long swallow and leaned back in his chair. "You ever hear of a man named Cope?"

"The paleontologist?"

Holliday smiled. "You've heard of him."

"He's been digging not too far from Leadville, I understand," said Roosevelt. "Did you meet him there?"

"I've never met him," answered Holliday. "I assume you know of March, too?"

Roosevelt nodded. "Yale man. Probably not as brilliant as Cope, but he's got huge money behind him. I assume you've never met him either?"

Holliday shook his head. "Nope. But I suspect I'm about to, all thanks to our friend Geronimo."

Roosevelt frowned in puzzlement. "What's *he* got to do with this?"

"It seems that Cope and Marsh have gotten everything they want from the Colorado mountains, and now they're digging up the ground in Wyoming." Holliday paused. "*Sacred* ground."

"I didn't think there were any Apaches in Wyoming."

"It's sacred Comanche ground."

"Okay, it's sacred Comanche ground," said Roosevelt. "What's that got to do with you or Geronimo?"

"The Comanche want them off it."

Roosevelt shrugged. "That figures."

"And since they're loaded not only with scientists but with shootists, it's my job to convince them to leave peacefully."

"Or else the Comanche will go on the warpath?"

"Not exactly," said Holliday, toying with his whiskey glass.

"Doc, I can play guessing games all night," said Roosevelt. "But wouldn't it just be easier if you told me what's going on?"

"You know what dinosaurs are?"

Roosevelt nodded. "I've seen some of their bones at the Peabody and the Smithsonian."

Holliday sighed and shook his head slowly. "I guess I must be the only educated man who's never heard of them," he said ruefully. "Comes from living on this side of the river, I guess. Anyway, according to Geronimo, the dinosaur bones they're digging for are *beneath* the Comanche bones in the burial grounds. And rather than risk their warriors against the scientists' shootists, Geronimo says they'll resurrect the dinosaurs to kill them and preserve their sacred ground."

"Let me guess," said Roosevelt. "Geronimo thinks if that happens they won't be able to put the dinosaurs back, and they'll head for less populated land—like Arizona?"

"That's about it," said Holliday. "Sounds like a fairy tale to me."

Roosevelt seemed lost in thought for a moment, and finally spoke. "I've seen the bones back East, Doc. These creatures did exist once."

"As big as Geronimo says?"

"Some of them must have gone seventy, eighty tons."

"You're kidding!" said Holliday.

"No, I'm not. It's a fascinating new science. Doc, you can't believe the size of those bones! Mr. Cope and Mr. Marsh are filling up entire museums with their finds. I'd love to spend some time with them, learning about this new science."

"Anyway," Holliday continued, "Geronimo told me where I'd find these scientists, and he gave me back my health—well, *some* of it—for a year in exchange for stopping them. He also told me I'd meet a mutual friend along the way. I guess that's you."

"I'd almost say he arranged for me to referee this match, but it was set up a year ago, and he wouldn't have waited this long to send you here to try to stop them. I hope you—make that *we*—can talk reason to them, but if they haven't seen what power the medicine men wield, they'd never believe it."

"I agree," said Holliday. "I think this is a lost cause from the start. I'll talk to them, they'll laugh in my face, if I can keep my temper nobody'll get hurt, and then when the Comanche have had enough, we'll all run like hell." He took another swallow, draining his glass. "There's no reason for you to get involved, Theodore. This proposition is a loser from the start."

"That's all the more reason why I'm coming along," said Roosevelt.

Holliday stared at him. "Even though I probably can't convince them to pack up and dig somewhere else?"

"Precisely because of it."

"You don't seem to be listening to what I'm saying," persisted Holliday. "If Geronimo's right, the whole area could get overrun by these monsters."

"I know," said Roosevelt, flashing Holliday a toothy grin. "And we'll be the first men to see them. It'll be bully—just bully!"

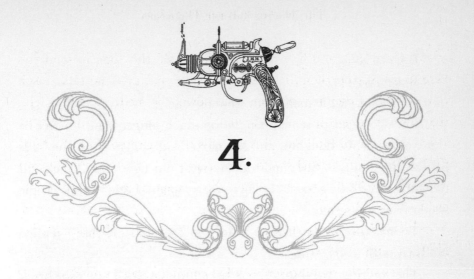

4.

"**S**O, WHAT HAVE YOU BEEN DOING FOR THE PAST YEAR?" asked Roosevelt as he and Holliday rode north and west. Neither was happy with their steeds. Holliday hated all horses, and Roosevelt felt that the gelding he'd bought at the Cheyenne stable was far inferior to his beloved Manitou, a fact that became increasingly apparent as the land began getting hillier and more heavily forested.

"Dying, mostly," answered Holliday. "And you?"

"You are not the cheeriest man I ever met," said Roosevelt.

"Or the healthiest."

"Granted," said Roosevelt. "Anyway, I've been dividing my time between my ranches in the Dakota Badlands and finishing Sagamore Hill."

"What's that?" asked Holliday.

"The New York home where I plan to spend the rest of my life," replied Roosevelt. "I've been working on it—well, having it worked on—on and off for the past two years. It should be just about ready in a few more months."

"Big place?"

"Reasonably."

"And you a single man again. Sounds lonely."

"I don't intend to remain single too much longer. And I won't be alone anyway. My daughter and her nursemaid will be with me." He paused and smiled. "She's more than a year old now. That'll help fill the house. And," he added, "I plan to marry again. I don't think people were meant to live alone."

"Try hooking up with Kate Elder and then tell me that," replied Holliday with a wry grin.

"The notorious Big-Nose Kate?" asked Roosevelt. "Didn't she break you out of jail when you were incarcerated on a trumped-up charge?"

"She couldn't nag and curse at me while I was in jail," answered Holliday. "I'd rather face John Wesley Hardin any day."

Roosevelt laughed. "All right," he conceded. "*Some* men weren't meant to live alone. And I'm one of them."

"Got anyone picked out?"

Roosevelt nodded. "My childhood sweetheart." He chuckled. "I say that as if a ten-year-old knows what a sweetheart is. Anyway, she's Edith Kermit Carow, and as soon as I get the Dakota ranches sorted out, and finish a pair of books I've contracted to write, I plan to ask her hand in marriage."

"So are you going to be a writer now?"

"Too limiting," said Roosevelt.

"So you're going to go back to ornithology and taxidermy, too?"

"I never went away from them," answered Roosevelt. "You know, I was the youngest minority leader in the history of the New York legislature. I think I may try my hand at politics again."

"I'd vote for you," said Holliday.

"Not until I ran for President and you moved to a state that was part of the Union," replied Roosevelt with a laugh. "But all that's for when I go back East. Right now what I'm most interested in is learning about paleontology."

"I'd never heard of it till last week," said Holliday.

"With all due respect, you don't speak to a lot of college-educated people out here."

"True," admitted Holliday. A vision of Johnny Ringo crossed his mind. "And I killed the only one I knew."

"I heard about that," said Roosevelt. "Anyway, I want to talk to one or both of these men. For example, there's a femur—a leg bone—that's taller than I am. How did they know where to look for it? How did they figure out what the dinosaur looked like just from that one bone? How long did these creatures live, and when? And given how powerful they were, what could possibly have killed them? I mean, a lion could do them about as much damage as a toothless puppy could do to you."

"You make it sound sort of interesting," acknowledged Holliday. "And truth to tell, not a lot interests me these days. I'd like to live long enough to learn some of the answers to all those questions."

"So would I," said Roosevelt, grabbing his binoculars to study a red-brown bird that was flying overhead.

"It's just a bird."

"And Abraham Lincoln was just a man, and Hindoo is just a race-horse, and John L. Sullivan is just a boxer," replied Roosevelt. "It's an endlessly fascinating world we live in," he continued, watching the bird until it was out of sight, "and the dinosaurs are among the most fascinating things."

"In *my* world, it's the fascinating things that keep shooting at you," said Holliday.

"Still, whoever would have heard of Doc Holliday if you were just a dentist in Georgia?"

"I could do with a little less notoriety," remarked Holliday.

"Nonsense," protested Roosevelt. "You've made a mark on the mountain of history. People will be talking about those thirty seconds at the O.K. Corral for the next century or two."

"*Near* the corral," muttered Holliday irritably, so softly that Roosevelt didn't hear him.

"By the way, we're being watched," noted Roosevelt.

"Off to the left," said Holliday. "Yeah, I spotted them a couple of minutes ago."

"*Them?*"

"Yeah, two of 'em."

"Damn!" said Roosevelt. "I only saw one."

"The other's not moving," answered Holliday. "There! Now he is."

"Yes, I see him now. Comanche?"

"I assume so," said Holliday. "Just between you and me, I've never seen a Comanche before, but this is their territory."

"Are they just going to follow us?" asked Roosevelt.

"Probably," replied Holliday. "If they meant us any harm, they'd have done it by now."

"Good!" said Roosevelt. He pulled his horse to a halt, placed two fingers between his lips and whistled shrilly. The sound made both their horses uneasy, but while Roosevelt's was prancing nervously, he turned in his saddle, faced the two Comanche, and signaled them to join him and Holliday with a waving motion of his hand. The two Indians sat motionless, staring at him.

"What the hell's got into you, Theodore?" demanded Holliday.

"You say they don't want to kill us," answered Roosevelt. "So why not have them take us to their medicine men and see if we can reach an accommodation?"

"I said they *probably* don't want to kill us," growled Holliday. "And

44

you can't make any deals for Cope or Marsh until you talk to them and get them to okay it."

"Geronimo's not worried about Cope or Marsh," said Roosevelt. "He's worried about the Comanche medicine men, so the sooner we find them and open a dialogue, the better."

"You've been out East too long, Theodore," replied Holliday. "You've forgotten how things work out here."

"I'm more concerned with making sure they *do* work," said Roosevelt. He peered off at the Indians, who had retreated behind some trees and shrubbery. "Ah, well, it was worth a try," he added, his face reflecting his disappointment.

"I've just been given a year," said Holliday, urging his horse forward again. "I'd hate to lose the last fifty-one weeks of it."

"All right," said Roosevelt. Then he shrugged. "They're gone anyway. We might as well keep going."

"In five minutes," said Holliday, pulling his horse to a stop and dismounting. "The goddamned horse may not need a rest, but I do." He reached for his flask, then shrugged and pulled his canteen off his saddle horn instead.

"You *do* know where their camps are, right?"

"I know the general area. I figure they'll keep moving around, but they're not hiding their presence, so we'll find enough signs to follow."

"Good. It'll give me a chance to practice my tracking skills," said Roosevelt. "In the meantime, since this thing they sold me is a pretty spiritless trail horse . . ." He reached into his saddlebag and pulled out a book.

"Don't you ever rest or relax?" asked Holliday.

"Reading relaxes me."

"I'm sure it relaxes a lot of people—but not on horseback, in enemy territory, when we're almost certainly being watched or followed."

"Being watched and followed in enemy territory is practically a given," answered Roosevelt. "If they start shooting, I'll put the book away."

It comes back to me, thought Holliday. *I admired your brain and your energy and your courage, but I never really* liked *you. You are not only the most accomplished man I've ever met; you can also be the most irritating. I'm so annoyed now that I might as well climb back up on this goddamned horse.* Which he did.

They rode in silence until it was too dark to read. Then Roosevelt pulled some beef jerky out of his saddlebag, offered a piece to Holliday, and carefully replaced his book in a different compartment.

"What were you reading?" asked Holliday, washing down a bite of jerky with a swig from his flask.

"*A Tale of Two Cities,*" answered Roosevelt. "By—"

"I know," interrupted Holliday. "Better than *The Pickwick Papers,* not up to *David Copperfield.*"

"Right," said Roosevelt. "I keep forgetting that you're one of the literate shootists."

"It gave me something to do while my patients were screaming in agony," replied Holliday.

Roosevelt threw back his head and laughed. "You can be a very witty man when you forget that you're mad at the world."

"Oh, I forgive it most of its transgressions. I just wish it would leave me alone." He grimaced. "And I guess it will, in a year at the outside."

"I wouldn't bet on it, Doc," said Roosevelt.

"That was my deal."

"I know, but Geronimo's an intelligent man. He'll find more uses for you."

"Well, next time I'm going to insist on a full recovery," said Holliday, coughing into a blood-stained handkerchief.

They decided not to build a fire or rest for the night. They couldn't be sure all the Comanche warriors would be content merely to watch and follow them, and the sooner they reached one of the paleontologist's camps the sooner they'd stop being easy targets should the warriors have a change of heart.

It was in mid-afternoon of the next day that they began seeing unmistakable signs of a white man's camp. Half an hour later—it should have taken ten minutes, but Roosevelt kept stopping to watch birds and sketch unusual plants and trees—they came upon a dozen tents, which would only provide shelter for another month or two before the nights became too cold, and a hastily constructed log building. Though empty, the camp showed signs of recent habitation, so the two men dismounted, turned their horses loose in a primitive corral, and sat down by the remains of the morning's fire.

"That log building has to be where they're keeping whatever they pull out of the ground," remarked Roosevelt.

"You could always find out for sure and take a look," said Holliday.

Roosevelt shook his head. "I don't mind being rude and not waiting for them to come from their dig to show me, but I have absolutely no idea what I'd be looking at."

"Yeah, I suppose that *does* make a difference," agreed Holliday.

"How big can this burial ground be?" mused Roosevelt.

"Well, the one back in Arizona, where we had them move the train tracks, was at least twenty miles long, and maybe three or four miles wide," said Holliday. He thought about it, and shrugged. "Hell, for all I know, it was fifty miles long. All I know for sure is that we had them move it."

"And was that the only burial ground?"

"You mean for the Apaches?" asked Holliday. "No, I know of at least three or four more."

"So Cope and Marsh could be fifty, maybe a hundred miles apart, not desecrating the same burial ground, but digging in different ones," said Roosevelt, poking the fire with a long stick to get it going again.

"I suppose so," said Holliday. "It all depends on what signs they look for, where they know to dig for these bones they're after. Maybe Wyoming's loaded with them from one border to the other, or maybe they're all concentrated within a few miles of where we're sitting."

"I wonder what this landscape looked like when the dinosaurs roamed the land," mused Roosevelt, staring off toward the mountains to the west.

"You'd better have a damned good reason for being here, or you're about to find out," said a cold voice from behind them.

Roosevelt and Holliday turned to face the speaker, a lean man with unkempt black hair and a beard of black stubble. Roosevelt, seeing a gun pointed at them, raised his hands, but Holliday just smiled.

"Well, hello, Cole," he said. "When did you become a scientist?"

The man stared at him, clearly surprised. "Doc?" he said. "What the hell are you doing here?"

"Mostly, hoping you won't shoot me," said Holliday.

The man holstered his gun. "Same old Doc!" he said with a laugh.

"Theodore," said Holliday, "say hello to the notorious Cole Younger."

"I've read about you," said Roosevelt.

"Lies, mostly," said Younger. "And you are . . . ?"

"Theodore Roosevelt."

Younger's brow furrowed in thought. "You're the guy who made the treaty with Geronimo?" he said at last.

"I had that honor." Roosevelt studied him. "I must say that you don't look like your picture."

"I've been shot full of holes and served a lot of jail time since I posed for any pictures," answered Younger. "I used to be able to stand up straight. These days I walk kind of hunched over—but at least I'm still here."

"And what *are you* doing out here on a dinosaur hunt?" asked Holliday.

"Originally I was riding shotgun to keep the Indians at bay," answered Younger. "But then they hired a couple of other shootists. I don't know if they're any good, but they look like they know what they're doing—and I got put in charge of guarding all the bones." He laughed again. "Can you imagine what the dime novels will make of that? Cole Younger, guarding a bunch of bones!"

"We could have walked away with them any time in the last thirty minutes," said Holliday.

"I doubt it," said Younger. "First, you couldn't lift most of the bones we got in that shed. And second, that's where I was taking my afternoon siesta."

"Point taken," said Holliday.

"Excuse me, Mr. Younger—" began Roosevelt.

"Just Cole'll do."

"Cole," corrected Roosevelt. "But whose camp is this—Mr. Cope's or Mr. Marsh's?"

"This is Professor Cope's camp, though he don't much care if you call him 'Mister'," answered Younger. "I'm told not calling Marsh 'Professor' is a firing offense. Unless you happen to be one of his shootists, that is."

"And when is Cope due back?"

"Maybe half an hour before sunset," said Younger. "He's got about thirty men out digging with him, plus a couple riding shotgun, and at least one or two trying to foul up Marsh's dig."

"Marsh is nearby?" asked Roosevelt.

"I haven't seen him myself," answered Younger. "But they say he's about thirty miles north of here . . . or at least he was four days ago."

"How has Mr. Cope's dig been going?" asked Roosevelt.

"Pulling out a lot of bones, some of which have got him real excited," said Younger. "But we've got some trouble too."

"Oh?"

Younger nodded. "Marsh has hired a damned good saboteur—that's the real reason I'm watching the bones—and the Comanche have picked off three of our men, and also indulged in a little sabotage against a couple of our wagons." He paused for a moment. "At least, I *think* it's them, but it could be Marsh's doing."

"I see," said Roosevelt.

"So we got one or more of Marsh's guys trying to stop us, and the Comanche picking off a man or burning a wagon whenever they think can get away with it—and this ground looks pretty soft, but a couple of our horses have gone lame."

"I got a feeling all that's going to be the least of your problems," said Holliday.

5.

"SO TELL ME," said Holliday, as they sat on a pair of tree stumps by the dead fire, waiting for Cope and his party to return, "how the hell did you let a little twerp like Jesse James talk you into that Minnesota thing?"

"You mean the Northfield raid?" asked Younger.

Holliday nodded his head. "It's been written up in enough dime novels."

"It even made the papers back in New York," added Roosevelt.

Younger lit a hand-rolled cigarette. "And they all say it was the Youngers and Jesse James?"

"The Younger Brothers and the James Brothers," said Roosevelt. "It's one of the most famous robbery attempts in our history."

"Don't know how a story like that gets started," replied Younger. "Jesse and Frank were nowhere near Northfield. Hell, I'll bet whatever Mr. Cope's paying me that Jesse's never set foot in Minnesota in his life."

"So who was it?" asked Roosevelt.

"Me and my brothers Jim and Bob, and a couple of other guys.

They got killed, and all three of us brothers got shot up pretty bad." Suddenly he grinned. "Just as well that they caught us and tossed us in jail. They made it their business to keep us alive until the trial. If we'd have gotten away, filled with lead like we were, all three of us would have died within a week or two."

"You don't sound at all bitter," noted Roosevelt.

"Well, we'd much rather have gotten away clean with the money instead of loaded down with lead, but we're rough men, we took a gamble, we lost, and we paid our debt."

"They let you all out?"

"Me and Jim did nine years each and got paroled. Bob never did recover from all them bullets, and he died in jail."

"Sorry to hear it," said Holliday. "He's the only one I never met."

"Well, you can read all about him," said Younger.

"I know," said Holliday. "Same place I read all those phony stories about me."

Younger shook his head. "No, I wrote my autobiography while I was in jail. Had to do something to kill all that time. And," he added with a happy smile, "I sold it last month. Some New York publisher that your pal Bat Masterson showed it to."

"He's not exactly my friend," said Holliday. "We just seem to be on the same side of issues out here."

"Well, he's *my* friend," chimed in Roosevelt. "And as good a sportswriter as the *Telegraph* has on its staff." He turned to Holliday. "How did you meet Cole and Jim?"

Holliday grinned and looked at Younger. "You tell him, Cole."

"Me and Jim needed some quick cash, so we hired on as lawmen back in Dallas a couple of years before the Minnesota raid. I can't believe Doc didn't tell you the story about how the sheriff gave him something like ten hours to clear out of town after he shot a man at a gaming table."

"Yes, I heard it," replied Roosevelt with a chuckle. "The sheriff had an abscessed tooth, Doc was packing his gear and was the only dentist still awake, so the sheriff came in, Doc put him under with laughing gas, and then"—Roosevelt uttered a hearty laugh—"he pulled all the sheriff's teeth before he woke up, and high-tailed it out of town."

"That's the story," agreed Younger. "But Doc wasn't leaving town because of the sheriff. Doc could have taken him without drawing a deep breath."

"Even back then I couldn't draw a deep breath," interjected Holliday with a smile.

"Anyway, the reason Doc left in a hurry was so he wouldn't have to face Jim and me."

"I didn't want to kill you," said Holliday.

"You wouldn't have," replied Younger.

"Anyway," concluded Holliday, "you try to avoid gunfights with your friends—especially when you have as few as I do."

"So Jesse wasn't involved in that robbery," said Roosevelt, still dwelling upon the Northfield, Minnesota, raid.

"He'll never deny it—if you knew Jesse, you'd know why—but no, he wasn't there," said Younger. "Wouldn't have helped if he'd been with us. He ain't the best shot you ever saw, and he can be damned unpleasant when you disagree with him. Frank is the James brother I like. We're talking about getting together and putting on a Wild West show once we get a grubstake together."

"*The James and Younger Show*," said Roosevelt. "I like it."

"*The Younger and James Show*," Younger corrected him unsmilingly. "At least it'll keep that bastard who's working for Marsh on his toes."

"That bastard?" repeated Roosevelt, frowning.

"He's just a goddamned publicity hound," replied Younger. "Hell, I'll bet his fee isn't money, but one of them twenty-foot-high leg bones."

"Who are you talking about?" asked Holliday.

"Bill Cody," answered Younger. "He left his Wild West show to work for Marsh for half a year." He paused and snorted in contempt. "The man's no threat. I don't know how the hell he convinced Marsh he's a shootist."

"Well, he did kill something like a thousand buffalo," remarked Roosevelt.

Younger pointed a forefinger toward Roosevelt's ear and pretended to fire it with his thumb. "Riding up and sticking the muzzle of your rifle in a buff's ear when he's grazing ain't the same as shooting someone who's aiming a gun or an arrow at you," said Younger decisively. "But I figure the real reason old man Marsh got Cody is publicity. There've been three times as many stories about him and his finds than about Mr. Cope and what he's dug up."

A happy smile spread across Roosevelt's face.

"What are you grinning at, Theodore?" asked Holliday.

"After spending time with a bunch of politicians who would even hedge their bets before declaring that night follows day, you have no idea how pleasant it is to be out here with a pair of shootists who call a spade a spade."

"You a politician?" asked Younger.

"One of the best," said Holliday before Roosevelt could answer.

"Really?" said Younger. He paused and thought about it for a moment. "Well, I don't suppose it's much worse than being a shootist."

"You're going to hear a lot more about this young man if you live long enough," said Holliday. "He's not only a successful politician, but he's one of the country's leading ornithologists and taxidermists."

"Whatever *they* are," said Younger.

"And when he was a volunteer deputy in the Dakota Badlands, he went out unarmed in a blizzard and brought in three armed killers."

Younger stared at Roosevelt. "I'm starting to get impressed."

"He's also written some books about the opening of the West," continued Holliday.

"If one of them says Jesse James was on the Northfield, Minnesota, raid, I'm less impressed," said Younger with a smile.

"I haven't gotten to that yet," said Roosevelt.

"Good," said Younger decisively. "Now you'll write the true story."

"He also wrote the definitive treatise on naval warfare," said Holliday.

"Okay, okay, he's a good writer. I hear you." He paused and flashed a smile at Roosevelt. "That makes two of us."

"He was also the lightweight boxing champion at Harvard," concluded Holliday.

"Lightweight? That was a few pounds ago," noted Younger.

"Want to go a few rounds with him?" asked Holliday with a smile.

Younger took a good look at Roosevelt, his barrel chest, his muscular arms, the muscles in his neck, and shook his head. "No, I wouldn't want to hurt him."

"Oh, that's a very good answer," laughed Holliday. "I guess I'm sitting with *two* politicians."

All three men laughed at that.

"So what exactly *are* you doing here, Doc?" asked Younger at last.

"It's a little difficult to explain," said Holliday, "but basically I'm here to get your boss and this Marsh fellow to go dig for bones elsewhere."

Younger frowned. "You know a better spot?"

"Nope," answered Holliday. "But I know a lot of safer spots."

"I can handle any trouble that shows up here," said Younger.

"I don't think so," interjected Roosevelt.

Younger turned to Roosevelt. "Is this *your* idea?" he demanded pugnaciously.

"No, Cole," said Holliday. "He's just a friend who I talked into coming along with me. This is Geronimo's idea."

"Geronimo?" repeated Younger, frowning in puzzlement. That just don't make any sense," he complained. He turned to Roosevelt. "I know he signed his treaty with *you*." And back to Holliday. "And I heard that you did him a favor or two, But does he want these bones for himself?"

Holliday shook his head. "He doesn't want 'em at all."

Younger frowned. "Then I truly don't understand what the hell he's got to do with this."

"You know where you are right this minute?" asked Holliday.

"Right here, talking to you two."

"And do you know where 'right here' is?"

"Wyoming territory," said Younger, frowning.

"Close but no cigar," said Holliday. "You, and Cope's whole expedition, and Marsh's whole expedition, are standing on some sacred Comanche burial grounds."

"How the hell do you know?" said Younger irritably. "Indians don't plant no crosses."

"*I* don't know," replied Holliday. "But Geronimo does."

"Are you trying to get me to believe that old bastard has made peace with the Comanche?"

"No, he doesn't give a damn about them."

"I know I spent a lot of years in jail," said Younger, not trying to hide his exasperation, "but my brain hasn't stopped working, and you're just not making any sense."

"The two expeditions have to dig through the burial grounds to get to the fossils," interjected Roosevelt.

"Fossils?" repeated Younger.

"Dinosaur bones."

"Okay, they have to dig through the small bones to get down to the big ones," said Younger. "So what? They're all dead."

"Dead isn't necessarily a permanent condition," said Holliday. "Don't forget: the combined powers of something like fifty-five medicine men kept the United States from expanding across the Mississippi until Geronimo went against their wishes and signed the treaty with Theodore. He's the most powerful of them all, but they haven't lost their powers."

"Okay, everyone's powerful," said Younger irritably. "What's that got to do with anything?"

"He's mostly concerned with the Comanche medicine men," continued Holliday. "If Professor Cope and Professor Marsh desecrate enough graves, he's afraid the medicine men might magic up some of the creatures the bones come from to either scare you off or kill you."

"And he's worried about the Comanche turning their critters loose on *us*?" snorted Younger in disbelief. "You'll have to do better than that, Doc."

"He doesn't give a damn about you," agreed Holliday.

"Then I still don't—"

"He isn't worried about their supernatural creatures, because they can control what they create," said Holliday.

"You'd better make some sense soon," grumbled Younger. "I'm getting ready for dinner and so far you've used a hell of a lot of words to say nothing."

"They created a creature to kill Theodore a year ago," said Holliday. "He's still here. They resurrected Johnny Ringo a few years ago and sent him to Tombstone to kill me. I'm still here."

Holliday took a swallow from his flask. "Their creatures can be awesome, and they're certainly deadly, but they're not perfect. And if you and Cody live long enough, like for another month or two, you'll figure out how to beat them. So Geronimo thinks they may have the power to resurrect hundreds of creatures, not from inside their heads, but from the bones your two expeditions are digging up."

"Either way we die," said Younger, "so why does Geronimo care?"

"Because he doesn't think the medicine men can kill as many monsters as they resurrect, and if they *do* resurrect them to drive you off, they'll start roaming away when they're done with you, and some of them will wind up in Apache territory."

"Bullshit!" said Younger. "If they make it that far, and he's half as powerful as you think, he'll just order them to turn back."

"I believe I can answer that, Mr. Younger," said Roosevelt, who'd been sketching a pair of prairie dogs in the dying light while he listed to the two shootists.

"Cole," Younger corrected him.

"Cole," Roosevelt amended. "I'm no expert, but from what little I've read about these dinosaurs, they are about ninety-nine percent instinct and one percent brainpower. It may be that their brains are so small the medicine men, including Geronimo, *can't* control them."

Younger considered what Roosevelt said for a moment, and then responded. "If you know it, and Geronimo knows it, then surely the Comanche medicine men know it."

"They know they'll endanger a lot of Comanche lives," agreed Roosevelt. "But what we don't know is how important that is to them. If the ground is truly sacred to them, maybe it's more important for them to chase the expeditions away or kill them, so the Comanche who die at the same time will find peace in the sacred burial ground." Roosevelt grimaced and shrugged. "Or maybe they've already resurrected one or two and learned that they *can* control them. Geronimo's powerful, but he's not infallible."

"What do *you* get out of this, Doc?" asked Younger. "What's Geronimo paying you to do his dirty work for him?"

"My health."

Younger stared at him and frowned. "Bullshit," he said. "You move like everything hurts, I can hear you breathing from where I'm sitting, and I saw you cough some blood into your kerchief a few minutes ago. I'd hardly call that health."

"Everything's relative," said Holliday with a rueful smile. "A few days ago I was in a sanitarium, waiting to die. I couldn't sit up without help, and I couldn't walk even *with* help. I was going to die in less than a day. Geronimo gave me a year in exchange for my coming here and trying to get the two expeditions to go east to Dakota or south to Colorado."

"That Apache sure as hell did a half-hearted job of restoring your health," noted Younger.

"He explained his reasons to me." A grim smile. "Needless to say, I thoroughly disagree with them."

"So you're here to convince Professor Cope to pack up and leave?"

"Cope and Marsh both."

Younger stared at him for a moment before replying. Finally he said, "You want an honest opinion?"

"Always happy to have one," replied Holliday.

"You got more chance of getting Geronimo to convert to Christianity," said Younger with a smile. "The most important thing in either of these guys' lives is digging up some new bone before the other one can. I don't know what started it, but I don't think I've ever seen two guys hate each other as much as these two."

"Those are comforting words," said Roosevelt.

"Doc," said Younger, "your friend's as crazy as *they* are."

"Anything's possible," answered Holliday. "But he usually has a reason for what he says." He turned to Roosevelt. "Theodore?"

"Cole, you said it yourself," said Roosevelt with a smile.

"Said what?"

"The most important thing in both their lives is digging up some bone before the other one does."

"So?" demanded Young.

"So we only have to convince *one* of them to leave," continued Roosevelt. "The other will follow him because he'll be sure he's found a better spot to dig, and he'll want to be there to pull out the better specimens before his rival can."

A slow grin spread across Younger's face. "You know, he's got a point."

"He usually does," agreed Holliday.

Younger looked off to his left, where a cloud of dust seemed to be approaching them. "You'll have your chance pretty soon. That'll be the Professor."

6.

EDWARD DRINKER COPE WAS A LEAN MAN with a carefully trimmed brown mustache and clear blue eyes. Holliday estimated his age at forty-five, give or take a couple of years. It was clear from his appearance that he'd been digging in the earth all day, and just as clear that he'd cleaned himself up as best he could before returning to camp.

There were some thirty men with him, and as he dismounted he issued orders to them as they began unloading the wagons and unhitching the horses. He watched them for a few minutes; then, satisfied that they were doing their jobs the way he wanted, he turned and walked toward the log building that held most of the huge bones. He stopped when his gaze fell on Holliday and Roosevelt.

Holliday remained seated, but Roosevelt got to his feet.

"Professor," said Younger, also getting up, "we got ourselves a couple of famous visitors."

"I believe I recognize one of them," said Cope. "Mr. Roosevelt, isn't it?"

"At your service," said Roosevelt.

"I certainly hope so," said Cope. "I'd like you to use your connections to stop that thieving bastard Marsh from sabotaging my dig and stealing fossils that are rightly mine."

"I'll certainly talk to him," said Roosevelt easily.

"Do you know that son of a pig has some of his fat rich friends in Congress trying to pass a bill that would restrict where I can carry out my explorations?" continued Cope, spitting on the ground to show his contempt for Marsh.

"Explorations?" said Roosevelt curiously.

"For fossils."

"Since Wyoming's not a state, I hardly think the Congress of the United States has any authority here," said Roosevelt.

"I'm here because they harassed me when I was digging on the other side of the Mississippi," said Cope angrily.

"I'll look into it," said Roosevelt.

Cope turned to face Holliday. "Who's your friend, who doesn't seem to feel obligated to get to his feet when we're introduced?"

"Get up, Doc!" said Younger urgently.

"I'm comfortable right where I am," replied Holliday, making no effort to stand.

"Mr. Cope . . ." began Roosevelt.

"I prefer Professor," interrupted Cope.

"Professor Cope, say hello to Doc Holliday."

Cope stared at Holliday as if comparing him to the mental picture he'd formed of the legendary hero of the O.K. Corral. "You're really him?"

"Sure am," replied Holliday easily. "If you've got a toothache, I'll prove it to you."

"And you've killed thirty men?"

"Probably not," said Holliday.

"But you *are* the famous shootist?"

"Well, I'm a shootist when I'm not being a dentist or a gambler. How famous I am is probably a matter of some debate. There are certainly towns where I've got a little more fame than I'd like."

"Well, I'll be damned!" said Cope, obviously impressed. "Doc Holliday has come to *my* camp! I couldn't have asked for anything better!"

Holliday stared at him curiously.

"That bastard Marsh is no more than fifty miles from this spot," continued Cope. "What'll it cost for you to kill him?"

"I'm not an assassin for hire, Mr. Cope."

"Professor," said Cope.

"Professors don't hire killers, Mr. Cope," replied Holliday.

"Cole, get ready to earn your pay," snapped Cope, suddenly tense.

"I don't quite follow you, Professor," said Younger.

"If he won't kill Marsh, then it's obvious that Marsh has sent him here to kill *me*!" said Cope.

Holliday turned to Roosevelt. "And they say *he's* the reasonable one," he said sardonically.

"We're just here to make sure nothing untoward happens to *either* expedition," said Roosevelt to Cope.

"Other than sabotage, murder and Indian attacks, you mean?" said Cope.

"Actually, yes," said Holliday.

Cope stared at Holliday as if he might start foaming at the mouth momentarily. "All right," he said at last. "I'm not an unreasonable man. Suppose you tell me what's worse than what I just said."

"Whatever it is," said Holliday with a smile, "you're not going to stab it to death with that dagger you've got in your coat pocket."

"Dagger?" said Cope with a puzzled frown. Then, suddenly, he smiled. "Ah! You mean this!" He withdrew a whitish, foot-long pointed object. "You're the dentist. Why don't you tell me what it is?"

Holliday got painfully to his feet, then walked over.

"May I?" he asked, holding out his hand.

"Be my guest."

Holliday took it and studied it for a long moment. "If it's what I think it is, I'd hate to see the mouth it came out of."

"That's a *tooth?*" exclaimed Roosevelt, taking the specimen from Holliday and examining it eagerly.

"An allosaur tooth," answered Cope. "Not one of its canines, either."

"Can I see it?" said Younger, holding out his hand. Roosevelt reluctantly passed it over. "You know," continued Younger, "you could make a hell of a dagger out of this."

"What the hell kind of critter is an allosaur?" asked Holliday, suddenly interested.

"A carnivorous dinosaur," answered Cope. "Probably about the size of an Indian elephant, maybe a little bigger—and a *lot* faster."

"Something with a mouth that held a tooth like that actually existed?" persisted Holliday.

Cope smiled. "Now do you know why we dig."

"What could it possibly have fed on? Surely it would eat its habitat out in a matter of weeks."

"How much does an Indian elephant weigh, Mr. Roosevelt?" asked Cope, replacing the tooth in his pocket.

"Call me Theodore—and I'd guess four and a half tons on average, maybe five at the outside."

Cope nodded. "I think the allosaurs weighed about the same. What do you suppose their prey was?"

"I'm a believer in Mr. Darwin," answered Roosevelt, "so I know the elk and moose of today are the end results of evolution. I assume the owner of that tooth fed on an earlier version."

"And they would weigh what?" asked Cope.

"Maybe a ton," said Roosevelt. "A ton and a half at the outside."

"Well, I hate to disillusion you, Theodore," said Cope, "but so far we haven't found the remains—the fossils—of any mammals anywhere on Earth that are as old as the dinosaurs." He paused and shook his head. "No, our friend the allosaur almost certainly went after other dinosaurs for his dinner." He paused thoughtfully. "In fact, they very possibly hunted in packs."

"Excuse me for butting in," said Holliday, "but why would a four-ton carnivore need to hunt in packs? Seems to me he'd run out of food soon enough as a lone predator."

"Let me show you," said Cope, squatting down and using the tooth to create a rough drawing of a sauropod in the dirt. "We call this one a brontosaur, but he had a lot of similar-looking relatives."

"For a prey animal, he sure doesn't look like he's built for speed," opined Roosevelt.

"He isn't," answered Cope, still amused. "How much do you think he weighs, Theodore?"

Roosevelt shrugged. "Thick legs, all that neck and tail," he mused. "I'd say three thousand pounds."

"Doc?" asked Cope.

Holliday studied the drawing for another moment. "If he's really got the belly you gave him, maybe two tons."

"Cole?"

"I'm with Doc on this," answered Younger. "Maybe four thousand pounds."

Cope laughed.

"What's so damned funny?" asked Holliday.

"The smaller adults weighed a hundred thousand pounds," said Cope. "Based on the bones we've unearthed, the big ones, the bulls so to speak, went about seventy-five tons, maybe a little more."

"You're kidding!" exclaimed Holliday.

"Not at all," replied Cope. "Now do you understand why the allosaurs hunted in packs? One swipe of that brontosaur tail would cripple any allosaur that ever lived . . . and these brontosaurs weren't the biggest. They have a relative, the diplodocus, that measured more than one hundred feet in length."

"Well, now I know why you're digging," said Holliday, opening his flask, and taking a swallow. He offered it to Cope and Roosevelt, but both refused it. Younger reached out and grabbed it before it could be offered.

"I have a question, Professor," said Roosevelt.

"Yes?"

"How did something that big, that awesome, ever die out?"

"That's something we hope to find out."

"It'd take a lot more than my Winchester to bring something like that down, I'll wager," said Roosevelt, shooting Holliday a meaningful glance.

"Yeah, I think even cannon fire might just irritate him," agreed Holliday.

"No need to worry about it," said Cope. "These babies have been gone for millions of years." He stared from Roosevelt to Holliday and back again. "You want to see something *really* interesting?"

"Happy to!" said Roosevelt enthusiastically.

"Sure, why not?" said Holliday.

"Follow me," said Cope, leading them to the door of the log cabin. "I think it's still light enough that we won't need a candle."

He opened the door and entered, followed by his two visitors, and walked directly to a huge bone that extended the length of the cabin.

"What the hell *is* it?" asked Holliday.

"I'm not sure," said Cope. "It's clearly the femur—the leg bone—of one of the sauropods, but this fellow must have stood twenty, maybe twenty-two feet at the shoulder. We came up with it two days ago, and I'm not leaving this site until we find the rest of him."

"If you stay in one spot, won't the Comanche be better able to plan an attack, if indeed they're going to attack you in any kind of force?" asked Roosevelt.

"We haven't come upon any human remains there, so maybe they'll realize that it's not part of their burial ground," answered Cope.

"Wait a minute," said Roosevelt sharply.

"Yes?" asked Cope.

"You *knew* that this was a burial ground and you came here anyway?"

"I would go to hell itself in the interest of science, sir," said Cope harshly.

"Besides," said Younger, "we're digging up dinosaurs, not Indians. Haven't come to a human skeleton yet."

"That's not the way it works," said Holliday.

"Oh?" said Younger.

"I got the train to change its route around a sacred Apache burial ground back in Arizona," replied Holliday. "If you laid every Apache who'd ever lived end-to-end, you couldn't have reached from one end to the other, but the whole thing was still sacred."

"Then I'm sorry," said Cope, "but I can't let that stand in the way of the quest for knowledge. Besides, that's what I've got Cole Younger for."

"When we got here, he was guarding the bones you'd already found," noted Holliday, "not the bone-hunters who were out searching for more. I don't think you realize just what kind of danger your expedition is in."

"It's not a problem," said Cope with a sudden smile.

"Oh?" said Holliday. "Why not?"

"The notorious Doc Holliday is here now," said Cope. "One of you will guard the bones and the other will guard the men!"

"That's not what I'm here for," said Holliday, as Younger gave him an *I-could-have-told-you-so* grin.

"Name your price!" said Cope.

"Just a minute, Professor," said Roosevelt. "Let me confer privately with my friend, and perhaps we can work something out."

Cope nodded his agreement. "I'll be in here, cataloguing some of the finds."

Roosevelt put an arm around Holliday's shoulders and escorted him out in to the open air, stopping only when he was sure they were far enough away that Cope couldn't hear them.

"What the hell's this about, Theodore?" demanded Holliday. "You know why I'm here."

"I know."

"Well, then?" persisted Holliday.

"You heard him, Doc," said Roosevelt. "What'll you do if one of these flesh-eaters shows up right now?"

"Seriously? Run like hell, I suppose."

"I don't think there's a weapon in the world that can stop one, or do more than annoy it," said Roosevelt. "Now, it seems Cope has taken a liking to you, or at least has a use for you . . . and we both know you're not the easiest man to get along with, even on your good days. So it makes sense that you stay here, and that I go ingratiate myself with Marsh—but before I do that I'll stop by Cheyenne and send a telegram to Tom and Ned, telling them what we may be facing, and that if it comes to pass we're going to need something that will even the odds."

"No matter how you make it sound, the end result is that I'm riding shotgun for this guy," complained Holliday.

"Would you rather ride to Cheyenne in a day, and then approach Marsh on your own?" asked Roosevelt.

Holliday took another swallow from his flask, emptying it. "You know, this project was a lot simpler when it only had me thinking about it," he growled.

"Is that an agreement?" asked Roosevelt, flashing him a grin.

"I'd sooner let the Indians and the dinosaurs eat the whole fucking state than ride another day on that goddamned horse," muttered Holliday.

"Good!" sad Roosevelt. "We'll tell Cope that you agree, and that I've got business elsewhere. Both statements will be true, too."

"Temporarily," said Holliday.

"Temporarily," agreed Roosevelt.

The two men returned to the cabin and informed Cope that he had an extra shootist on his staff after all. It was all Younger could do not to laugh at what he considered Holliday's capitulation. Roosevelt decided to leave at daybreak—he gave Cope a story about some business he had in Cheyenne, which was almost true—and after dinner they sat around the campfire listening to Cope expound on some of the finds he'd made and others he planned to make. His intellect was apparent, and his enthusiasm was boundless, broken only when the topic of Marsh or one of Marsh's finds came up. Finally, since he had a hard day of digging ahead of him, Cope went to the tent he'd set up behind the cabin.

Roosevelt and Younger sat up another hour, then walked to the cluster of tents where the men slept.

Holliday found that he wasn't so much sleepy as thirsty, and since his flask was empty he walked to where he'd left his horse, planning to refill his flask from one of the two bottles he had tucked in his saddlebag.

As he approached his horse, he caught a flicker of motion out of the corner of his eye. Since the horse wasn't nervous, he decided it couldn't be a mountain lion or a bear, and that meant it was a Comanche, here to kill Cope or somehow destroy the cabin.

Holliday began humming aloud on the assumption the warrior

wouldn't think people hummed when they were aware of his presence, and began fiddling with the saddle bags.

A few seconds later there was a savage scream designed to startle him into immobility, and a Comanche brave leaped out from the thick shrubbery and came at him with a tomahawk. Holliday ducked and stepped under the horse, and the Comanche raced around the horse to confront him. He calmly pulled his pistol and fired point-blank at his attacker, who gave a surprised grunt and fell to the ground with a bullet between his eyes.

Roosevelt, Younger and most of the men raced out of their tents toward the sound of the gunshot, followed by Cope, who had clearly been awakened and looked like he was still half-asleep.

"Nice shot," said Younger as he examined the body.

"Theodore," said Holliday, "I don't know how many more I can kill before you-know-what happens. You'd better start riding to Cheyenne right now."

Roosevelt seemed about to protest, then thought better of it and nodded his agreement.

"We're sitting ducks out here in the dark," said Younger. "Let's go back to the cabin. Doc, you and I will take turns standing watch."

"First let's go hide this body in the woods," said Holliday, indicating a forest about a mile northeast of camp. "No sense letting his friends know what happened."

It took them about ten minutes to cart the corpse off, hide it under some leaves and branches, and return to camp. Roosevelt had already left.

"I'll sit watch if it's all the same to you," said Holliday.

Younger agreed, leaving Holliday to sit out by a fire, wondering just *what* he was watching for.

7.

OLLIDAY AWOKE TO THE SMELL OF BEEF cooking over a fire. He wrinkled his nose, tried to go back to sleep, but couldn't shut out the voices coming from his left.

Finally he sat up, realized he'd been sleeping on a blanket stretched beneath him on the floor of the cabin. He looked around, saw that he was the only person remaining in the cabin, got to his feet, and made his way painfully to the doorway, where he winced at the brightness of the scene before him.

Half a dozen of Cope's men—three white, one black, two Chinese—were squatting around the fire while a Mexican tended to the meat. Cole Younger was standing by the door.

"Good morning, Doc," he said.

"Never saw one yet," growled Holliday.

"Cheer up. We'll have breakfast ready in a couple of minutes."

"Meat?"

"Steaks," said Younger.

"I think I'll drink my breakfast, thanks," muttered Holliday.

"I'll tell Jorge to put on some coffee."

"Don't bother," said Holliday, inhaling the odor of frying meat deeply and fighting back the urge to vomit. "I've got my breakfast right here." He tapped the pocket that contained his flask.

"Too early in the day for me," said Younger.

"Too early in the day for me, too," replied Holliday. "That's why I need a drink."

Younger laughed and gave Holliday a friendly slap on the back. "You're a right funny man! I'm glad we never had to face each other down in Texas."

"Whack me on the back one more time," said Holliday, placing his handkerchief to his mouth and coughing, "and we may face off right here and now."

"Like I said, you're a damned funny feller," said Younger.

"Am I smiling?" replied Holliday. He looked around. "Where's the boss?"

"The Professor?" repeated Younger. "Said he wanted to scout out a site to the north and east of here. He'll be back soon."

"North and east?" said Holliday sharply.

"Yeah."

Holliday pointed. "That way?"

"Right."

"And you let him go?"

"Why not?" asked Younger. "I'm not his keeper."

"That's where we hid the body last night. They've got to know he's missing, and you let Cope go off alone in that direction. I assume he's alone?"

"I never thought of that, Doc," admitted Younger, frowning.

"I also assume he's no marksman?"

"He doesn't even carry a gun."

"All right," said Holliday. "I'll go after him."

"I'll come with you," said Younger.

Holliday shook his head. "Probably nothing'll happen—but if it does we need someone who they'll listen to in order to organize a defense."

Younger nodded. "Yeah, you got a point. We haven't heard any gunfire, so he's probably okay—but if he's not . . ."

"If he's not, he's dead, and this figures to be their next target," concluded Holliday. "Where the hell's my horse?"

Younger told one of the Chinese to fetch it while Holliday checked his pistol and gun belt.

"You need three or four more bullets, Doc," noted Younger, studying his belt.

"Makes no difference. If I've used so many that I have to reach behind me for the missing ones, I'm already dead."

The man arrived with Holliday's horse.

"Give a sick old man a hand up," said Holliday. The man cupped his hands, Holliday placed his foot in them, and the man helped boost him to the saddle.

"You can't imagine how much I hate horses," were Holliday's parting words as he rode off to the north and east.

It took him about five minutes to reach the spot where they'd left the Indian, but when he got there he couldn't find any sign of the corpse.

"Shit!" he growled. "Either you're collecting human bones too, or the Comanche found their warrior and took him off to bury him, hopefully where you won't dig him up again while he's still fresh."

He dismounted, tied his horse to a small tree, and began examining the area. From the moccasined footprints, he concluded that three Comanche had come across the body. It would have had to be since sunrise, since the corpse was too well-hidden to have been found in the dark.

Holliday frowned. Why had three braves been just five minutes away—at a slow walk—from the camp in the daylight?

He heard a horse whinny off to his left, he turned, and there, perhaps sixty yards away, was a row of some twenty Comanche warriors.

"I hate mornings!" said Holliday as he turned to face them.

He stared at the warriors, who sat motionless on their horses, staring back at him.

"Let's go," he muttered, flexing his right hand. "Or are you just killing time until lunch?"

One of the Comanche put an arrow in his bow and let it fly. It hit the ground twenty yards short of Holliday. He wanted to throw back his head and laugh at such a futile and misguided action, but he was afraid if he did it would bring on a coughing fit and he didn't want to show any weakness.

Instead he pointed his finger at the warrior in the middle, pretended to shoot him, and then went through the pantomime of holstering his finger.

A burly warrior from the right side of the line began moving his horse forward. Holliday considered his options. The one thing he didn't want to do was show them how short a firing range his pistol had before the bullet lost both accuracy and velocity. He decided that if he faced the brave with his hand poised above his holster they would see how puny his weapon was at even thirty yards. Finally he decided to fold his arms across his chest as if he was totally unconcerned and was just biding his time before drawing and firing his weapon, which in a way was true, though not for the reasons he hoped to imply.

The warrior was fifty yards away, then forty, and then two more warriors began urging their horses forward.

Suddenly they stopped and looked at something Holliday couldn't see, well off to his left.

"Don't worry, Doc," said Cole Younger's voice. "We'll be there in another half minute."

Holliday turned in the direction of the voices, and suddenly saw a column of some thirty men—Younger, the six from the campfire, and close to twenty-five more—approaching him in single file. They fanned out on either side of him, brought their mounts to a stop, and faced the Comanche warriors, who held stock-still, staring back at them.

"What the hell are you doing here?" said Holliday. "Not that I'm not glad to see you."

"I got to thinking," said Younger. "I'm being paid to ride shotgun and keep the Indians at bay, not to guard a bunch of bones. And you've seen those bones. It'd take four of them to lift one of the big ones, and most of their ponies couldn't carry 'em anyway, so even if they wanted the damned bones they'd still be there trying to load them for the next couple of days—and I knew you weren't going more than a mile or two from camp, so why the hell not ride out, just in case they'd arranged this very type of reception for you?"

"That's some pretty smart thinking," said Holliday, never taking his eyes off the warriors. "Just keep on doing it while I'm around."

"You'd think being a soon-to-be famous author would make thinking easier," complained Younger wryly. "If we fire even a single shot, we're probably going to get in a shootout that'll kill all of one side and two-thirds of the other, and truth to tell I ain't ready to hobnob in hell with Jim and Bob just yet." He paused. "On the other hand, if we don't do anything, sooner or later the Professor is going to come back this way, and if they see him first . . ."

"They won't know it's Cope," said Holliday. "He's not wearing a uniform or anything."

"True," agreed Younger. "But I've seen what they do to lone white men."

"Not just white men," chimed in one of the Chinese. "They got my brother two weeks ago."

"Well, we can't just spend the day staring at each other," said Holliday. He frowned as he stared at the Comanche. "You know," he continued, "if they're hunting for Cope they know he's not here, and it makes sense that they'd go to wherever they thought he was. So I think they were here because of the dead Indian. Either the guys who found him brought some of their friends and relations back to show them where it happened, or reconstruct it, or else they were all in the area, not looking for a fight but just because it's Comanche land, and they found the body and before they could figure out what to do next, I showed up."

"What are you getting at, Doc?" asked Younger.

"I think if we ride back to camp, they're going to turn around and go home. They're not looking for Cope, and since no one's started shooting yet, they're not out for revenge—at least not here and not now."

"And what about the Professor?"

"He'll come back when he's found whatever the hell it is that he's looking for."

Younger stared at the Comanche for a long minute, then turned back to Holliday. "It's worth a try."

"I'm not guaranteeing it'll work," said Holliday, "just that it makes sense. But tell them that nobody draws a gun or aims a rifle until *you* do, and you don't do it until *I* do."

It took Younger only a moment to pass the word up and down the line. Then, on his signal, they turned and began walking their horses back to camp. Holliday climbed onto his own horse and brought up the rear.

They reached camp without incident, split up into small groups, and awaited Cope's return. He showed up an hour later, looking very excited.

"I believe I've found a nest of fossilized eggs!" he enthused.

"Good," said Holliday. "Beats the hell out of having steak for breakfast."

Cope stared at him but said nothing.

"By the way, Professor," said Younger, "did you see any Comanche while you were looking for . . . for *eggs?*" He couldn't hide his disillusionment in any grown man who would go searching for eggs.

"Not a one," said Cope. "I think they've cleared out of this area." He went into the cabin to scribble in one of his notebooks.

Younger shook his head. "How the hell can he find eggs that have been buried for a million years, but not see Indians who were on the warpath an hour ago?"

"Just lucky, I guess," said Holliday.

"*Lucky?*" repeated Younger incredulously.

"Two men leave camp an hour apart. One finds ancient eggs that'll make him famous. The other finds a Comanche war party." Holliday allowed himself the luxury of a grim smile. "Who'd you rather be?"

8.

OLLIDAY SPENT TWO MORE DAYS in Cope's camp and decided to leave. Cope hadn't paid him, so he didn't consider himself an employed bodyguard—or a fossil guard either—and he made up his mind to ride to Marsh's camp and make sure that Roosevelt had sent the telegram to Edison and arrived healthy and whole. The truth of the matter was that he found Younger boring and Cope all but incomprehensible.

He offered to buy one of Cope's wagons so he wouldn't have to ride the whole distance, but the expedition needed them and his offer was politely but firmly refused. He stopped by the supply tent long enough to pack a couple of meals of beef jerky, which he devoutly hoped he wouldn't have to eat, and then he was off in the general direction of Marsh's camp.

He'd gone about ten miles along a high, rocky trail and found that every single joint in his body hurt, so he pulled his horse up, dismounted, and sat down with his back against the broad trunk of a solitary tree. He fingered his deck of cards and wondered if he had time for a half hour of solitaire—after all, since he didn't know exactly where Marsh's camp was, he might be just two or three miles from it. But then he decided that it was just as likely that he was two or three days from it, and he wanted to scout out a better place to spend the night, so he sat for another ten minutes and then painfully mounted his horse.

He covered a few more miles, the trail leveled out and the landscape became greener, and as he reached the outskirts of a forest he realized that he was getting hungry. He didn't relish the effort of chewing on the beef jerky, but while he was sure there were all kinds of edible things growing around him, he had no idea which they might be. He dismounted, pulled out the jerky, took one bite of it, and made a face. He didn't know which leaves or grasses might be harmful, but then, he'd been poisoning his system with alcohol for as far back as he could remember, so what further harm could a little more poison do?

It occurred to him that if his horse ate it, it was probably safe for humans. Not necessarily tasty, but safe. So instead of tying his horse to a tree or a bush he led him to the shrubbery and watched to see what the animal ate.

He was still watching his horse when he heard another horse snort twice, and became aware that he was no longer alone. He turned and found himself facing a grizzled man who was pointing a gun at him.

"Nice day, ain't it, neighbor?" said the man.

Holliday merely stared at him.

"'Course, it could be a little warmer," continued the man. "I'm afraid you might freeze your ass off once the sun goes down."

"I'll be fine," said Holliday.

"Well, maybe you will," agreed the man. "But you'll be without your horse and your gun and any money you got with you."

"I didn't see you at Cope's camp, so you must be working for Marsh," said Holliday. "Why not just take me to him?"

"Never heard of neither of 'em," said the man. "The gun first, I think."

"Whatever you say," said Holliday, raising his left hand in the air while very gently, very carefully withdrawing his pistol from its holster with his right hand. He made a production of pointing it butt first to the grizzled man, and as the man reached for it, Holliday spun it in his hand so that the muzzle was pointing at the would-be thief. He fired point-blank at the man's belly, blowing him off his horse.

"You aren't exactly the brightest bear in these woods, are you?" said Holliday contemptuously, standing over the fallen man.

"Who the hell *are* you?" gasped the man as Holliday leisurely aimed the gun between his eyes.

"When you get to hell, which'll be any second now, tell the gatekeeper that Doc Holliday has sent him another one. You'll have plenty of company."

He fired the gun, and the man shuddered convulsively, then lay still—

—but both horses panicked and began running off before Holliday could grab the reins of either. The effort brought forth another coughing fit that lasted almost three minutes, and left his chin and his shirtfront covered with blood. He spent another minute gasping for breath, coughed again, and finally had to lean against a tree in order to stay on his feet.

"Wonderful," he muttered. "Just wonderful."

He surveyed his surroundings and saw a number of birds, some still screeching in response to the noise of the gunshots, others settling back down after flying up in alarm.

He waited until he had recovered enough strength to speak in his normal voice. "You'd damned well better be one of these critters," said Holliday, "because I can't walk from here to either camp."

Holliday looked into the trees. None of the birds was paying him the least attention.

"I mean it," he said. "We renegotiate our deal, or I quit here and now."

A squirrel approached him, and when it was about ten feet away it slowly grew and morphed into Geronimo.

"You are a killer," said the Apache, "but you are a man of your word. And you gave me your word you would keep these two grave robbers from further desecrating the Comanche burial ground."

"Use your eyes, damn it!" snarled Holliday. "I can't walk twenty paces without coughing my lungs out, and I'm miles from both camps."

"You made a bargain," said Geronimo.

"You misled me," replied Holliday. "You said you'd restore my health."

"I have explained that," said Geronimo. "And in case it has already escaped your memory," he added, pointing to the robber's corpse, "you just killed that man, which demonstrates that you can still function as you always did."

"That man had the brains and foresight of a demented toad!" snapped Holliday. "I want a new deal. A year of pain and a lifetime in hell isn't much of a bargain."

Geronimo stared at him for a long moment. 'We have an agreement," he said at last.

"It doesn't make any sense anyway," growled Holliday. "You opposed all the other medicine men who acted in concert against you and lifted the spell that kept white men east of the Mississippi. Why the hell can't you deal with two goddamned bone collectors?"

"You are just a man, using the arguments and threats of men to make them stop and go elsewhere, and that is clearly in the interest of the Comanche. But I made the agreement with Roosevelt. They believe that I am their enemy, and if they know that I am involved in any way, even though I want the same thing that they do, they will eventually do exactly what you are here to prevent them from doing."

"Can they even hurt you?"

"They can," confirmed Geronimo. "But more importantly, they can hurt my people—and before I will let that happen, I will sacrifice myself if need be. But this can all be avoided if you and Roosevelt can make the grave robbers go elsewhere."

"You'd really die for your people?" said Holliday.

"When one is a leader, one must accept the responsibilities of leadership."

"That's one good reason never to run for office."

"Speak to your friend Roosevelt," said Geronimo. "The day will come when he bears far greater responsibilities than you can imagine."

"He's not exactly my friend," said Holliday. "Hell, I've only had two friends since I came out here. They were both Earps. One's dead and the other's no longer speaking to me."

"He is a better friend than you have ever had."

"Because he likes me?" asked Holliday curiously.

Geronimo shook his head. "Because he is Roosevelt."

"I don't understand."

"That is why you have only had two friends, and one of them will not speak to you," answered Geronimo.

"Touché," said Holliday wryly.

"The sun will set in another hour," noted Geronimo. "What will you do, Holliday?"

"Die, probably," answered Holliday. "I've got no food, no shelter, and no horse."

"I will help you this one time," said Geronimo. "It would serve neither of our interests for you to die here and now."

"I could surely use a buckboard, a team of horses, and a bottle of whiskey," suggested Holliday.

"No, Holliday. You would surely misuse them."

Holliday was about to reply when he felt a sudden dizziness. He thought he was about to black out and collapse, but somehow he found that he couldn't. He shook his head to clear it, then realized that far from standing, he was seated atop his horse. He checked his saddle bags and found to his annoyance that Geronimo had reunited him with his horse but had removed his liquor.

He realized that his surroundings had changed. The forest was no longer there, the land was flat, not much was growing except grass and weeds, and a small creek ran off to his left. He could hear noises up ahead—voices, axes chopping wood, even a man playing a banjo.

He urged his horse forward, anxious to reach Marsh's camp and get some food. Then he saw something unusual off to his left, and rode a little closer.

It was a dead man, hanging by his neck from a makeshift gallows, and attached to his foot was a sign that contained a single word: *Saboteur*.

"Yep, we're here," said Holliday grimly, urging his horse forward.

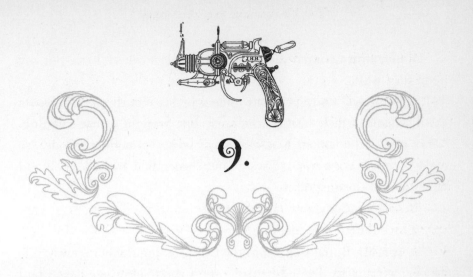

9.

OLLIDAY RODE INTO THE CAMP, which was larger—and, he noted, better kept—than Cope's. There were three main buildings. He assumed one was a storage house, one a bunkhouse, and he had no idea what the third might be.

A tall man with a neatly trimmed beard and flowing blond hair that reached down to his shoulders emerged from one of the buildings and approached him.

"Mind if I ask what your business is, stranger?" he asked.

I wonder what your reaction would be if I told you I was retired? thought Holliday. Aloud he said, "I'm looking for my friend, Theodore Roosevelt."

Suddenly a huge smile spread across the bearded man's face. "Well, I'll be damned. I thought we might never meet. You're Doc Holliday, right?"

Holliday nodded his head. "Right."

The man extended a hand. "And I'm Bill Cody! Buffalo Bill at your service."

Holliday dismounted carefully. "Got a place where I can put my horse for a while?"

"Absolutely." Cody put two fingers in his mouth and emitted a shrill whistle, which startled the horse but brought a man running. "This here is the famous Doc Holliday's horse," announced Cody, "so make sure he's got grain and water and shade. Take his saddle off and wipe some of the dust off it."

"Yessir, Mr. Cody, sir," said the man.

"That's Buffalo Bill, damn it!" snapped Cody.

"Yessir, Mr. Buffalo, sir," said the man, leading the horse away.

"It's getting harder and harder to find good help these days," said Cody to Holliday. Then he shrugged. "Oh, well, I suppose he's good with a shovel."

"Is Theodore around?" asked Holliday.

"I believe he's out hunting for dinner," replied Cody. "Remarkable man. Never slows down, never stops. He's got damned near the equivalent of a college education in bones from Professor Marsh, he runs to and from the dig site twice a day just to keep fit, he brings back enough deer and elk to feed the whole damned camp, and when everyone else is sleeping you can see the lantern burning in his tent while he sits there reading his books."

"That's Theodore, all right," agreed Holliday. "Where's Mr. Marsh?"

"Mucking around with his bones in there," said Cody, jerking a thumb in the direction of the largest building. "And let me give you a hint: Don't call him Mister."

"Yeah, I know," said Holliday. "Same with Cope."

"What is it with these geniuses?" laughed Cody.

Holliday shrugged. "Beats the hell out of me."

"Ah, well, the pay is good, and the rewards are even better," said Cody, lighting up a cigar.

"Rewards?"

Cody smiled. "Why do you think I closed my Wild West show down? If the Professor digs up anything besides bones, like, say, the mummified corpse of one of these dinosaurs, I get to exhibit it in my show for a year."

"Not a bad deal," agreed Holliday.

"Oh, it'll be a hell of a draw," enthused Cody. "But there's something that could draw even better."

"Oh?"

Cody nodded. "Doc Holliday. Hell, every man and boy from here to Maine has read about the O.K. Corral, and how you tracked down Billy the Kid."

"I'm a dying man," answered Holliday. "I don't plan to spend my final days being gaped at by a bunch of strangers."

"Well, if you change your mind, the offer's open, and I think you'll like what I'm willing to pay."

"You don't want a skinny, used-up, consumptive shootist who's got one foot in the grave," said Holliday. "Get this Annie Oakley I've heard about. Give the people something to look at."

Cody grinned. "I'm ahead of you, Doc. I've already signed her, and as soon as this excursion is over, I'm going after Calamity Jane too."

"She's no shootist," said Holliday.

"True," agreed Cody. "But she's the best damned storyteller you'll ever run across. Even gave the scribes some cock-and-bull story about how she had Bill Hickok's baby, and they bought it." He chuckled. "Not a one of them could count."

"How about Belle Starr?" asked Holliday. "From all I hear, that lady *is* a shootist."

"But a dumb one," replied Cody. "They arrested her again just before I came out here."

"Well, two out of three won't be bad."

"I'd still rather have Doc Holliday."

Holliday shook his head. "Some other lifetime."

A burly, bearded, balding man walked out of the largest building, wearing a dust-covered suit and tie, and Holliday knew that this must be Othniel Charles Marsh.

"If that's a saboteur, Mr. Cody, you should have shot and hung him up the minute he arrived," said Marsh. "And if he's a visiting dignitary, then you should have brought him to me and introduced us."

"I'm no saboteur, and I'm sure as hell no dignitary," said Holliday.

Marsh frowned. "Then what are you?"

"Just a used-up old dentist."

Marsh turned questioningly to Cody.

"Say hello to the most famous dentist in the West," said Cody with a grin. "Doc Holliday, this here gentleman is the most famous paleontologist in the country, Professor Othniel Charles Marsh."

"Pleased to meet you," said Holliday.

Marsh frowned. "If you are, then extend your hand like a gentleman."

Holliday frowned, but reached his hand forward for Marsh to clasp it in his own firm grip.

"You'll stay for dinner, of course," said Marsh.

Holliday nodded. "Thanks."

"Mr. Roosevelt—another visitor—should be back with the main course any time now."

"I know," replied Holliday. "He's who I've come to see."

Marsh glared at him for a moment, then turned on his heel and re-entered the building without another word.

Holliday stared at the spot where Marsh had been. "Is he like that all the time?"

"This is one of his good days," replied Cody with an amused grin. "I assume you've come from Cope's camp. How is *he* to deal with?"

"Pleasanter," answered Holliday. "Though I'm told that the easiest way to put him in a foul mood is to mention Professor Marsh."

"Marsh is always in a foul mood," said Cody, pausing to pull out a cigar and light it. "But if you want to put him in a killing rage, just mention Cope."

"You know," said Holliday thoughtfully, "I've seen my share of altercations, even been in a few of 'em, but I can't recall any two men ever hating each other quite like these two."

"You want to know the crazy part?" asked Cody. "They were actually friends right after the War Between the States. Even went out on a couple of digs together."

"Hard to imagine," said Holliday.

"They've been at each other's throats for maybe fifteen years now," continued Cody. "I think Professor Cope has used up most of his fortune on this . . . I don't know what you call it, a contest or a feud. Professor Marsh is getting close to broke, too, but he's got some college and museum money behind him."

"Damned waste of money, if you ask me," offered Holliday, backing up a step as the breeze changed and began wafting Cody's smoke toward him.

"Oh, I don't know. When they started, only three species of dinosaur had been found in the country. Last I heard, we're nearing eleven hundred and twenty species, all but those first three and maybe twenty others due to Professors Marsh and Cope. Maybe if they didn't hate each other's guts we'd still have only three species."

"Well, just speaking from one minute of personal experience," said Holliday, "I can sympathize with Cope. I don't have any problem at all hating Marsh's guts."

"He doesn't know he's being rude or mean," said Cody. "He just doesn't think about anything but dinosaurs."

"And Cope," said Holliday.

"And Cope," agreed Cody.

Suddenly the stillness of the afternoon was broken by a single rifle shot.

"Dinner," said Cody with a smile.

Holliday nodded. "I can't remember Theodore ever missing what he aimed at, or needing two shots to bring down a deer or an elk."

"He's a remarkable man, like I said," remarked Cody. "I'd love to get him in my show, but somehow I know he's destined for more important things than that."

"With him the sky's the limit," agreed Holliday. "I imagine someday he could even be Mayor of New York City."

"I wouldn't be at all surprised," said Cody. His cigar went out and he re-lit it. and offered one to Holliday, who refused.

"Wish I could, but my lungs aren't up to it," said Holliday. "On the other hand, if you've got a bottle stashed somewhere around here . . ."

"You know, I just happen to," said Cody with a smile. "Let's mosey over to the bunkhouse and . . ." He stopped and looked off to his right. "Ah, hell—too late. Here's Theodore."

Roosevelt rode into camp, leading a pack horse that had a dead deer sluing over its back. Cody whistled again, four different notes this time, and a crew of men emerged from the bunkhouse to unload the deer.

"Glad we weren't digging this afternoon," said Cody, "or you and I would have had to skin and gut the damned thing. Welcome back, Theodore."

"Thanks," said Roosevelt, joining them. "Hello, Doc. What are *you* doing here?"

"Just making sure that you sent the telegram," said Holliday.

Roosevelt frowned. "Do I strike you as irresponsible?"

"No, of course not," said Holliday. "I also wanted to make sure the Comanche hadn't paid you a surprise visit along the way. And to tell you the truth, I was getting tired of Cope's camp."

"You're going to get tired of this one a lot quicker," said Roosevelt.

"I know."

"Ah!" said Roosevelt with a grin. "You've already met Professor Marsh."

"Yes."

"What do you think of him?"

"He's probably not a lot worse than Johnny Ringo when he was mean drunk."

Roosevelt threw back his head and laughed.

"I'm glad *somebody* finds it funny," said Cody.

"Any trouble with the Comanche here?" asked Holliday.

"They watch us from time to time, from a distance," answered Cody. "But that's about it."

"None at Cope's camp either," replied Holliday. "Though we came close the other day." He turned to Roosevelt. "That's why I wanted to make sure you sent it."

"I think our mutual friend may have overestimated the problem," said Roosevelt.

"I hope so," said Holliday. "But . . ."

"But?"

"But I saw him a few hours ago, and *he* doesn't seem to think so."

"I have absolutely no idea what you two are talking about," complained Cody.

"And with a little luck, you never will," said Roosevelt. "Now let's go start a fire so we're not eating raw deer."

"We've got men to do that, Theodore."

"Got to keep fit," said Roosevelt, heading toward a pile of firewood. "Besides, why should they have all the fun?"

Cody turned to Holliday. "Your friend has a very odd notion of fun."

"If you think *that's* odd," said Holliday, half-smiling, "you ought to see his notion of relaxing."

10.

THEY WERE SEATED, all forty of them, at a long wooden table which hadn't been anywhere to be seen when Holliday arrived. He, Roosevelt and Cody were invited—it sounded more like *ordered*, to Holliday—to sit at the head of the table with Marsh, who spent the first half hour explaining how he had put together the scattered remains of a stegosaurus and offering his opinion as to the reason its back and tail looked the way they did. Like Cope, he seemed unable to go more than a few minutes without explaining what a vile blaggard his mortal enemy was; and like Cope, he seemed to have only two interests in his life—unearthing fossils and destroying his rival.

"So how many species have you discovered?" asked Roosevelt.

"It's difficult to say," replied Marsh. "There are certain sauropods that *may* be different species, or there may simply be an enormous variation of size within one species. Same with the carnosaurs. I've got one I've tentatively called a Utahraptor that we found a few hundred miles from here, but until I can get back to Yale and really go to work, I can't be sure that it's not simply an undersized version of another carnosaur species."

"So you really have no idea how many species you've discovered?" suggested Holliday.

"Of course I have an idea," said Marsh irritably. "Somewhere between six hundred and six hundred fifty. How many does that Pennsylvania liar claim?"

Holliday shrugged. "I don't know. But I know he's written and submitted more than a thousand scientific papers."

"Hah!" snapped Marsh contemptuously. "If he killed an ant by stepping on it, he'd publish a paper on squashed ants."

"It's too bad the two of you can't work together," said Roosevelt.

Marsh stared coldly at him for a full minute. Finally he spoke. "If you suggest that again, I shall have to ask you to leave my camp."

Cody flashed an I-told-you-so grin at Holliday.

"So, Doctor Holliday," said Marsh, "tell me about the O.K. Corral."

"Not much to tell," replied Holliday. "It's maybe ten yards by twenty, nothing much to recommend it. And please call me Doc."

"I meant the gunfight at the O.K. Corral," said Marsh, trying to hide his irritation.

Holliday resisted the urge to explain, for maybe the hundredth time, that it took place in an alley *behind* the corral. "It was over pretty fast," he said. "There was me and the Earps on one side, and two Clantons, two McLaurys, and a kid called Billy Claiborne on the other. Someone fired the first shot—it could even have been me, but things happened so fast I can't be sure—and in maybe thirty seconds both McLaurys and Billy Clanton were dead, Morgan and Virgil Earp were shot up, and Ike Clanton and the Claiborne kid were running for their lives."

"Details," said Cody. "How about some details?"

"Bill, you've fired guns," said Holliday. "You know how much smoke just one gun makes. Imagine maybe a dozen of them firing again and again, all within twenty feet of each other, with buildings on each side so the smoke couldn't float away."

"Shit!" said Cody with a grin. "How'd you know when it was over."

"When we didn't hear any more shots on the other side of the smoke," answered Holliday truthfully.

"It sounds terribly inefficient," opined Marsh.

"We didn't choose the fight or the venue," said Holliday. "Besides, I'd have said picking one spot instead of another to dig for something that lived a million years ago was inefficient."

Marsh chuckled. "I study the terrain and try to reconstruct what it was like, not a million, but many millions of years ago. Were those always cliffs, or were they once the bed or bank of a huge river ten or thirty million years ago? You try to get a picture of what the land looked like when the dinosaurs lived, and then you pick the likeliest place to dig. You estimate where the ground was softest, where a corpse would sink in a few days, because if it didn't, then the ancestors of ants and scavengers like hyenas and vultures would eventually consume it, bones and all." He stared at Holliday. "You look dubious. Let me suggest that my record—and even that Pennsylvania bastard's record—gives proof that it works."

"Can't argue with that," replied Holliday, who was fast losing interest. He let Roosevelt continue questioning Marsh on the basics of paleontology long after most of the men had left the table, and, as usual, was impressed by the New Yorker's seemingly endless thirst for knowledge of any kind.

Suddenly there was a commotion at the edge of the camp, and then a familiar voice called out, "Damn it, Doc! Tell these assholes that I ain't a Comanche!"

Holliday got up and, joined by Cody and Roosevelt, walked over to see the cause of the disturbance. They found Cole Younger seated atop his horse, hands in the air as half a dozen guns were pointed at him.

"He's okay," said Holliday. "Put your guns away."

"We don't even know if *you're* okay," snapped one of the men. He turned to Cody. "What do you say?"

"It's Cole Younger, all right," said Cody. "Last I heard he was riding shotgun for Cope. At any rate, he sure as hell ain't no Comanche."

The men holstered their guns and drifted away.

"What the hell are you doing here?" asked Holliday.

"Professor Cope sent me," replied Younger.

"I'm not working for him, and I'm not going back there, at least not for a while," said Holliday.

Younger shook his head. "You got it wrong, Doc. He don't care if you come back or not."

"Then why—?"

"We found the body of the white man you killed," continued Younger, "and he sent me ahead to see if you were okay. There were no tracks, no signs, no nothing, so I guessed that your Apache friend stepped in, and I figured if you were still alive you'd be here with Teddy."

"Theodore," Roosevelt corrected him.

"Too hard to spell," offered Cody. "You run for office again, they're going to call you Teddy."

"I'll worry about it when the time comes," said Roosevelt. He looked up at Younger. "In the meantime, you might as well dismount and give your horse a rest. You're surely not going back in the dark, not with all these Comanche around."

"I was hoping for an invite," said Younger, climbing down from his horse.

"Nobody tried to bother you along the way?" asked Holliday.

"You mean like the one who clearly bothered you?" asked Younger with a smile.

"I meant Indians."

"Never saw a one," answered Younger. "You got any idea who it was that you killed?"

"Just some poor bastard who was down on his luck," said Holliday.

"Well, yeah, he was," agreed Younger. "But once upon a time he was a helluva gambler named Ace High McGregor. Owned his own casino and even was a partner in a hotel back in Denver."

"What happened?" asked Roosevelt.

"What do you think happened?" replied Younger. "He knew there were better hands than a king-high flush, but he didn't figure anyone would get one on the same deal. Lost the casino and the hotel, and before long he lost his friends, his wife, and his health, one after the other."

"Ace High McGregor," mused Cody. "I've heard of him."

"I haven't," said Holliday.

"I'm a stranger here myself," added Roosevelt.

"So where's the drinkin' stuff?" asked Younger as one of the men led his horse off to the stabling area.

"We've got some where we keep the foodstuffs," replied Cody, leading them off. "Professor Marsh doesn't like to see anyone drunk when he's paying their wages, but he makes the occasional exception when they come up with something real valuable."

"Like gold?" asked Holliday.

Cody and Younger both laughed in amusement.

"You don't know these madmen at all," said Younger.

"Something valuable is something that'll get 'em in all the papers back East," said Cody.

"And shove the other guy out," added Younger.

"Here we are," said Cody as they reached the table where they'd recently eaten, and which was now lit by lanterns. "Looks like the boss has gone back to his tent or his bones. Either way I don't figure he'll be coming back right soon, so let me pull out a bottle."

The others seated themselves on the wooden benches some distance from the tents and the fossil-holding buildings, and Cody returned a moment later with a half-full bottle of whiskey and four glasses. He poured one for himself, Holliday and Younger, and was preparing to pour one for Roosevelt until the Easterner signaled that he didn't care for any.

"See any Comanche on the way in?" asked Holliday.

"A couple," answered Younger, downing his drink and pouring another.

"No problems?" said Holliday. "I assume we'd have heard gunfire if there'd been any."

"Know what I think?" said Younger. "I think they're afraid of your Apache friend."

"What friend?" asked Cody, also emptying his glass and refilling it.

"I doubt it," said Holliday, ignoring Cody's question.

"It makes sense," persisted Younger. "There are twenty, maybe thirty thousand of them, and less than a hundred of us when you put both expeditions together. Why the hell haven't they killed us all?"

"When we annoy them enough, they probably will," said Holliday.

"I agree with Doc," said Cody. "We're going about this all wrong, and sooner or later it's going to lead to trouble."

"How can we be doing it wrong?" asked Younger. "I mean, hell, we're digging in the dirt. You know of any other way to dig up these monsters' bones?"

Cody shook his head. "You're not following me."

"Enlighten us all," suggested Roosevelt.

"You want to make sure the Comanche leave us alone?" said Cody. "Put 'em on salary."

"What?" said Younger unbelievingly.

"Pay 'em. They may be savages, but they're bright enough not to bite the hand that feeds them."

"They're *not* savages," said Roosevelt adamantly.

"Pay them with *what?*" demanded Younger. "They don't use money."

"Now that we've crossed the river they're going to start," said Cody with conviction.

"That figures, coming from you," said Younger angrily.

"Why would you say that?" asked Cody with a dangerous edge in his voice.

"You're no shootist," said Younger. "You're a wheeler-dealer who's looking for a fast buck."

"What difference does it make? Maybe I can't beat Doc Holliday to the draw, but so what? Hell, the graveyards are full of men who couldn't beat him to the draw. And before you get too high and mighty, Cole Younger, don't forget that you didn't win the only famous gunfight you were in, up there in Minnesota. They shot up your whole damned family."

"And you're the guy Mr. Marsh is paying to hold off the Indians!" snarled Younger.

"He's *Professor* Marsh," shot back Cody, growing red in the face, "and what the hell difference does it make to you whether I shoot his enemies or buy them off with money or women or a chance to be in my Wild West show?"

"Goddamn it, Bill Cody!" roared Younger. "You're giving shootists a bad name!"

"Well, let's walk away from the table and see if I can't give 'em a better name," said Cody.

They both walked about fifty feet from the table and stood there, facing each other.

"We'd better do something," said Roosevelt to Holliday.

Holliday sighed deeply. "I know," he replied, getting to his feet and walking over until he stood between the two men.

"You really mean to do this?" asked Holliday.

"Damned right!" growled Younger. "I've had enough of the famous Buffalo Bill. He's just a goddamned hustler!"

"You backshoot a couple of people and get thrown into one jail after another and people think you know how to handle yourself in a fight," said Cody. "I'm sorry I ever offered you a job in my show. The only thing you'd be good for is cleaning up after the horses."

"Get ready to die, you son of a bitch!" shouted Younger.

"I'm not afraid to die," said Cody. Suddenly he sneered. "Especially not when I'm facing *you!*"

"All right," said Holliday. "You've been drinking, and you aren't as used to it as I am. Your blood's up, and nothing's going to stop you from having it out here and now."

"Right!" growled Cody.

"Damned straight!" said Younger.

"Okay, if I can't talk you out of it, I can't talk you out of it. But there's one thing you should know." Holliday paused and they both turned to him expectantly. "I'm challenging the winner."

"*What?*" demanded Younger.

"This is some kind of joke, right?" said Cody nervously.

"No joke at all," said Holliday. "If you're too drunk and too dumb to call it off, then you're no use to Cope, Marsh, or me, and I'll take great pleasure into lowering both their payrolls.

Younger turned to Roosevelt. "Is he kidding?"

"I hope not," answered Roosevelt.

"Well, I for one didn't sign on to draw against Doc Holliday," said Cody. "I'm going back to my tent." He turned and started walking. As he passed Holliday, he whispered, "My show could use a sharpshooter when this dinosaur silliness is done. Let's talk later."

Holliday smiled and didn't say a word.

"Would you really have done it, Doc?" asked Younger curiously as the tension began seeping away from his body.

"Get a good night's sleep," said Holliday, "and you can ponder it all the way back to Cope's camp in the morning."

Younger seemed about to argue, then thought better of it, and walked off into the gathering darkness.

Holliday pulled out his flask, took a swallow, and watched the two men walk away until they were out of his range of vision.

"Truth to tell," he said, "I've never seen either of them in action. I wonder what the result would have been?"

"That's easy to answer," said Roosevelt.

Holliday turned to him. "Oh?"

Roosevelt nodded.

"Okay," said Holliday. "Who'd have won?"

"The Comanche," said Roosevelt.

11.

"**S**O WHAT HAVE WE LEARNED?**" asked Roosevelt. He and Holliday sat beside a dying fire after all the others had sought out their tents or any available shelter and gone to bed.

"Other than that Cope and Marsh are both about ready for the lunatic asylum, you mean?" responded Holliday.

"Other than that," said Roosevelt with a smile.

"Well, they know their stuff. You could fill a couple of freight trains with the bones they've dug out of the ground." He grimaced. "What I don't think anyone can do is make them stop."

"Or work together," added Roosevelt, as one of the lanterns ran out of fuel and flickered out.

"Or work together," agreed Holliday.

"Well, none of the things Geronimo was worried about have happened yet," said Roosevelt, "except for someone taking a shot at you. Maybe the old gentleman was overreacting."

"I don't think anyone ever referred to him as a gentleman before," said Holliday. "When the white men talk about the Indian they most want to see dead, Geronimo beats Sitting Bull by a comfortable margin." He frowned. "More to the point, I've never seen him overreact before. I just wish I knew what the hell he expects us to do about it."

"Maybe Cody had a point," suggested Roosevelt.

"Oh?"

"Hire them all."

Holliday shook his head. "They might take money rather than go to war with you over most of their land, but not their burial grounds. I don't know why that should be, because to the best of my knowledge none of the tribes believe in resurrection or reincarnation, but they'll kill to keep people from messing in their burial grounds."

"But they *haven't*," Roosevelt pointed out. "From what I've been able to tell, there have been some sporadic attacks, usually by lone warriors, but they've kept their distance."

"I know," said Holliday, pulling out his flask. "The only answer I can come up with is that their graveyard may well be eighty miles by fifty, but they've only using a couple of hundred acres so far, and neither Cope nor Marsh has desecrated the ground that's in use as opposed to the ground that's earmarked for future use."

Roosevelt considered Holliday's statement. "It *sounds* reasonable, Doc," he said at last, "but somehow I don't believe it."

"For what it's worth, neither do I," admitted Holliday, taking a swallow from the flask. "Just clutching at straws."

"Well, as long as the most dangerous situation so far is a lone outlaw who thinks he can beat you to the draw, I suppose we'll have a few pleasant weeks—well, as pleasant as they can be around Marsh and Cope—and then we'll go back East with their treasure and see how they reconstruct them in their various museums." Roosevelt leaned forward, his enthusiasm obvious even in the dark. "It's really a fascinating science, Doc. Imagine a creature that could kill an elephant for lunch, or one that could give a pronghorn buck a half mile lead and run him down in another half mile." He offered his trademark grin. "It makes you wonder what the world was like back then—and more to the point, how Man ever got a foothold here, let alone became the dominant species."

"I imagine any preacher'd be happy to explain it to you," said Holliday. "Of course, they might have a little difficulty explaining what happened to the dinosaurs." Suddenly he smiled. "They'd probably say that they were too big to fit in the Ark."

Roosevelt sighed deeply. "This science is too new. I doubt that we'll ever know the answer during our lifetimes. That's damned frustrating!"

"I'll be hobnobbing with Satan in less than a year," replied Holliday. "I'll ask him when I get there, and try to get word upstairs to you."

"Don't talk like that, Doc," said Roosevelt.

"You don't like to think about dying?"

"I don't like to think about you winding up in hell, or accepting it so casually."

"Not to worry," said Holliday, taking another drink from his flask. "I'll be surrounded by damned near every friend I ever had except you, and certainly I'll be rubbing shoulders with every man I ever killed." His face suddenly distorted in a grimace. "I hope Kate gets religion. I do *not* look forward to spending an eternity with her."

"She broke you out of jail," noted Roosevelt.

"Only so she could try to kill me a few more times."

"It's an unusual relationship, I'll grant you that."

"*Was*," Holliday corrected him. "It *was* an unusual relationship."

Roosevelt flashed Holliday his familiar grin. "Texas Jack Vermillion writes me the occasional letter," he replied. "He says she still visits you regularly at the hospital."

"Of course she does," growled Holliday. "Those metal chippies she's got working for her don't feel a thing when she slaps 'em or whacks 'em with a gun barrel. If she wants blood, she has to come to me. Admittedly, I've got a limited supply of it, but still . . ."

"So she's still running a house of ill repute?"

Holliday shook his head. "Actually, it's a house of excellent repute. Those metal chippies Tom and Ned built never need a break or a meal—not that Kate would give 'em either even if they *did* need them."

"You two would have produced a hell of a child," said Roosevelt.

"A hot-tempered sadistic shootist with consumption," retorted Holliday. "You have peculiar taste in kids, Theodore."

He paused and took a final swig from his flask, emptying it. "In fact, there's those who'd say you have a peculiar taste in, if not friends, at least allies—a dying shootist and the most powerful medicine man alive."

"You're both primaries," said Roosevelt. "I'm drawn to that."

Holliday frowned. "Primaries? Like elections? I don't understand."

Roosevelt smiled. "No, like colors. Most people are pastels. They can't help it, and it doesn't make them any better or worse. There are very few primaries, but they stand out for better or worse, and they seem to be the ones I'm attracted to, or at least the ones I keep running into."

"So I'm a primary, cough and all?"

"Doc, they'll be arguing about who were the good guys and who were the bad guys at the O.K. Corral for another century, but the one thing they'll all remember is that you came to the aid of Wyatt Earp and his brothers and risked your life solely for friendship, with no thought of recompense."

"I suppose so," said Holliday without much enthusiasm.

"Answer me this," continued Roosevelt. "Have you ever shot a man who wasn't trying to kill you?"

"No, never."

Roosevelt grinned again and bowed his head to an imaginary audience. "There you have it."

"Some of them thought they had pretty good reasons for trying to kill me," continued Holliday.

"Now you're just being Doc," said Roosevelt.

Holliday blinked in confusion. "What are you talking about?"

"You've emptied that flask, and if I say you're a terrible man who'll be remembered as a cowardly backshooter, you'll argue with me, just as you're arguing when I'm praising you."

There was a brief pause while Holliday considered the statement. Then he uttered an amused laugh. "Well, I'll be damned!"

"Probably," replied Roosevelt with a smile. "But what was that in reference to?"

"You know me even better than Wyatt did." Suddenly he frowned. "I wish he'd known I was just bullshitting the last time we spoke."

"That was when you said the wrong thing?"

Holliday nodded. "About his wife."

"Perhaps he'll forgive you."

"Wyatt's not the forgiving kind," said Holliday, shaking his head. "Can't blame him for that. Neither am I." He turned the flask upside down, just to make sure it was empty. "Besides, I got you now, and truth to tell, I don't think I can handle more than one friend at a time."

"You're a very unusual man, John Henry Holliday," said Roosevelt.

"Out of all the millions of white men on this continent Geronimo will treat only with you, and you think *I'm* unusual?"

"I'm not qualified to judge myself."

"Well, *I* am," said Holliday firmly. "Geronimo thinks you're going to be king of America if you live long enough."

"America will never have a king," said Roosevelt firmly.

"King, emperor, chief, president, it's all the same to him," continued Holliday. Then he smiled. "Probably the best title is Boss."

"I'm flattered than he should think so," replied Roosevelt, "but I've been elected to the State Assembly of New York, nothing else—and I left it when Alice died. I've never been a mayor, a governor, a Senator, a—"

"You've been a deputy marshal," interrupted Holliday. "You brought in those three killers in the Dakota Badlands during that blizzard. I heard all about it from Bat Masterson."

"The Winter of the Blue Snow, they called it," acknowledged Roosevelt. "And yes, I was a deputy—but it was a volunteer position. I was unelected and unpaid."

"You're young yet," said Holliday, shaking his head. "You'll learn."

"I'm twenty-seven," answered Roosevelt.

"See? You've got your whole life ahead of you."

"How old were you at the O.K. Corral?" asked Roosevelt.

"What's that got to do with anything?" demanded Holliday.

"Just asking."

"Maybe thirty."

"And before the afternoon was over your reputation, for better or worse, was made for all time to come," said Roosevelt.

"What are you getting at, Theodore?"

"Just that while it's nice to have most of one's life still ahead, the incidents that posterity will judge you by are few and far between, and you can rarely spot them in advance, so you can't procrastinate, you can't loaf, you have to live each moment as if this is the moment that posterity will remember."

"It sounds exhausting,' said Holliday.

"It does require one to believe in the vigorous life," chuckled Roosevelt.

"I'm glad you feel that way, Theodore," said Holliday, slipping his flask into a coat pocket and gently moving his coat back to expose his gun. "Because I think we're about to put it to the test."

"What do you see?" asked Roosevelt, his voice tense but his posture unchanged.

"Over your left shoulder," said Holliday. "It could be a deer or even a bear, but it could also be a Comanche."

Roosevelt paused a moment in thought before he spoke. "If it's a Comanche, and he's not threatening us, pretend you don't notice him. If he's just scouting the camp, let him go back and report what he sees, which is just you and me. His leaders know where the camp is, so it won't do us any harm. But if we kill or capture him, they're going find out, and then they'll have no choice but to retaliate."

A grim smile crossed Holliday's face. "I could have killed him in the time you spent telling me not to."

"Is it definitely a Comanche?

"Unless deer or buffalo have taken to wearing beads," answered Holliday. Suddenly he smiled. "Take that back. Couldn't be a buff, or Cody'd be out here blasting away with his rifle."

"What's he doing?" asked Roosevelt.

"Trying not to let us know he's here," replied Holliday in amused tones. "He's never going to step out into the open while we're here, and having gone to all the trouble to sneak this close I don't imagine he's returning to his camp without whatever information it is that he's after."

"So he'll just stand there until we go to sleep," said Roosevelt. Suddenly he grinned. "And if we sit up all night . . . ?"

"Then none of the three of us is going to get any sleep." Holliday frowned. "I wonder what he *is* here for?" he mused.

"There can only be two reasons, and it's the wrong time of day for one of them."

"Which one is that?"

"Counting our guns. I assume not everyone here carries one."

"Yes, they do. Marsh insists."

"It will just antagonize the Comanche," said Roosevelt disapprovingly.

"I don't think he gives a damn about the Indians," Holliday pointed out. "My guess is that the guns are in case we run into Cope's party."

"He told you that?"

"I haven't been here long enough to ask."

"Then—?"

"Because every one of Cope's men goes armed for the same reason," said Holliday.

Roosevelt shook his head in wonderment. "Can you imagine what these two men could do if they worked *together?*"

"I gather they tried that once. That's how they came to be mortal enemies."

"I'm inclined to say 'What a waste!'" said Roosevelt. "Except that I wonder if they'd be so fiercely motivated, so willing to spend every last cent of their fortunes and every last minute of their days, if they *didn't* have such a rivalry."

"Beats me," said Holliday.

"It's getting chilly, and I'm getting stiff and uncomfortable. Is the warrior still there?"

Holliday nodded. "Bet he's getting kind of stiff and uncomfortable himself. It's a hell of a lot easier to pretend we don't see him than for him to pretend that he's not there."

"I think I might as well go to my tent and do a little reading," said Roosevelt.

"The light will attract him," said Holliday.

"I doubt it. He's not here to kill anyone, because as far as he knows we haven't spotted him and he could try to do it right now. He's just counting guns, as you say . . . or maybe he plans to sneak into the bone shack and make sure we don't have any of his ancestors in there. Either way, he doesn't want to kill me, and as long as I convince him I don't know he's there he won't bother me."

Roosevelt stood, keeping his back to the warrior, stretched his arms, bade Holliday a good-night, and walked off to his tent. A moment later the canvas wall and top were illuminated by a reading lamp.

Holliday remained where he was for another half hour, then decided Roosevelt had a point and he'd prove nothing by sleeping out here. He got to his feet, faced the bushes where the Comanche was hiding, took off his hat in a sweeping motion, bowed from the waist, and walked to the outbuilding that housed the cot he'd been assigned, a smile on his face as he tried to imagine the warrior's confusion.

12.

YOUNGER WAS GONE by the time the rest of the camp awoke. Holliday began the day by coughing up blood, as usual. When he recovered, he got up—he'd slept in his clothes, like almost all the men—and looked around for Roosevelt but couldn't find him.

He saw Cody seated at a table, munching on some venison, and decided it was too damned early in the day for meat—or for eggs or any other solid or semisolid food, for that matter. He settled for his flask, refilling it when Marsh was busy studying maps of the area, and starting in on it again.

"Here he comes!" noted Cody. "A little earlier than usual. Usually he misses breakfast."

Holliday looked in the direction indicated and saw a shirtless Roosevelt trotting toward their table, shadow-boxing all the way, his torso drenched in sweat.

"Good morning!" said Roosevelt enthusiastically. "Beautiful day, isn't it?"

"It's too damned early to tell, but I'd lay odds against it," grumbled Holliday. "What the hell are you doing, Theodore?"

"My morning run," answered Roosevelt. "Just keeping fit, and working up an appetite—which, for a change, it looks like I'll be able to assuage before noontime."

Cody laughed. "Oh, come on, Theodore—I always keep a couple of pieces of bread for you."

"Clearly our Buffalo Bill is one of Nature's noblemen," said Holliday sardonically. "Why, I'll bet if you asked he'd be happy to share his deer with you."

"No need to," said Roosevelt before Cody could object. "The mess tent's open. I'll just get something there and be back to join you."

He headed off, and Cody turned to Holliday. "You knew the mess tent was open," he said accusingly. "Do you delight in ruining other people's digestion?"

"I never gave it any serious thought," admitted Holliday, "but now that you mention it . . ."

"Damned lucky for you you're so good with *that*," muttered Cody.

"Yeah," agreed Holliday. "If I wasn't so good at killing men, I suppose I'd have to spend most of my time fixing their teeth."

"I know you were a dentist," said Cody. "Why did you stop?"

Holliday was suddenly wracked by another coughing spasm. When he finished he put his bloody handkerchief back in his pocket. "You were asking . . . ?" he said.

"Never mind," said Cody, looking at the blood that remained on Holliday's fingers. "I do hope you'll consider joining the *Buffalo Bill Wild West Show* when this foolishness is done."

"You don't want me," said Holliday. "I can't tell stories like Calamity Jane, because I'd have coughing fits in the middle of them. And I'm no sharpshooter like Annie Oakley."

"But look at all the men you've killed!" protested Cody.

"Most men have more vital areas than you can imagine," answered Holliday, toying with a biscuit but finally pushing it away. "Stick to your ladies; people will flock to see them."

"Jane's a drunk," replied Cody.

"I heard she'd killed some notorious men," said Holliday.

"Oh, she has," said Cody. "But not with a gun." Holliday stared at him curiously. "With a social disease. *That's* why she's *Calamity* Jane."

Holliday laughed at that. "Not to worry," he responded. "The history books'll clean it up."

"Getting back to you . . ."

Holliday shook his head. "I'm living on borrowed time—and the guy I borrowed it from wants it back at the end of the year."

"I'm not quite sure what you're referring to," said Cody. Suddenly he learned forward. "I hear you're pretty tight with Geronimo. You think he'd be interested?"

Holliday stared at him. "Are you willing to have every member of your audience check their guns at the ticket office?"

It was Cody's turn to frown. "What are you talking about, Doc?"

"You let armed white men walk into a tent where Geronimo's performing, and how many seconds do you figure it'll take before they start shooting at him? Surely not a whole minute."

Cody considered what Holliday said, and finally shrugged. "You've got a point. I'll wait another eight or ten years. By then they'll have so many more recent enemies that they'll have forgotten why they were mad at him in the first place."

"I suppose you have to think like that if you're going to be an entrepreneur," said Holliday, taking another swallow of whiskey as Roosevelt, with almost a pound of venison and a pair of fried eggs on his plate, joined them.

"Lovely day!" he said enthusiastically.

Holliday looked out across the sunlit campsite and winced. "Oh, shut up, Theodore," he muttered.

"You'll have to excuse my friend," Roosevelt said to Cody. "He's not at his best before mid-afternoon."

"I haven't been at my best since 1869," growled Holliday.

"Damn!" said Roosevelt, getting up. "I forgot the coffee!"

As he trotted off to the mess tent, Cody turned to Holliday. "Does he *ever* slow down?"

"Theodore?" replied Holliday. "He even goes to sleep energetically—if he *does* sleep. Personally, I've never seen him go to bed without a book in his hands."

"Remarkable man!" said Cody.

Holliday nodded his agreement. "That's why Geronimo chose him."

Roosevelt trotted back with a pot of coffee and a trio of empty cups. "I thought someone else might like some too," he announced.

"No, thanks," said Cody.

"Too strong for me," said Holliday, taking a swallow from his flask. "I'll stick with this weak stuff."

"Well, what the schedule for today?" asked Roosevelt.

"This is going to come as a shock to you, Theodore," said Holliday, "but I have a feeling that they're going to dig for fossils."

"I meant where, and for what?" replied Roosevelt with a smile.

"You'd have to ask Professor Marsh," said Cody.

"I think I will, once I finish my breakfast," said Roosevelt. "As long as I'm stuck here until Tom and Ned show up, I might as well help with the digging."

"Tom and Ned?" repeated Cody.

"A couple of friends," said Holliday. He turned to Roosevelt. "You're really going to dig in the dirt for a bunch of bones?"

Roosevelt nodded enthusiastically. "Both Cope and Marsh think this was a prime feeding territory of the triceratops. Might as well find out sooner than later."

"The tricera-*what*?" said Holliday.

"You know, I've heard Marsh use that term," interjected Cody. "Recently, I think."

"It's like a rhinoceros," said Roosevelt. "Only bigger. *Much* bigger."

"I've seen drawings of a rhinoceros," allowed Holliday. "How big do they get?"

"There are three species," answered Roosevelt. "Well, two species and one sub-species."

"Of course," said Holliday sardonically.

"The black rhinoceros is the most prevalent, and weighs maybe a ton and a half. The white rhinoceros goes about three tons." A pause. "I don't know if they can interbreed."

"Might be damnably awkward," said Cody.

"They're actually black and white?" asked Holliday. "The few drawings and descriptions I've come across make 'em all sound kind of gray and colorless."

Roosevelt grinned. "The big one has a square jaw and lip, which prompted the Boers to call it the *vid* rhino, for *wide*, not white." He picked up a stick and drew the foreface of a white rhino in the dirt next to his chair. "And once the British heard its name—well, *mis*heard it, the other became the black rhino just to differentiate it." He proceeded to draw a black rhino's foreface to demonstrate the difference.

"What's the third?" asked Cody. "The puce, or maybe the mauve?"

"The third is the Indian rhinoceros, bigger than the black, smaller than the white, and looking for all the world like it's armored."

"How do you kill it if it's armored?" asked Holliday.

Roosevelt shook his head. "It *looks* armored, but it's not."

"Is this all from books, or have you actually seen one?" asked Cody.

"I've seen the remains of a couple at the Smithsonian," answered Roosevelt. "Someday I'll get to Africa and see the white and black species for myself."

He said it with such conviction that no one challenged him.

"So how big is the tri— tricer— this rhino's uncle?" asked Holliday.

Roosevelt shrugged. "We won't know until Cope or Marsh has enough bones to identify one and reconstruct it, but from what I've read and heard, maybe eight to ten tons."

"So you're saying that it's maybe six times bigger than the most common rhinoceros, the kind that all the hunters write about?"

Roosevelt nodded his head enthusiastically. "Thrilling, isn't it?"

"Mostly I'm thrilled that they're extinct," answered Holliday. He paused, frowning. "What the hell could kill something like that?"

"Whatever it was," said Cody, "just pray you never have to meet one of them."

"Could turn a man to religion," agreed Holliday.

"Relax," said Roosevelt, wolfing down his breakfast. "They've been dead for a few million years, maybe more."

"Let's just hope they *stay* dead," said Holliday meaningfully.

"You really mean to help dig?" asked Cody, pulling out one of his pistols and making sure every chamber except the operative one had a cartridge in it—like everyone with a six-shooter, he left that empty so he didn't accidently blow his foot off—and then went through the same procedure with the other pistol.

"Might as well," answered Roosevelt. "What else is there to do?"

"You might help me ride shotgun against the Comanche."

"They haven't bothered you yet, and we *are* desecrating their sacred burial ground," said Roosevelt.

"So you plan to help desecrate it further," noted Holliday.

"There are times," Roosevelt said, "when your sense of humor isn't as rib-tickling as you think it is."

"So I've been told," replied Holliday.

Roosevelt downed the last of the venison and drained his coffee cup. "All right," he said, getting up. "I'm ready."

"Let's go see Professor Marsh and find out what he has in mind for today," said Cody. He turned to Holliday. "You coming along, Doc?"

"Ride a horse so I can dig in the dirt when I finally climb off him?" said Holliday. "I admire your notion of a joke, but it's a little early in the day for humor."

Cody seemed amused. "Sorry I asked."

He joined Roosevelt and the two walked over to what Cody called the bone building, where Marsh was plotting out the day's dig. They returned a few minutes later and approached Holliday.

"Well?" asked Holliday.

"He's got a spot about three miles from here," answered Roosevelt. "He's found a femur bone that he thinks may have belonged to a triceratops, and he wants to continue digging in that location."

"And you're really going to help dig?"

Roosevelt grinned. "Why not? After all, I've already got my shirt off."

Holliday turned to Cody. "And you're going to hold off the Indians?"

"If need be," answered Cody.

"Just out of curiosity, how many have you killed so far?"

"None. But if any of them attack us, I'm ready." Cody paused. "I *have* killed a saboteur."

"I saw him as I rode in here," said Holliday.

Cody shook his head. "No, that was a different one. The one I nailed was five days ago. The one you saw was killed by Chan Lee, one of the Chinese diggers."

"Excuse me for demonstrating my ignorance, but just what the hell does a saboteur *do* on a dinosaur dig?"

"Well, if they know we've got something *really* rare, they'll try to destroy it. But the clever ones do other things."

"For instance?"

"About two months ago Professor Cope found a couple of leg bones that belong to a huge creature, maybe seventy-five tons, that he calls a brontosaur, and he shipped them back East, along with some vertebrae."

"And your guy wrecked the train?" asked Holliday.

"No. He found the remains of a skull maybe two hundred miles from here. A *huge* head, but not big enough to eat what a brontosaur needs to sustain it. He had some confederates sneak the skull onto the train with the other bones. When they reconstruct it back East, Cope's going to become a laughing stock for giving them a head that couldn't possibly consume enough to support that body if it had thirty hours a day to do nothing but eat." Cody threw back his head and laughed.

"It's creative, I'll give it that," admitted Holliday.

"Of course, now that Theodore's heard it, he'll be the one to expose it once he goes back to New York," said Cody.

Roosevelt shook his head. "That was privileged information," he said. "I plan to keep it to myself. Someone else can expose it."

"And if no one does?" asked Holliday.

"Then you're going to have the damnedest-looking dinosaur you can imagine!" laughed Cody. He turned to Roosevelt. "They're saddling the horses and getting the wagons ready. We'd better be going."

Roosevelt nodded his agreement, then turned to Holliday. "See you at dinnertime," he said.

"I don't think so," answered Holliday.

Roosevelt frowned. "Why not?"

"We've got some friends who are arriving in Cheyenne in a couple of days. Someone should be waiting for them to guide them back here."

"I was so enthused about the dig I hadn't even thought of that," admitted Roosevelt.

"Neither had I," replied Holliday. "But I'm almost out of liquor, and I needed an excuse to go to Cheyenne to replenish my supply. Besides, it'll be nice to sleep in a real bed again."

"I understand Frank James was seen there a couple of months ago," said Cody. "If you run into him, tell him I've got an offer he can't refuse."

"That he can't refuse?" repeated Holliday.

"Right."

"Must be different from all the other offers you've been making."

"You go to hell, John Henry!" growled Cody. "Come on, Theodore. Let's go find some bones."

13.

IT WAS HOT IN CHEYENNE, hot and dry. Holliday couldn't do anything about the heat, but he made it his business to take care of the dry, He headed straight to the Plains Hotel, rented a room, then sat down in the shadiest corner of the bar and ordered a beer. It arrived warm but wet, he downed it, and then ordered a bottle of whiskey and a glass.

A good-looking young woman looked in through the window from the sidewalk, and a moment later entered the bar and approached Holliday's table.

"You're him, ain't you?" she said.

"Anything's possible," replied Holliday. "Have a seat."

She shook her head. "You're the one who murdered my pa."

"I object to the term 'murdered,'" he said. "I never shot anyone who didn't have a weapon in his hand."

"Oh, I suspect he had one in each hand and three or four more tucked in his belt and his boots." She paused. "He was a real son of a bitch, my pa."

"Let me make sure I've got this straight," said Holliday. "You're not accusing me of killing your father. You're *thanking* me?"

"Ain't many people deserved it as much as he did," she said. "He used to beat the hell out of me."

"I'm sorry to hear it."

"If you've got a room here, and can buy a girl dinner and a few drinks, I'd be happy to show you how grateful I am," she said with a smile.

He signaled the bartender to bring another glass to the table. "Pour yourself a drink," he said. "But I'm afraid dinner is out of the question. I have a previous engagement, always assuming the Bunt Line is on schedule."

"Ah!" she said, her face lighting up. "Someone's coming from back East to hire you! Who're you going to be killing?"

He returned her smile. "All I'm killing is this bottle, Miss . . . ?"

"I've had lots of names," she said. "This month I'm using Amanda."

"And your father was?"

"A bastard who deserved killing."

Holliday shrugged, his interest waning. He poured himself another glass.

"Strong stuff," she said, finally taking a swallow.

He nodded. "That's the best kind. It'll kill your memory and put hair on your chest."

She threw back her head and laughed. "I *like* you, Doc Holliday!" she said. "Hell, if the old bastard was still alive, I'd have been proud to pay you to blow him to hell and gone."

"I hate to disillusion you, Amanda," said Holliday, "but I'm not for hire."

She frowned. "That's not what I've heard."

"I can't help what you've heard," he replied. "I'm not a professional killer."

"You mean you shot all them men just for the fun of it?" she asked.

124

Holliday just stared at her for a long moment. "I hate to disappoint you again," he said at last, "but I never shot anyone without a reason, and I never shot anyone who didn't deserve it."

"I'll vouch for that, at least as far as my pa was concerned," she said, taking another swallow of her drink. "You know, this stuff ain't so bad when you get used to it."

"A discovery I made half a lifetime ago," said Holliday.

"You *sure* you got company for dinner?"

"I'm sure I'm supposed to." He pulled out his watch. "They're due in about twenty minutes, if they're on schedule."

"Well," she said, getting to her feet, "maybe some other time. I still owe you."

"You do?" he said curiously.

"For killing my pa."

"Oh, right."

She turned and walked back out into the street, leaving Holliday idly wondering who her father was and why he had killed him.

He was still wondering and still drinking half an hour later, when Tom Edison and Ned Buntline entered the hotel, with a couple of young men carrying a large trunk between them. He got up and walked over to the foyer to greet them.

"Set it down right here," said Buntline, handing a coin to each. He turned to see Holliday approaching him. "Hi, Doc!"

"Hello," added Edison, who was signing the guest book at the front desk.

"Good trip, I hope?" said Holliday.

"Absolutely," said Buntline. Suddenly he grinned. "And even if it wasn't, I'll never say a word against the Bunt Line."

Holliday chuckled. "Well, it's been a long trip, so you'll want to rest up for a night, but tomorrow morning we'll head off for Cope's and Marsh's camps. The way these guys are pulling up bones, added to the way the Comanche are leaving 'em totally alone, leads Theodore and me to think the Comanche have something in mind that won't cost them any warriors. And you know what that'll be."

"I know," said Buntline. "And just in case it does happen, I brought a really good camera along."

"Okay, gentlemen," said Edison, handing a room key to Buntline and tucking the other into a pocket, "let's unpack and then think about dinner."

"If you want to eat first, no one's going to run off with that trunk," said Holliday. "Hell, it took two strong young men to lift it."

"It's not the trunk we're protecting," answered Edison. "It's what's in the trunk, and if you couldn't lift it by yourself, it wouldn't be very practical to use against"—he looked around to make sure no one was listening—"what it was created to use against."

"Will it work?" asked Holliday.

"I think so," answered Edison. "I hope so."

"If the best you can do is hope, *you* can use the damned thing," said Holliday.

"We'll test it out before you carry it into battle," said Buntline. "Now let's move this equipment to our room, and then get something to eat. The Bunt Line has a lot of virtues, but food isn't one of them."

They had the desk clerk summon a pair of young men to carry the trunk to their suite, while they followed with their suitcases.

"Where's *your* luggage, Doc?" asked Edison when they reached their rooms and he unlocked his door.

"I'm wearing it."

"No change of clothes?"

"I'm in a battle, not a fashion contest," answered Holliday. "Besides, I just got here a couple of hours ago, and I'm heading back to one of the camps tomorrow."

"Which camp are we going to?" asked Edison as the two men set the trunk down and left.

"Cope's, probably."

"It's closer?" said Buntline.

"It's pleasanter," replied Holliday. "Minimally."

"I don't understand."

"They each hate each other's guts," said Holliday. "You know that, of course, but I don't think anyone realizes the full extent of it. I think either would be happy to spend eternity burning in the pits of hell as long as the other starting burning one minute sooner. When I say Cope's camp is minimally more pleasant, I just mean that his hatred of Marsh doesn't slop over to other people as much as Marsh's hatred for him does."

"That's pretty much what we've heard," said Buntline, sitting down on a leather couch. "I guess hearing about it doesn't really bring it home like experiencing it."

"That's okay," said Holliday. "None of us is working for either of them. Neither is Theodore. We'll do what we have to do *if* we have to do it." He stared at the trunk. "You *sure* whatever you've got in there will work? You won't believe the size of these damned leg bones until you see them yourselves."

"They *should* work," said Edison, seating himself on a high-backed wooden chair. "Hell, there's no reason why a properly placed bullet from Theodore's Winchester won't work." Holliday made no comment, but his skepticism was clearly written on his face.

"Trust us, Doc," said Buntline. "If we could light all of Tombstone and Leadville, we can turn the lights off on a dinosaur or two."

"I hope so," said Holliday, who was still uncomfortable from his long ride and elected to remain standing, leaning against the only section of wall that didn't have a print or a painting on it.

"What the hell does that mean?" asked Buntline.

"I hope your weapon will turn their lights off, and I hope if they're resurrected there are only one or two, since I think you could have a few thousand buried there."

"How crazy can the Comanche be?" said Buntline. "One allosaur could wipe out an entire village in a matter of minutes. And from what I hear, a brontosaur could flatten it in even less time."

"Let's hope they're not quite that crazy," said Edison.

"I'll drink to that," said Buntline. "Or at least I will once we get up to our rooms and I unpack a bottle."

"Well, gentlemen," said Edison, "before the thought of my being mistaken spoils our appetites, shall we go down for dinner?"

"Why not?" said Buntline, getting up.

"The hotel can watch your luggage until we're through with dinner," said Holliday opening the front door and starting to step outside. "We can eat in the hotel, of course, but I hear there's a nice restaurant on the next block called the Wheel."

"Not The Wagon Wheel, or the Some-other-kind-of Wheel?" asked Buntline.

"Just the Wheel," replied Holliday.

"Why not?" said Edison. "Let's give it a shot."

Holliday had no knowledge whatsoever of the Wheel. He'd passed it coming into town, and since he was sure that Amanda would be lurking for him by the hotel's restaurant he'd quickly come up with a reason to eat elsewhere.

He was pleasantly surprised when the Wheel actually served up some pretty good steaks, and doubly so when they returned to the hotel and there was no Amanda there to praise him in front his friends for murdering her father.

Edison and Buntline had begun their day at sunrise and went up to their room to sleep, and Holliday spent an hour in the bar, then spent two more hours breaking even in a poker game at a casino down the street.

When he returned he found that he wasn't sleepy, so he looked around for something to do while drinking from his flask. The only thing he found was a copy of the Bible, so he picked it up, took it to the bed, propped himself up against the headboard, and began reading it by the light of a kerosene lamp.

He hoped it was right, that everything had started with Adam and that Edison and Buntline were wasting their time, as were he and Roosevelt, but somehow he couldn't quite convince himself that things were that simple or that easy.

When he awoke after a restless sleep he still had very little faith in the Bible as an accurate historical document, and was anxious to get back to one camp or the other so he could try out Edison's new weapon.

14.

THERE WAS NO WAY THAT A HORSE, or even a pack mule, could carry the trunk, so Holliday rented a wagon and a team of horses to pull it, attached his own horse to the back of the wagon with a long lead shank, and happily climbed onto the driver's seat.

"You know how to drive one of these things?" asked Buntline dubiously.

"I drove one in Tombstone," replied Holliday.

"I know," said Buntline, frowning. "That's why I'm asking."

"Nothing to it," said Holliday. "You just aim them in the direction you want to go, yell 'Giddyap!' and off you go." And indeed, as he said the word the horses bolted forward.

"Very good," said Buntline, frowning. "Now let's go back and get Tom."

"Damn!" said Holliday. "Wasn't he aboard?"

He turned the team around, went back for Edison, and soon they were heading westward again.

"Which camp are we going to?" asked Edison.

"Cope's," answered Holliday. "He's three or four hours farther than Marsh, but he's five or six hours pleasanter."

"Which camp is Theodore at?"

"Marsh's, if he's still in the country."

"I don't understand," said Edison, frowning.

"Last I saw of him, he was preparing to show them how to dig. Knowing Theodore, I figure it's no worse than a fifty-fifty proposition that he's dug down to China."

Edison sighed and nodded. "That's our Theodore, all right."

"Well," said Buntline, "I suppose we'd better have a list of the species they've uncovered, so if worse comes to worst we'll know what we're up against."

"I get the distinct impression that they're making up names as they go along," answered Holliday. "After all, nobody's ever seen any of these things before."

As they were leaving town on a westbound trail Holliday suddenly pulled the team to a stop.

"What is it?" asked Edison, looking around.

"Maybe nothing," said Holliday, not taking his eyes from an owl that perched on a dead limb of a dying tree, staring at him. Holliday stared back, and the two remained motionless for the better part of a minute.

"Is something wrong?" asked Buntline nervously.

"I don't know yet," replied Holliday, ignoring a pair of flies that circled around his face.

Finally the owl spread its wings and took off in an easterly direction, and Holliday clucked to the horses, which began walking again.

"Well, *that's* a relief," said Holliday, finally brushing the flies away with the back of his hand.

"What did you think it was?" asked Edison.

Holliday shrugged. "I wasn't sure. Geronimo, maybe, or perhaps one of the Comanche medicine men."

"It was just a bird," said Buntline.

"It was an owl, five hundred miles from where it belongs, and out in the noonday sun," said Holliday. He shrugged. "Well, at least it wasn't Geronimo, and if it was a Comanche, he's probably just watching to see who I'm bringing back with me. No way he could know what's in the trunk." He paused. "Probably," he added.

They rode in silence for an hour, then came to a small creek where Holliday let the horses drink.

"I wonder why they picked Wyoming," said Edison, looking around. "With the Rockies, at least you can gauge the strata and know where to dig after you've pulled out your first dinosaur. This strikes me as too much guesswork."

Holliday shook his head. "There's not much guesswork involved, not with those two. Either one of them points at the ground and says 'Dig here!' and you can bet the farm they'll dig up some bones right there." A quick smile. "Always assuming you own a farm to bet," he added.

"Well, what we've got in here ought to work on just about anything," said Edison, patting the trunk.

"First, I hope we don't need it, and second, I hope you're right," said Holliday.

"It's been a year or more since we've seen Theodore," said Buntline. "What's he been doing? I was sure he'd be running for office by now, but I haven't seen anything about him in the papers."

"Building a home, probably making arrangements to divest himself of his Dakota properties, getting ready to get married again," answered Holliday.

"That'd be a lot of any normal man," said Edison with a smile. "Somehow it seems like slow motion for Theodore."

"Well, he *has* written a few books in the past year, and who the hell knows what else?" said Holliday. "He's going to have to be a little less modest about his accomplishments if he's really going to run for office again." A sudden smile. "Right now I imagine he's busy getting the equivalent of a college course in paleontology. It's amazing how he can put up with Marsh's manners as long as he can learn from him."

Edison nodded. "That's our Theodore, all right."

They rode another hour, then stopped for the lunch Buntline had bought in the hotel's restaurant. While Buntline was pulling it out, Edison hobbled the horses, removed their harness, and let them graze in a nearby glade.

"Okay," said Holliday. "If you're going to spill your drinks, or drop food on your chests, or forget to button up your pants after you sneak behind the bushes to relieve yourself, this is the time and place to do it."

"What are you talking about?" asked Buntline.

"This is the last meal where I cannot absolutely guarantee that you'll be watched by one or more Comanche. They *might* be watching us now, but I think we're still a little too far for them to give a damn about. We don't pose a real threat until we go another twenty or twenty-five miles. Five or six hours ought to do it."

"But they haven't attacked anyone yet?" said Edison.

"Not so's you'd notice it."

"What the devil does that mean?" asked Buntline, pulling out a pipe and lighting it.

"They haven't attacked anyone while they were digging," replied Holliday. "I can't vouch for the fact that they haven't killed the occasional white man who wandered off, or maybe some who weren't part of the digging parties but were just passing through."

"What kind of weaponry do they use?"

Holliday grimaced as a change in the wind blew some of Buntline's smoke into his face. "About what you'd expect," he answered, moving a few feet to his left to avoid the smoke. "Bow and arrows, rifles, the occasional six-shooter or spear."

"Where did they get the rifles?" asked Edison.

Holliday stared at him. "Where do you think?" he said at last.

"Sorry," said Edison. "I've got to get used to being out here again."

Buntline pulled a bottle out of the woven basket that had contained their lunch. "Water, Doc?" he offered.

"I'm not dirty," replied Holliday, pulling out of his flask and draining it. "Okay," he said, getting to his feet, "now we *have* to get there by sunset. I left a couple of spare bottles in Cope's camp."

"And some in Marsh's, I would guess," said Edison with a smile.

Holliday shook his head. "No, if he found them, he'd confiscate them."

"He's a drinker?"

"No. He just doesn't like anyone else to be."

They harnessed the horses again, climbed back into the wagon, and began heading west toward the two camps.

About three hours into the ride Holliday made a wide semicircle around where he felt was the farthest Marsh's crew might be digging from their base camp. This took them to some rocky, uneven ground, which was hard on the horses and especially on the wagon wheels, but finally it became reasonably flat again, just as a coyote's howl broke the stillness of the afternoon.

"A real one, do you think?" asked Edison.

"I doubt it," said Holliday. "If Cody wants a real attraction in his show, he'll hire a bunch of Indians and have them mimic the growls and cries and chirps of every damned animal out here."

"Well, they were giving coyotes a bad name back when I was in Arizona," said Buntline. "Every time you heard one, someone would wind up with an arrow sticking out of him a minute later."

"Until Mr. Morse's telegraph lines run out to the Arizona desert, it's a hell of a lot better communication system that anything we've devised," said Edison. "You work with what you've got."

"Point taken," acknowledged Buntline as two more coyote calls came to their ears.

"I'd say they're half a mile to the north," offered Holliday.

"You're sure they're just *watching* us?" asked Buntline.

"If they were doing anything more than watching us we'd know it by now," answered Holliday. "You've got nothing to worry about."

"I was curious, not worried," said Buntline. He patted the trunk. "If we can kill a dinosaur with what we've got in here, there's no sense worrying over a couple of Indians."

"Dinosaurs can fire rifles from a quarter mile away, can they?" asked Holliday in amused tones.

"Okay," growled Buntline. "I'll just keep my mouth shut."

Holliday and Edison chuckled at that, and about ten minutes later the coyote howls ended.

"What does the silence mean?" asked Edison.

"That they recognized me," answered Holliday. "They know I'm connected with the digs, so they figure I'm heading to Cope's camp— after all, I'm giving Marsh's a wide berth—and they'll have warriors posted along the way, watching us. You won't hear another howl unless I change directions, or . . ."

"Or?" asked Edison.

"Or a real coyote is calling to his ladyfriend."

They passed three abandoned digging sites in the next two hours, and reached Cope's camp just before twilight. Not much had changed. It was still in the same clearing, with the same configuration of tents spread across it. The more permanent structure, which held the fossils, had been expanded since Holliday had left.

Cope was there, cataloging the day's finds, and his men were scattered around the grounds, some working, some just loafing before dinner, which was cooking on a large fire.

"Mr. Edison," said Cope after Holliday made the introductions. The paleontologist extended a dirt-covered hand. "This is a great pleasure. And Mr. Buntline; I've read about your work, sir."

"The pleasure is all ours," replied Edison.

"What brings you to my humble camp?"

Edison looked surprised. "Didn't Doc tell you?"

Cope looked puzzled. "No, sir. Not a word."

"They expressed keen interest in seeing your discoveries and meeting you," said Holliday promptly.

"That's very flattering," said Cope. "I've been keeping a bottle of fine French brandy for a special occasion. I think this qualifies as such. Excuse me for a moment while I get it." He turned and walked off toward his tent.

"What the hell was *that* all about?" asked Buntline.

"Why tell him that some of these monsters may be resurrected by Comanche magic?" replied Holliday. "He'd probably post ten of his men as guards. Much better to have them dig, and maybe we can get the hell out of here before anything happens."

"I agree with Doc," said Edison. "Why alert them to something that even now, even after we've seen some of the things Geronimo and other medicine men can do, seems impossible to believe?"

"Okay," said Buntline. "Let's just hope the next location he picks isn't another piece of sacred ground." He frowned. "Why the hell couldn't they dig in, oh, I don't know, Michigan or Arkansas, someplace back East?"

"Maybe we should ask him," said Edison. "I'd be curious to know."

"Maybe we should," repeated Buntline.

Cope returned from his tent, carrying a bottle and four coffee cups. "This stuff really deserves crystal goblets," he said apologetically as he walked to a crude wooden table, "but . . ."

"Not a problem," said Holliday. "We're drinking the brandy, not the containers."

Cope smiled. "I'm glad you understand."

He took the top off the bottle and began pouring.

"Smells good," said Buntline.

"Smells divine," Edison corrected him with a smile.

"Well, gentlemen," said Cope, holding his cup up. "To my world-famous visitors."

"And our world-famous host," said Edison.

Suddenly three shots rang out.

"What the hell was that?" asked Buntline.

"I think it may have been our world-famous enforcer," said Holliday wryly.

They drained their cups as another shot echoed through the camp.

A moment later Cole Younger appeared atop his horse, blood streaming down the side of his face.

"What the hell happened?" demanded Cope as the four men ran the greet him and the rest of the staff began gathering around him.

"I don't know," growled Younger, dismounting and wiping his ear with a handkerchief. "Four Comanche blocked my way and started yelling at me. I don't speak no Comanche, so I just signaled them to get the hell off the trail. One of them aimed his rifle at me and damned near took my earlobe off." He paused. "That's four Comanche that ain't ever gonna bother us again."

"How far away did this occur?" asked Holliday.

Younger shrugged. "Maybe half a mile." He turned to Cope. "Right at the spot you had picked for digging tomorrow, Professor."

"You mind if we take a look?" asked Holliday.

"Ain't nothing there but three dead Indians," said Younger.

"I was asking Professor Cope," said Holliday.

"I'll come with you," said Cope.

"So will we," said Edison as he and Buntline stepped forward.

"What the hell," said Younger. "I'll come along too."

"You stay here and get someone to help you stop the bleeding," said Cope.

"You sure?" asked Younger. "Them Comanche probably had friends."

"We're sure," said Cope. "We'll have Doc with us."

Younger went off to get help with his ear. Cope waited until Holliday had gotten his horse and his two other visitors had saddled the horses that had pulled the wagon, then began leading them just to the north and east of the camp. After a few minutes they came to the bodies of the three Comanche warriors; one had died fast, two slowly, but all three were definitely dead.

Holliday studied the tracks and pointed to the spot where they had confronted Younger.

"Right here," he said. "Doesn't look any different from anything else around here. I wonder what the hell they had in mind."

Cope shrugged. "Who knows? Shall I send someone out to bury them? I mean, after all, it *is* their burial ground."

Holliday shook his head. "I'd let the Comanche do it themselves."

"Very well," said Cope. "Well, we might as well get back to camp before it's totally dark."

"You go along, Ned," said Holliday. "I have something I need to discuss with Tom."

Buntline frowned, but began riding alongside Cope.

"What is it?" asked Edison.

"Something's wrong," said Holliday.

"I know," said Edison, looking at the bodies with some distaste. "Three men are dead."

Holliday shook his head impatiently. "But *why?*" he said. "Marsh and Cope have been digging here for more than a month, and no one's bothered them. Suddenly three warriors try to kill Cole Younger just because he's standing—well, riding—right at this spot. What's changed?"

"I don't have any idea," said Edison.

"Well, *I* have an idea, and I don't like it much." He looked around. "Shit!"

"What is it?"

"I have a feeling that if we each had a shovel and started digging right here, we'd come to a stash of bones a lot closer to the surface than Cope thinks . . . and that they won't be dinosaur bones.'

Edison stared at Holliday. "You really think so?"

"It makes sense."

"Then what do you think we—" Edison froze. "Doc?"

But even as the word left his mouth, he closed his eyes and prepared for his death as Holliday drew his pistol and fired two shots.

Before Edison could yell, or collapse, or ask Holliday why he was shooting at him, he was almost knocked of his feet as a dead warrior, tomahawk in hand, fell against him as he tumbled to the ground.

"I thought you were shooting at *me!*" breathed Edison.

"He sneaked up right behind you," said Holliday, holstering his gun. "Another second and he'd have buried that damned hatchet between your ears."

Edison stepped aside, then turned and looked at the fallen Comanche.

"Thank you for saving my life, Doc," he said sincerely.

"Happy to," said Holliday. He walked over to the dead Comanche, and saw that he had been shot in the belly by Younger, "He was ninety percent dead already." He scanned the area for more lurking warriors. "If I'm right about what this means—that they're finally digging at an actual burial site—you just may get a chance to save us all."

15.

OLLIDAY WAS AWAKENED BY THE CURSING OF A MAN who had burned his hand grabbing a too-hot frying pan. He experienced a coughing seizure, sat on the edge of his bed for a few minutes until he felt strong enough to face the day, considered shaving, decided he'd lost enough blood in the past five minutes and he'd wait until his hands were steadier, and wondered, for the hundredth time, why he was risking a life that almost had an expiration date on it.

Finally he got up, looked around for his boots, then realized he'd gone to sleep with them on. He sighed, shook his head, and emerged from his tent into the sunlight. He winced, held a hand up to shield his eyes, and tried to remember why he'd gotten out of bed in the first place.

"Good morning, Doc," said Ned Buntline, who was half-sitting and half-squatting on a log, a cup of coffee in his hand.

Holliday muttered something unintelligible, yawned, suppressed a cough, and slowly wandered over to Buntline.

"I hear you had a little adventure last night, you and Tom," said Buntline.

Holliday shrugged. "Nothing very adventurous about it." Suddenly he smiled. "Interesting expression on Tom's face just before I fired my gun."

"Yeah, he told me," said Buntline with a chuckle.

"He still sleeping?" asked Holliday, squinting and scanning the area.

Buntline uttered a hearty laugh. "Only shootists who drink too much sleep this late, Doc. He's off with Cope, looking at some finds—or maybe looking *for* some."

"He ought to know better," said Holliday. "Cole and I shot those warriors awfully close to camp."

"You know nothing scares him," said Buntline. "Hell, if he was inclined to run, he'd have done so when the Apaches blew his arm off."

"Yeah, I know," answered Holliday. "What the hell time is it anyway?"

"Maybe an hour before noon. They've been gone for close to four hours. Those that are coming back for lunch should show up before too much longer."

"And what are you doing here?"

"Do I look like a paleontologist?" asked Buntline with an amused smile. "I'm a builder, and I figure someone ought to stay here guarding my invention, since it may save us all one of these days."

"Does it bother you that Tom gets all the credit?" asked Holliday, finally adjusting to the light enough to stop shading his eyes with his hand.

"Hell, no," said Buntline. "We're like the President and the Congress back East. He proposes, I dispose."

"I don't know what the hell you're talking about."

"He gets the idea and designs the mechanism, but I'm the one who builds it. If he didn't dream up the Buntline Special, you couldn't have used it on Johnny Ringo . . . but if I don't make it, it remains nothing but an idea." He paused. "Besides, I've got other interests as well."

"Oh?"

Buntline nodded. "Those dime novels about you and Wyatt and the other shootists are so damned popular that—"

"You're going to publish one?" interrupted Holliday.

Buntline shook his head. "No, there are more than enough people publishing them already."

"You're going into competition with Cody?" suggested Holliday. "I know Cole Younger plans to start a show, him and Frank James."

"How the hell many wild west shows does the public need?" replied Buntline. "No, I plan to write about you and the others, not for magazines, but for the theatre. Can you picture it? A play about—"

"Say the O.K. Corral and we just may do a rehearsal right here," said Holliday grumpily.

"How about the alley behind the Corral?" asked Buntline with a smile.

"Okay, you get to live," said Holliday, returning his smile. "Though what may happen here if the Comanche get mad enough might be even more dramatic."

"Perhaps," agreed Buntline. "Show me how to get a seventy-five-ton brontosaur on stage and I'll consider it."

"I thought they were the harmless ones."

"Tell me that after he steps on you, or you get in the way of his tail."

"Point taken," acknowledged Holliday.

"On the other hand, maybe—"

Holliday suddenly motioned him to be silent.

"What is it?" whispered Buntline.

"One lone man, not making enough noise. Could be a Comanche."

Buntline began looking around, frowning. "Where is he?" he whispered. "I can't see a thing."

Holliday folded his hands in his lap and pointed to his left with his right index finger.

"I don't see a damned thing," said Buntline.

"Try keeping your mouth shut and using your ears," said Holliday.

"Sorry."

Holliday seemed relaxed and indeed appeared half-asleep. Buntline tried to appear nonchalant, and did a terrible job of it.

Finally Holliday raised his voice. "Okay, you can come out now!"

A white man wearing a large Stetson broke from cover and entered the camp.

"Should'a known I couldn't sneak up on you, Doc," he said.

Holliday turned to stare at him. "You better go back while you can," he said in level tones.

"I can't," said the man. "This is my job."

"He's not paying you enough for this," said Holliday. "One more chance—go back."

"Who the hell is he?" demanded Buntline. "You talk like you know him."

"I've seen him," said Holliday, never taking his eyes off the man. "He works for Marsh."

"Doing what?" asked Buntline.

"He's here and he's armed," said Holliday. "What do you suppose he does?"

"There's no reason for anyone to get hurt," said the man. "You're not on Cope's payroll, Doc. Let me swipe a couple of bones and I'll go back and tell Marsh I destroyed a wagonload of them, and brought these to prove I'd been here."

"You're working for the wrong side," said Holliday. "Theodore would just beat the shit out of you, and then probably nurse you back to health." He got to his feet. "One last chance. Leave while you still can."

"I can't, Doc," said the man, tensing. "This is what I get paid for."

"Whatever he's paying you, it's not enough," said Holliday.

"I don't want to kill you, Doc," said the man.

"We're on the same page. I don't want to die."

"Don't try to stop me, Doc. I'm going to pick up some bones now."

"You're a very foolish man," said Holliday.

The man took a step forward, and Holliday drew his pistol and fired three quick shots. Two went into the man's chest; the third lodged in his stomach.

The man fell to his knees and stared at Holliday in disbelief. "You drew first," he said accusingly.

"Damned right I did," said Holliday. "It's a gunfight, not a sporting contest."

The man fell face first in the dust, dead before Holliday finished his sentence.

"Well, *that* ought to get them back for lunch on the double," said Buntline, staring at the dead man.

"You know, we could save a lot of trouble by locking Cope and Marsh in a room together and letting the survivor take charge of both digs," said Holliday, his face registering his disgust with the situation. "We've got a million Comanche who don't want us here, we've got medicine men who will do what they can to kill us, and all they can think of is sabotaging each other."

"You okay?" yelled Cole Younger's voice.

Holliday turned to Buntline with a grimace. "If we weren't, alerting whoever's threatening us by telling them that you're on the way probably isn't the brightest thing in the world to do."

"You've got a point," said Buntline.

"Yell back that we're all right," said Holliday.

"Me?"

"If I took a deep enough breath to yell, I'd be coughing for the next five minutes."

"We're fine!" hollered Buntline.

Younger, followed by half a dozen men, all with weapons drawn, burst into the clearing. "What the hell's going on here?" he demanded, staring at the body.

"Saboteur," said Holliday.

'Looks like his sabotaging days are over," said Younger, rolling the corpse over with his foot. "Anyone know this man?"

"That's Jed Wilkes," said one of his companions. "He used to work for Professor Cope. I guess Professor Marsh bought him away."

"No wonder he knew when and where to look for bones," said Holliday. "A couple of you men get some shovels and bury him."

"Hell, no!" said Younger.

"He's not going to turn into any nosegay," said Holliday. "Best to bury him now."

Younger shook his head adamantly. "I'll stick him across a horse and lead him up to Marsh's camp with a note on him, a note that'll say something like 'You want bones? Try these on for size!' Something like that. I'll whack his horse on the rump, and head back here while they're running him down and figuring out what happened."

Holliday shrugged. "It's your war. I'm just here to look at the animals."

"What animals?" demanded Younger.

"Who knows?" said Holliday noncommittally. He pulled out his flask. "Defending the camp against fools is thirsty work."

Cope arrived a couple of minutes later, accompanied by Edison and most of his men. Buntline briefly explained what had happened.

"Damn!" he said, turning to Younger. "I was right to leave you here, guarding our finds. Though now that we've got Doc . . ."

Holliday held his hands up, palms out. "You don't have me. I'm just passing through." He turned to Edison. "Any sign of anything bigger than a Comanche?"

"Like what?" interjected Cope.

Holliday saw Edison shake his head almost imperceptibly. "Like two Comanche," he answered.

"The four bodies were gone," said Edison.

"Makes sense," replied Holliday. "No sense burying 'em right where the Professor's digging."

"Okay, men," said Cope, turning to his crew. "Let's start moving the bones we brought back."

Holliday walked to the edge of the camp opposite where the men were bringing the bones, accompanied by Edison and Buntline.

"What was that all about?" he asked.

"The man's a fanatic, Doc," said Edison. "If he had even a hint that something he did might get the Comanche to resurrect some dinosaurs, he'd do everything he could to precipitate it."

"So would Marsh, come to think of it," agreed Holliday.

"So the trick is *not* to let them know why we're here, and maybe they'll find everything they're looking for and pack up their gear and go somewhere else to dig."

"You've got a real head on your shoulders," said Holliday. Suddenly he grinned. "I'll take a wild guess that you've been told that before."

Edison chuckled. "Once or twice."

"Well, let's keep a low profile, urge Cope to do the same, hope Theodore's having some luck getting Marsh and Cody to behave, and maybe we can all die in bed, wondering what dinosaurs really looked like."

"Do you believe it'll be that easy?" asked Buntline.

Holliday sighed deeply. "Of course not."

16.

ROOSEVELT SHOWED UP JUST BEFORE DARK, dismounted, and walked to the center of camp.

"Welcome back, sir," said one of the men who were preparing dinner.

"I'd like some coffee, please," said Roosevelt. "It's been a long ride."

Roosevelt waited until they'd poured him a cup, then looked around the camp. Men were starting to come in from the afternoon dig, but he soon spotted the men he wanted and walked over to them.

"What the hell are you doing here?" asked Holliday

"I'm pleased to see you too," said Roosevelt, flashing him a toothy grin.

"Damn it, you know what I mean," said Holliday. "I thought you were keeping an eye on Marsh's camp while I watched this one."

"I have a feeling this one's in more trouble," said Roosevelt, sitting down on a tree stump.

"What are you talking about, Theodore?" asked Buntline.

"I was out hunting for the camp's dinner, as usual," began Roosevelt.

"They're currently about twenty miles east of you, maybe a little more. Anyway, I was tracking a pronghorn buck when I heard a pretty hideous noise, not like anything I've ever heard before . . ."

"What did it sound like?" asked Buntline.

"He just told you he'd never heard it before," noted Edison mildly.

"I mean, was it like an animal, or some kind of machine like—I don't know—like a train or something."

"Probably closer to a scream," said Roosevelt, frowning. "But it wasn't like any scream I've ever heard."

"Besides," added, Edison, "pronghorns are mute. Go on, Theodore."

"I came to the buck about five minutes later," continued Roosevelt. "Half of it was missing."

"Missing?"

"Something *big* had killed it and taken a couple of bites of it, and I found what was left." Roosevelt grimaced. "It was a mess. I mean, I've hunted grizzly and puma, but I've never seen anything with a bite like that. So I figured maybe what we were afraid of was coming to pass, and I decided to follow the creature's trail and see what we're dealing with here."

"And what *are* we dealing with?" asked Holliday.

Roosevelt shrugged. "I don't know. I never caught up with it. But in another three or four miles I came to what was left of a really big grizzly that didn't get out of its way fast enough."

Edison smiled a satisfied smile. "Ned was afraid we'd made this trip for nothing. I'm glad to see he was wrong."

"I think you'd have been much happier if he was right," responded Roosevelt. "Believe me, Tom, I've spent a lot of time in the wilderness, and I never saw anything that can do the damage this thing did—not as much, and certainly not as fast."

"You've left out the most important thing, Theodore," said Holliday.

"Oh?"

Holliday nodded. "Why do you think we're in more danger than Marsh's camp?"

"Because I followed whatever it was to within about five miles of here, and then I came upon some more tracks, just as big but clearly *different*. So right at the moment I don't know for a fact that any of these creatures are in Marsh's immediate vicinity, but I know for a fact that you've got at least two of them within five miles of you."

Holliday nodded again. "I *knew* this was going to happen when they started digging in the wrong spot."

Roosevelt frowned. "How can you tell the difference?"

"Because suddenly the Comanche stopped watching us and started trying to kill us." Holliday turned to Edison and Buntline. "Maybe you'd better show us what you've brought and how it works."

Edison nodded. "Maybe we'd better." He paused. "We don't have enough for the whole camp. These are just prototypes. We've only created two."

"Let's keep this very quiet while we can," said Holliday. "Especially what you saw, Theodore."

"Don't want to panic the men, right?" suggested Buntline.

Roosevelt and Holliday both looked amused.

"You still don't know who we're dealing with," said Holliday. "You give either of these geniuses the tiniest hint that they might run into a hungry six-ton meat-eater and they'll race each other to get to it first."

"Doc's right," said Roosevelt. "I think Marsh would give everything he's got, probably including his life, for a close-up look at a live one."

"Okay," said Edison. "It goes no further."

"Until one shows up," added Buntline. "Then nobody'll keep it a secret—the two idiots who are rushing toward it, or the hundred intelligent men who are screaming and running hell-for-leather in the opposite direction."

"Well," said Edison, getting up off the log he was sitting on, "I think we'll go to my tent. If I do it out here, we're bound to attract attention, and then we'll either have to tell them what we've got or lie to men who trust us and have become our compatriots."

"Okay," said Holliday. "Let's mosey over there."

"All together or one at a time?" asked Buntline.

"The tent'll only hold the four of us," answered Edison. "Let's go."

The tent was at the far end of the camp, and Roosevelt returned his empty cup as they passed the fire in the center of the place. Buntline reached for a piece of meat that was cooking, swore when he burned his fingers, and stabbed it with a knife, carrying it along until it was cooler.

"Welcome back, Theodore," said Cope, emerging from where he'd been cataloging the day's finds. "I hope this means that son of a bitch is dead or disabled, but I suppose it doesn't."

Roosevelt grinned. "He sends his love to you, too."

Cope chuckled. "You know, I used to like him. Like and respect."

"So I've heard."

"Just goes to show I'm not perfect," said Cope. "Will you be staying with us for a while?"

"Looks like," answered Roosevelt.

"Good. I've been reading your history of the West, and I'd like to ask you some questions."

"I'll be happy to answer any that I can," replied Roosevelt. "If you don't mind my saying so, you seem so single-minded about fossils I'm surprised that my books interest you."

"I'm especially interested in some of the Indians' legends," continued Cope.

"Ah!" said Roosevelt. "Especially about giant monsters?"

Cope smiled. "Not that they'd ever have seen any," he replied. "But if they came upon some fossils, that could give birth to a legend or a superstition."

"Theodore was just telling us about some tribe in the Colorado Rockies that had just such a legend," interjected Edison. "Might be an interesting place to look for bones."

"I've been planning to get to Colorado," said Cope. "Maybe I'll move it up on my list." He paused. "Would you gentlemen care to join me for dinner?"

"In a few minutes," answered Roosevelt. "Tom wanted to ask me a few questions about New York politics, and I'm going to show mercy to your men by not boring them to death with my answers."

Cope laughed and headed off toward the fire. "Fine, I'll see you when you're done."

The four men continued walking to the tent, and a moment later Roosevelt was squatting in front of the trunk. Holliday found squatting or kneeling too uncomfortable, and simply stood there, hands on hips, waiting for Edison and Buntline to show him the weapon they'd devised.

"Well, as least you told him where to go," said Holliday. "Not where I'd have told him and Marsh to go."

Edison laughed at that. "You've always been the soul of discretion, Doc."

"On a hobnailed boot, maybe," responded Holliday.

Edison opened the trunk and pulled out the weapon he had devised and Buntline had built.

"Damned thing can't be a foot long," said Holliday, frowning. "That's not going to stop the kind of critter that can do the damage Theodore saw."

Edison reached over and pulled a cartridge out of Holliday's gun belt. "This tiny thing can kill a man, Doc. Add a few grains and a little speed to it and it can kill a lion or an elephant. Size has got nothing to do with it."

"That's sure as hell not what I've been hearing from Kate for the past ten years," muttered Holliday.

"How does it work?" asked Roosevelt.

"Just like a pistol," said Edison. "You aim it, and instead of pulling a trigger you press this firing mechanism here, and then you hope your aim was straight and true."

"Does it make much of a bang?"

"It doesn't make a bang at all," said Buntline.

"Enough powder behind the bullet to kill something bigger than an elephant, and it doesn't make a bang?" said Holliday, frowning.

"It doesn't fire bullets, Doc," said Edison patiently.

Holliday held the new weapon up, pointed it at his face, and looked down the barrel.

"There's some kind of hole here," he said. "What the hell comes out, if not a bullet?"

"Don't point it at yourself, just to be on the safe side," said Buntline, gently leaning on Holliday's arm until he lowered it.

"It emits—I like that word better than 'fires'—an invisible force that will play havoc with the creature's nervous system. He won't be able to stand, or balance, or even breathe," said Edison.

"Why not just a small cannon, something about the size of a rifle?" asked Holliday.

"A number of reasons," said Buntline. "Any weapon that fires a bullet or a ball capable of bringing down one of these monsters would break your shoulder the first time you fired it."

"Not only that," added Edison, "but where there's one resurrected dinosaur there's likely to be more than one. Any projectile—that's bullet or cannonball to you, Doc—that can kill one of these beasts, or even knock him down, will almost certainly cause an open wound, and believe me, you don't want a bunch of allosaurs catching the scent and rushing to the scene."

"Do they hunt in packs?" asked Roosevelt.

Edison shrugged. "Who knows? Lions do, tigers don't. It's all guess-work, but why take the chance?"

"If there's no bang and there's no discernible wound," said Holliday, "how do you know if you've merely wounded him or missed him altogether?"

Roosevelt chuckled.

"What's so funny?" asked Holliday.

"It's obvious you've never hunted."

"Okay," said Holliday. "Enlighten me."

"Being charged by a dinosaur has one thing in common with being charged by a grizzly," answered Roosevelt. "If you shoot and he's still charging, you don't waste any time worrying about whether you missed him or wounded him. You fire again."

"Makes sense, at that," admitted Holliday.

"That one's yours, Doc," said Edison. "I've got another one for Theodore."

"How do we load the things?" asked Holliday, moving the gun from hand to hand, aiming it and lowering, getting the feel of it.

"Ah!" said Edison. "I'm glad you asked. You see this trunk?"

"Of course I see it."

"Have you been wondering why we needed such a huge and obvi-ously heavy trunk to bring two relatively small weapons with us, cer-tainly smaller than the Buntline Special that Ned made for your friend Wyatt?"

"Not until you mentioned it," admitted Holliday. "The Buntline Special that you made me back in Tombstone, the one I used against the thing that used to be Johnny Ringo, wasn't exactly a simple weapon either."

"It's got to be a battery," said Roosevelt.

"How did you know?" asked Buntline.

"Tom's the Electricity King," answered Roosevelt. "It figures that he'd use it to power our weapons."

"Right," said Edison, opening the top of the trunk again so they could see the battery. "The guns plug in *here*," he pointed to a pair of small connections, "and you'll have to power them up at least an hour a day. Two hours would be even better."

"Shouldn't be a problem," said Holliday. "We can take turns plugging them in once we're all back in camp."

"All right," said Roosevelt. "Let's put these weapons back before Professor Cope comes looking for us."

They plugged in one of the weapons and Edison closed the top, then walked to the tent flap.

"Aren't you going to lock it?" asked Holliday.

Edison shook his head. "How will you get to the weapons if a raptor or an allosaur kills me while it's locked?"

"Good point," acknowledged Holliday. "Dinosaur hunting is new to me."

"Well, hunting men will be just as new to them," said Buntline.

"I know," said Holliday. "I figure the only advantage we got going for us is that they make bigger targets."

"True," said Edison. "Looks like it's going to be a moonless night. Let's just hope they're not nocturnal."

17.

HOLLIDAY DRAGGED HIMSELF OUT OF BED, slipped into his boots, blinked his eyes a few times, trying to focus them, pulled out his flask, found that he had drained it before he'd gone to bed and had to refill it, growled an obscenity, and walked out into the sunlight, wincing as it hit his eyes.

"Good morning!" said Roosevelt cheerfully. "I trust you're ready to seize the day."

"You go to hell," growled Holliday, heading off to where he'd concealed a bottle of whiskey in the bone shed. He took a long swallow, clumsily filled the flask, spilling some on the floor, tucked the flask into his vest pocket, and emerged into the open air once again.

"You'd better hurry, Doc," said Buntline, who was standing by the fire. "There's not much breakfast left."

Holliday merely glared at him.

"It wouldn't be a bad idea, Doc," said Roosevelt. "You might need all your strength before the day is over."

"How much fucking strength does it take to press a goddamned button?" muttered Holliday. He walked to a shaded area, looking around for something to sit on, found nothing, and finally sat down in the dirt.

"Maybe *I* should take the second weapon," said Buntline.

"Don't be silly, Ned," said Edison. "You couldn't hit the broadside of a barn—from the inside."

"Doc'll be all right," said Roosevelt with a smile. "Look at him. He's so mad at the world he doesn't need a gun to kill a dinosaur."

"Why?" asked Buntline.

"It's morning," answered Roosevelt, amused. "He'll be his usual unpleasant self come noon, and by nightfall he'll be almost pleasant."

"It's a wonder Wyatt or one of the other Earps didn't kill him one morning," said Buntline.

"Never underestimate him, even in the morning," said Roosevelt. "The reason the Earps lived long enough to make it to the O.K. Corral is because they *didn't* try to kill him one morning."

Cope came out of his tent carrying a large cloth bag.

"What have you got there, Professor?" asked Roosevelt.

"Goggles," answered Cope. "I should have passed them out sooner, but we've been digging in relatively soft earth. But before we quit yesterday we came to some bones that were, how can I express it, *affixed* to the still-buried sides of some rocky outcroppings. A couple of the men were cut by flying chips as we chopped away at the rocks, so it'll be mandatory to wear these things whenever we're digging through rocky ground. I don't want anyone losing an eye."

"Not a bad idea," offered Buntline.

Cope glanced at Holliday. "Is he okay?"

"He's as okay as he gets at this time of day," answered Roosevelt. "We'll be along in a few minutes."

"Fine," said Cope. "I'll see you there."

He signaled to a number of the men who'd been loading the wagons with digging equipment, and a moment later they were traveling north and east to the site they'd been working at the previous day.

"I've got a question, Tom," said Roosevelt.

"What is it?"

"I should probably be asking Cope, but there's no sense alarming him." Roosevelt looked around to make sure all the men had left the camp and there were no stragglers who might overhear him. "We know that there's at least one dinosaur wandering around, and based on the way the pronghorn looked, it wasn't killed by any herbivore. It was half-eaten."

"I know," said Edison. "So what's your question?"

"Just how much danger are we in?" said Roosevelt. "What I'm saying, or asking, is: the carnivorous dinosaurs have never seen a man before. Their prey weighed tons. So my question is this: will they recognize men as prey animals? Or will they simply ignore us?"

"That would have been a harder question to answer yesterday morning," replied Edison. "But based on your own observations one of them killed and partially ate a pronghorn, and I doubt that it had ever seen one of *them* either."

"I know," said Roosevelt. "But there may be a difference."

"Between two legs and four?" asked Edison dubiously.

Roosevelt shook his head. "The pronghorn ran away, and that probably indicated to the dinosaur that it was a prey animal. What if we just stand still or ignore it?"

"You might be able to, Theodore," said Edison. "And I don't doubt that Doc would be happier standing his ground than running from anything. But there are thirty impressionable men out there, and I don't think you can count on none of them breaking and running."

"Hell," said Holliday from where he was seated some fifty feet away, "Marsh and Cope would run right *toward* the goddamned thing."

Roosevelt chuckled. "You know, they probably would."

Holliday got painfully to his feet, coughed into a handkerchief that was covered with dried blood from the previous day, and began walking to Edison's tent.

"All right," he said. "Time to go to work."

"Yes, I suppose so," agreed Roosevelt.

"Stay there," said Holliday. "I'll get your gun for you."

"It's not exactly a *gun*," said Buntline.

"Will it work just as well or poorly if I call it one?" replied Holliday irritably.

"Go," said Buntline, waving him toward the tent. When he was out of earshot, Buntline turned to his two companions. "There are days when I can sympathize with Kate Elder."

"He's a sick man," said Roosevelt. "A *dying* man. He had less than a day left when he made his deal with Geronimo, and this was the best Geronimo would or could do for him. I'd be in an even worse temper if it was me."

"You've got a point," agreed Edison.

"I've known Doc for about five years," said Buntline, "and he's *always* like this in the morning." He paused, then continued. "Sometimes in the afternoons and evenings, too."

"He's been dying for a lot more than five years, Ned," replied Edison. "And he's accomplished five times as much as most totally healthy men." Suddenly he inclined his head toward Roosevelt. "Present company excepted, of course."

Roosevelt was about to reply when Holliday emerged from the tent, carrying a weapon in each hand. He walked up to Roosevelt and handed one to him.

"Damned things are too big for holsters," said Holliday.

"Yes, I see," said Roosevelt. "I suppose I'll just have to carry mine. I can't leave it with my horse. If a dinosaur actually appears, every horse figures to take off in the opposite direction."

"This could get damnably awkward, carrying it all day," said Holliday.

"Not much we can do about it," said Buntline. "I suppose I could try to fashion a holster, but I don't have any of my tools with me."

Holliday shook his head. "Not necessary. I'm carrying another weapon that's not in a holster or tucked in a book."

"Oh?"

Holliday opened his coat, revealing a knife that hung around his neck on a thin cord.

"Watch," he said, and in a single motion he grabbed the hilt of the knife, broke the cord, and hurled it into a small tree, all in the space of a second.

"Impressive," said Buntline. "I'll see what I can rig that will be strong enough to hold the weapon and yet break the second you tug on it." He paused. "But I won't be able to do it before tonight," he added apologetically.

"Then this'll have to do," said Holliday, walking to the tree and pulling the knife out of the trunk. He reached into his pocket for a new cord, and re-fastened it around his neck.

"You ever have call to use that?" asked Buntline.

"From time to time," replied Holliday.

"Well, let's get started," said Roosevelt. He turned to Edison and Buntline. "There's no need for you two to come along."

"Don't be silly," said Edison. "You've got the only two weapons that might bring a dinosaur down, we know there's one heading this way, and you're suggesting we stay a couple of miles away from the weapons?"

Roosevelt chuckled. "I hadn't thought of it in those terms. You're right to come along."

The four men walked to their horses, and a moment later they were riding toward the previous day's site. It took them about ten minutes to reach it over winding, uneven, frequently rocky trails. Finally they came to a large rock formation that covered a few acres, and saw thirty-two men, all wearing goggles, chopping away at various portions of it.

"Welcome," said Cope, looking up from the spot he was concentrating on. "Would you like some goggles too?"

Holliday shook his head. "*I'm* not hammering anything."

"And I've got my own spectacles," added Roosevelt.

Cope shrugged. "Suit yourselves."

Holliday and Roosevelt walked to a small rise. "You're the hunter," said Holliday. "Where's he likely to come from?"

"There are a couple of wrong assumptions there, Doc," said Roosevelt.

"Oh?"

Roosevelt nodded. "First, we have no idea what *is* coming. And second, I'm not the hunter. I'm just one of the prey."

"Okay, I concede both points," said Holliday, scanning the landscape. "But surely all predators have things in common."

"They kill and eat their prey, and that's about it, Doc," replied Roosevelt. "We don't know if this thing walks erect or on all fours. We don't know if he's a sight hunter or a scent hunter. We don't know if he's warm-blooded or cold-blooded."

"The other two I concede," said Holliday. "But why the hell does it make any difference if he's warm-blooded or cold-blooded?"

"A warm-blooded animal, like a lion, or even a dog or cat, eats every day if he can, and certainly every couple of days unless he's starving due to injury," explained Roosevelt. "But a cold-blooded animal, like a snake or a lizard, can get along just fine on one meal every few weeks."

Holliday nodded. "All right, it was a silly question." He paused.

"You saw what was left of the pronghorn. Was there any clue whether the killer was warm- or cold-blooded?"

"No, not from the body," answered Roosevelt. "If you want my best guess, it's warm-blooded."

"Why?"

"It should have gone to sleep, nearly comatose, after a meal like that if it was cold-blooded, but I tracked it for a few miles, and it wasn't slowing down."

"Wonderful!" muttered Holliday. He held his weapon up in front of him. "These damned things had better work."

"I'll second that," agreed Roosevelt. "You know, maybe we'd each better have one of them—Tom or Ned—with us, in case something goes wrong with the weapons."

"If I'm close enough to fire and it doesn't work, I don't imagine they're going to be able to fix it in time."

"Maybe not, but it can't hurt."

Holliday frowned. "You know, I never asked them a vital question."

"What was it?" asked Roosevelt.

Holliday indicated their weapons. "What's the range of these things?"

"You know, I never asked either."

"Maybe one of us ought to." Holliday looked around. "I don't see them."

"I thought I saw where they'd unearthed a cave, or at least a crevice out of the heat," replied Roosevelt. "If we can't see them, that's where they've got to be. I know where it was. I'll go ask."

"Fine," said Holliday. He looked around. "There's nothing to see here. I'll go back with you."

The two men turned and walked back to the digging sites. Roosevelt spotted the cave, walked over, and soon disappeared within it.

Holliday positioned himself just beyond where Cope and an assistant had unearthed portions of a small skeleton. He had no idea how many sizes dinosaurs came in, and he couldn't tell from looking at it if it was a juvenile or a full-grown one. There was no head, at least not in the immediate vicinity, but he saw a foot with powerful-looking claws. He concluded that it was an adult, because he was sure that no baby could have claws like that.

He mentioned his conclusion to Cope.

"Perhaps," replied the paleontologist. "But we'll have to examine them more closely to see if they belong to the same specimen." He smiled. "A lot of things have died on this spot over the last ten or fifty or two hundred million years, Doc. Sometimes the earth isn't all that good at separating them."

"Well, that explains some of it," said Holliday.

"Some of what?" asked Cope.

"How something this small could exists alongside of those forty and fifty-tonners."

"That's one possibility," replied Cope. "But of course there are others."

"For example?"

Cope shrugged. "It could be that they eat different things, and that they're not competitors for turf or food. Or if could be that they did live eons apart. The earth changes. What was a hospitable environment for one of them may have been anathema for another, but that doesn't mean they each didn't die here, separated by millions of years, and they were squeezed together by the movements of the earth." Cope smiled. "I could refer you to some papers I've written on that very subject . . ."

"I think I'll just take your word for it," said Holliday, returning the smile.

"Fine. I don't mean to be rude, but I really want to get these ribs and vertebrae back to camp tonight."

"Go ahead," said Holliday. "I didn't mean to disturb you."

Cope smiled again, and went back to chopping rock and dried mud away from the bone, and Holliday took a couple of steps back to give him more elbow room.

Then, since he found the sight of men carefully chopping tiny pieces of rock away with their hammers boring, he looked off to his left.

And blinked to make sure he wasn't imagining things.

And then muttered a heartfelt "Oh, shit!"

18.

"WHAT'S THE MATTER?" asked Cope irritably as he stopped hammering at the rock.

Holliday didn't answer, and the paleontologist looked up at him.

"What's wrong, Doc?" he persisted.

"We've got company," said Holliday grimly.

"If it's that bastard Marsh . . ." began Cope.

"We should be so lucky," said Younger, staring where Holliday indicated as most of the men began diving into the holes they'd dug for cover.

Two hundred yards away was a huge dinosaur, possessed of an enormous head, rows of razor-sharp teeth, tiny forelegs, massive hindquarters, and a large, heavy tail that it seemed to use for balance.

"Predator or prey?" asked Holliday, holding his weapon with both hands and aiming it at what he hoped was the creature's heart.

"My God!" said Cope excitedly. "It can't be!"

"It damned well is," said Holliday. "Do I try to kill it, or just stir up some dust at its feet—if this thing *can* stir up dirt—and try to scare it away?"

"Definitely a predator," said Cope, staring in rapt fascination. "It's too big to be an allosaur. There's a carnosaur that we've tentatively called a tyrannosaur. What a magnificent animal!"

"Theodore!" called Holliday, not taking his eyes off the creature. "You got a bead on him?"

"I'll take his head," answered Roosevelt from about seventy feet to Holliday's right. "You go for the heart."

"Tom!" yelled Holliday. "What the hell's the range on this thing?"

"At least a hundred yards," Edison hollered back.

"Doc!" called Roosevelt. "Don't shoot for a minute. I want to get my rifle, just in case these gadgets don't work."

"You think a rifle can stop this thing?" said Holliday dubiously.

"Do you think that toy you're holding can?" said Cope.

The dinosaur continued approaching them at a leisurely pace, stopping every couple of steps to test the air and survey its surroundings.

"Either he's not hungry or he's blind as a bat," said Holliday.

"Or else he's killed some Comanche and doesn't think we present any kind of a threat," suggested Cope.

The creature got within eighty yards of them, then seventy. Younger emptied his pistol into it without doing any appreciable damage, indeed without the beast even acknowledging that it was being shot multiple times.

"Theodore, what the hell's taking you so long?" growled Holliday to himself as a number of the men fired their pistols futilely at the dinosaur and others broke and ran for camp.

It was within fifty yards when Roosevelt called out: "Okay, Doc!"

"What kept you?"

"The wind shifted, and all the horses sensed a threat approaching. It took me an extra minute to get mine to hold still long enough to get my rifle."

"Don't you want a rifle too, Doc?" asked Cope. "Or perhaps a shotgun?"

Holliday shook his head without taking his eyes from the creature. "The condition I'm in, I could barely lift one—and if I fired it, I'd do more damage to me than to the dinosaur."

The dinosaur was thirty-five yards away now, and was clearly attracted by the scent of the men and the horses. The horses began screaming, and as it turned its head toward them, Roosevelt and Holliday both fired their weapons.

The creature emitted a hissing screech, fell backward, instantly got to its feet, and charged in Holliday's direction. Another shot from each of Edison's weapons slowed it down, and after two more shots it lurched to its right, and collapsed. It struggled to rise once, then fell over on its side and lay still.

"Well, I'll be damned!" said Holliday, staring at his weapon. "It could use a little more stopping power, but the thing actually works!"

"I've got to examine this!" cried Cope, racing toward the fallen dinosaur.

"Just a minute, Professor!" said Roosevelt as he approached the huge creature.

"What is it?" demanded Cope. "This is my camp. I have every right to—"

"Nobody's denying that," said Roosevelt. "But there's an old hunting term that you're probably not familiar with. We call it 'paying the insurance.'"

"What are you talking about?" asked Cope.

"Spending the price of an extra bullet—or whatever it is that these things shoot—to make sure your quarry is dead."

So saying, Roosevelt walked to within ten feet of the fallen dinosaur's huge head and pressed the firing mechanism on his weapon again. There was no reaction from the dinosaur.

"He was dead," said Cope. "Anyone could see that."

"There's another old expression," said Roosevelt. "It's the dead ones that get up and bite you." He turned to Cope. "Anyway, he's all yours now."

Cope raced up to the carcass and walked around it, prodding it here and there. "Definitely too big for an allosaur!" he said excitedly. "Definitely a tyrannosaur!" He pulled a notebook out of his pocket and began writing furiously. "Jim!" he cried to one of his men. "You and Travis start measuring him."

Those members of his crew who hadn't raced back to camp cautiously approached it, and Holliday and Roosevelt retreated to where Edison and Buntline had been watching the action.

"Well, they work," said Holliday.

"You don't sound too enthused," noted Buntline.

"Ned, we need more stopping power," said Roosevelt. "It took us six shots to kill it. Now, maybe we missed some vital areas, but either it's got remarkable vitality, or we'd better learn *exactly* where its heart and brain are in that huge body and cranium so we hit them the first time. If it had been twenty yards closer when it began its charge, it would have sunk its teeth into *some*one before we nailed it."

"I'll see what we can jury-rig," said Edison. "But you have to understand that we don't have much in the way or tools or facilities."

"Just making an observation."

"I'll make another," said Holliday.

"Oh?" said Edison.

Holliday nodded. "Did you see the expression on Cope's face? He's probably never been that happy in his life. And you know Marsh would be the same way."

"Well, he's a paleontologist," replied Edison. "This is his field of study. Of course he's happy. The one thing he never thought he'd see is one of these creatures in the flesh."

"I don't think you're following me," said Holliday. "This is the happiest and most excited he's ever been. When word reaches Marsh, he'll be the most insanely jealous bastard you ever saw, and of course he'll move heaven and earth to get his hands on his own specimen."

Edison frowned. "I'm not sure I follow you, Doc. I mean, that's obvious, but I don't know where you're leading."

"Our task wasn't to shoot dinosaurs, Tom," said Holliday patiently. "It was to convince Cope and Marsh to go dig somewhere besides the Comanche burial ground." He paused. "You think any power on earth could get either of 'em to leave now?"

"Ah!" said Edison. "I see!"

"Maybe news won't spread to Marsh's camp," suggested Buntline hopefully.

"That's the biggest killer to roam the world in millions of years," said Holliday. "How long do you think you can keep it secret?"

"If we tell our men to keep quiet about it . . ." began Buntline.

"Damn it, Ned," said Holliday irritably, "they send a saboteur here every couple of days—and we send one there."

"All right," said Buntline. 'All right. Try to remember that *I'm* not the enemy."

"You've been remarkably quiet, Theodore," noted Edison.

"Just thinking," answered Roosevelt.

"About . . . ?"

"What if we put together a small herd of cattle?" suggested Roosevelt. "No more than half a dozen head. And took them along on the digs?"

Holliday frowned. "As bait?"

Roosevelt shook his head. "Not to attract them. I'd be much happier if we never saw another one of those monsters, except perhaps in a zoo."

"Then I don't follow you."

"If they sense a tyrannosaur or any other huge predator, they'll start mooing in terror, and that should attract its attention. It means we'll sacrifice a cow or two to buy us a little more time, since as you point out these weapons don't have the stopping power of my Winchester, let alone a Lee-Enfield .303 or whatever else Selous uses on elephant."

"Selous?" asked Buntline.

"An African hunter I correspond with," answered Roosevelt. "When I finally get over there, he's offered to be my guide."

"Let's concentrate on making sure you live long enough," said Edison. He paused. "Won't the cattle be more likely to *attract* a dinosaur?"

"I don't think so," said Roosevelt. "Neither men nor cows are its natural prey. Until it gets close enough to panic them, I don't imagine the scent of cattle will attract it any more than the our own scent."

"Just one problem, Theodore," said Holliday.

"Oh?"

"You see any cows around here?"

"Where's the nearest place to buy some?" asked Roosevelt.

"Not for two or three days in any direction. This is Comanche country. You'd probably have to go to Cheyenne."

"We could send Tom and Ned," offered Roosevelt.

"Neither of us would know how to drive the herd from there to here," said Edison. "I learned to do a lot of things while I was out here, but being a cowboy isn't of them."

Roosevelt shrugged. "All right. It was a thought."

"If another dinosaur shows up," said Holliday, "how many more shots are these guns good for before they run out of power?"

"They should be good for another four to six shots apiece at full strength," said Buntline. "After that, they'll still sting for a few shots, but they probably won't kill something this big and with this much vitality."

"And then?"

"And then we have to re-charge them for the better part of a day."

"You should have brought more," said Holliday.

"Damn it, Doc!" snapped Edison, finally losing his temper. "These are *prototypes*! We made them on short notice, and couldn't possibly field-test them until we came here."

"All right, I apologize," said Holliday. He turned to Roosevelt. "Let's you and I go back and see if there's any way to see what harm we did—besides killing it, I mean."

"Makes sense," agreed Roosevelt. "If my shots bounced off the cranium and yours killed it, I'd like to know that before the next time we have to face one—and vice versa, of course."

"There were no open wounds and no blood, at least that I could see," said Holliday, "but Cope's been examining the damned thing for a few minutes now, so maybe *he* can tell us which shot was the fatal one."

He headed off to where the crew had gathered around the tyrannosaur, accompanied by Roosevelt. Cope was directing two men who were measuring the beast's head.

"Do you know what killed it?" asked Roosevelt.

"You two, of course," said Cope.

"I mean, which shot?"

Cope shook his head. "I never heard a shot, and as far as I can tell this lady here is totally intact."

"*Lady?*" said Holliday, surprised. "You mean this is the smaller, weaker sex?"

"No, Doc," replied Cope. "I just mean that this one is a female. As far as I can tell, and even that fraud at the other end of the burial ground would agree with me, there seems to be almost no size differential among the carnivores. Hell, if anything, the females are bigger than the males."

"Besides, size isn't everything," added Roosevelt. "The African lion is appreciably larger than the lioness, but it's the lionesses that make most of the kills."

"*Mea culpa*," said Holliday. "How could I live with Kate Elder all those years and not know that?"

"So there's no indentation, no wound of any kind, on the head?" persisted Roosevelt.

"See for yourself," said Cope.

"Just out of curiosity," said Holliday—*and for future reference*, he added mentally—"where is the heart located?"

"We'll have to cut her open to be sure," answered Cope, "but I think it'd be right about there." He pointed, indicating the spot.

Holliday nodded. "That's where I was aiming."

"I don't know what kind of weapons you were using," said Cope, "but they certainly did their job." He stood erect and looked off into the distance. "I wonder . . ."

"About what?" asked Roosevelt.

"If one of these creatures has survived all the way to the nineteenth century, I wonder how many others might have. And," he added, "I wonder what she's been feeding on to reach this size." He frowned. "And how she escaped notice is absolutely beyond me. There are a lot of questions waiting to be answered." He paused and sighed deeply. "At least *I'll* be answering them, rather than that bearded bastard from Yale."

Holliday and Roosevelt exchanged looks.

"All right," said Cope, clapping his hands to get his men's attention, "there'll be time to stand around later. We need skin samples, teeth, internal organs, even an eyeball. Let's get as much done as we can during the daylight. We'll skip lunch and eat a hearty dinner . . . and I want to leave two men here to ward off scavengers once night falls."

Cope began walking around the enormous body, pointing out the things he wanted each man to do, and Roosevelt and Holliday retreated to where Edison and Buntline stood watching the proceedings.

"Ah, well," said Buntline. "We might as well go back to camp."

"I don't know," said Edison. "I'm aware of Cole Younger's reputation, but there's no way he can protect them from another tyrannosaur, or even an allosaur."

"Doesn't matter," said Holliday. "We've got to go back to camp. We have our work cut out for us."

"Why?" asked Edison and Buntline in unison.

"We have to find a way to divide your battery in half," said Roosevelt.

"What are you talking about?" said Buntline, frowning.

"I've got to go to Marsh's camp as soon as possible," said Roosevelt. "And I've got to go armed."

"Are you sure that's necessary?" asked Edison.

"Tell him, Doc," said Roosevelt.

"They resurrected one tyrannosaur, and it wasn't enough," said Holliday grimly. "What do you think they're going to do next?"

19.

EDISON SPENT ABOUT FIFTEEN MINUTES fiddling with the battery, making notes and conferring with Buntline. Finally he stood up and turned to Holliday and Roosevelt.

"I'm sorry," he said, "but there's simply no way to divide the thing. Ned could build another, but we'd have to go Cheyenne, or possibly even a larger town, to get the materials we need."

"Okay, we can't divide the guns," said Holliday. He frowned. "That presents a problem."

"A major one," agreed Roosevelt. "One camp is going to be completely unprotected."

Holliday nodded. "And it's got to be Marsh's."

"Why?" asked Edison.

"If we take both weapons with us, it could take us at least half a day, maybe a whole one, to locate Marsh," said Holliday. "No sense leaving *both* camps unprotected for a day."

"Ah, I see," said Edison.

"So our main task now is to somehow convince Marsh to move his base of operations here. It's the only way we can protect everyone."

"So who will man the other weapon once Theodore's gone?" asked Buntline.

"Cole Younger will handle one," replied Holliday. "I'll have to trust him to pick the best shot to handle the other."

"The *other*?" repeated Buntline, frowning.

"Yeah," answered Holliday. "I don't relish the ride, but I've got to go with Theodore."

"Why?"

"Because all he'll have is his rifle, and based on our experience here I think it'll take more than one rifle to bring one of these creatures down."

"With a little luck we won't run into any," said Roosevelt. "Whatever it was that attracted the one we just killed to this camp may attract whatever comes next. Thirty men talking and breaking rocks make a lot of noise. "

"I'm perfectly happy to bet Marsh's life on that," said Holliday. Suddenly he smiled. "Wouldn't even mind losing."

"Doc!" said Edison, frowning.

"Seriously," said Holliday. "If they kill Cope and Marsh, maybe the Comanche will be happy and send 'em all back to hell."

"First, they won't stop with Cope and Marsh," said Roosevelt, "but will kill all sixty or seventy members of their staffs. And second, if they could make them vanish just like that"—he snapped his fingers—"then our Apache friend wouldn't be worried about them traveling a few hundred miles southwest to his territory."

Holliday frowned and pulled out his flask. "Don't you ever get tired of being right?" he growled. "I was really happy thinking of letting the dinosaurs have Marsh and Cope for lunch."

"I'll get the horses," announced Roosevelt, walking off to the stable area while Holliday turned both weapons over to Younger, and had Buntline begin instructing him on how to use them. Then Roosevelt was back, and the two men mounted their horses and headed off to the east.

"That was quite a monster," remarked Roosevelt as they rode along.

"Yeah, I'll be seeing him in my nightmares for years," agreed Holliday. "Well, for one year, anyway," he amended. He shook his head in wonderment. "Who'd ever have guessed that the day would come when I'd be standing side by side with a New York politician, shooting at something that dwarfs a grizzly bear and hasn't been seen on Earth for millions of years?" He paused. "I wonder how many more of them are out there."

"No sense worrying about it," said Roosevelt. "Your job is just to shoot straight when the time comes."

"That's been my job most of the past twenty years," replied Holliday. He sighed deeply. "I wonder what I'd have said in college if I'd known it would come to this."

"Did you enjoy college?" asked Roosevelt.

"Well, I could take a deeper breath then than I can now," answered Holliday.

"You know what I mean."

"I was never much for socializing," said Holliday. "I've had maybe three friends in my life, counting you."

"No sweetheart?" asked Roosevelt.

"I can think of better terms to define the meanest madam west of the Mississippi," said Holliday with a rueful smile.

"You must have loved her once."

"I will admit to being especially happy to see her the day she broke me out of jail," answered Holliday. "Well, until she tried to brain me with a rifle barrel a few hours later."

"All right," said Roosevelt with a grin. "I won't ask anything else about her."

"You seem to do all right in the sweetheart department, especially if you're marrying again," said Holliday. "What was your first wife like?"

Roosevelt stared off into the distance, and Holliday could see the muscles working in his face.

"Perfect," he said softly. "Absolutely perfect."

"In what ways?"

"The subject is closed," said Roosevelt with an air of finality.

They rode in silence for another hour, and the train led them down from the rocky hills to an increasingly forested area with a small stream off to the left.

"Stop!" said Holliday suddenly.

"What is it?" asked Roosevelt.

Holliday frowned and pulled out his pistol. "I'm not sure. But I heard something off to the left."

"Put that away," said Roosevelt, indicating the pistol. "If it's a dinosaur we'll need something more powerful, and if it's not, there's no danger."

"Could be a puma," said Holliday, scanning the trees and bushes.

"Forget it," said Roosevelt.

Holliday kept his gun poised and continued looking.

"Doc, trust me," said Roosevelt. "I'm a naturalist. I've made a study of our bigger mammals, and I'm telling you this is the wrong terrain for a mountain lion."

"It's the wrong terrain for a dinosaur, too," said Holliday without relaxing.

Suddenly some bushes began moving off to their left, and a minute later a dark face appeared.

"Just a black bear," said Roosevelt. "They're common out here. Put the gun away. He's not going to bother us."

"I know of a couple of men who got killed by black bears," said Holliday, training his gun on the bear.

"They probably irritated the bear beyond endurance, or maybe they ran into it when it had cubs," said Roosevelt. "Believe me, this is a land of plenty for black bears. They'll eat anything, animal or vegetable, and they're not going to risk getting hurt attacking us when there's so much edible vegetation and so many small animals around."

They urged their horses forward, the bear merely stared at them, and finally Holliday relaxed and holstered his gun.

The next ninety minutes went without incident. Then they stopped for lunch—Roosevelt picked his off the local flora, Holliday drank his—and two hours after that they pulled into Marsh's camp.

"Welcome back," said Cody, walking up and greeting them. "Glad to see you, of course, but you picked a hell of a time to come back."

"Oh?" said Roosevelt.

Cody nodded his head. "Yeah," he said with a grimace. "The Professor hasn't found anything worth a damn for three days now. Maybe you'll bring him a little luck." He paused. "Why do you keep looking behind you, Doc?"

"Just want to make sure we haven't brought him more luck than he bargained for," replied Holliday.

20.

It WAS A GLOOMY CAMP. The men took their mood from Marsh, and his mood was fouler than usual. They'd been coming up with finds so often that a three-day period without one almost made them feel that the area was played out.

"You know that book about the white whale, the one that Melville fellow wrote?" said Cody as he was explaining the situation to Holliday and Roosevelt.

"Sure," said Holliday. "*Moby Dick*."

"Magnificent novel," added Roosevelt. "As good as anything Mr. Clemens has written. Perhaps a bit better."

"You've *read* it, Doc?" said Cody. "Well, I'll be damned!"

"Probably you will be," replied Holliday. "But why does it surprise you that I've read one of the most popular American novels of the century?"

Cody shook his head. "I keep forgetting you've been to college."

"Not all shootists are illiterate, you know," said Holliday irritably. "Johnny Ringo could discuss the classics with the best of them."

"Didn't I hear that you killed him?"

"The one had nothing to do with the other," said Holliday.

Cody stared at him curiously for a moment, then continued speaking. "Well, getting back to what I was saying, I just want a peaceful, harmonious camp—but Marsh is obsessed as Captain Ahab."

"And Moby Dick is the fossil he can't find?" suggested Roosevelt.

"Sort of," agreed Cody. "Of course, his real white whale is Professor Cope, and I assume Cope'd be just as happy to toss a harpoon or two into Professor Marsh."

Holliday nodded his agreement. "Yeah, I'd say that about sums it up."

"Actually," added Cody, "I've been thinking about going out after my own white whale."

"Your own white whale?" repeated Holliday, frowning.

"*Buffalo Bill's Wild West Show*," replied Cody. "I thought I might pick up some new attractions out here. Hell, I even thought we might find a whole dinosaur skeleton to take on tour. But all I do is stand shotgun while thirty men I couldn't care less about dig in the dirt. Dullest job I ever had."

"Well, you never know," said Holliday. "It might get less dull in a hurry."

"Only thing that breaks the monotony have been the three saboteurs we've caught, and to be honest I didn't catch two of them, a bunch of the workmen did." He paused. "Yeah, I miss the crowds, the excitement, the ladies coming up to see the famous Buffalo Bill. You know, I ain't seen a woman in close to ten, eleven weeks now, not even a Comanche woman."

"I got one back in Leadville I'd be happy give you," said Holliday.

Cody threw back his head and laughed. "I heard about you and her. Hell, I think everyone has. Wouldn't mind seeing one of them metal chippies she's got. They properly friendly, Doc?"

"Sure are," said Holliday. "Any one of 'em could hug you on a Monday and not let go till Saturday night."

"No wonder you're so damned skinny," said Cody.

"Same reason you're so talky," answered Holliday.

"I don't follow you."

"I never met a meal I liked, and you've never met a word you didn't," said Holliday.

Cody laughed again. "By God, I'm glad you're here! Maybe I won't leave camp just yet after all."

"We're *all* leaving," said Roosevelt firmly.

Cody looked up at the sky. "Don't look like rain."

"Rain's got nothing to do with it," said Roosevelt. "I've got to talk to Marsh."

"You better call him *Professor* Marsh or it's gonna be a mighty short conversation," said Cody.

"I'll keep that in mind," said Roosevelt. "Where is he now?"

"Probably out digging," answered Cody. He pulled out a cigar, offered one each to Roosevelt and Holliday, who refused, and lit it. "I'm just here because I'm doing night duty."

"He's digging at night?" said Holliday. "No wonder he's not finding anything."

Cody shook his head. "No, I'm on what we call saboteur duty. A couple of other men are standing guard against the Comanche."

"When's he due back?" asked Roosevelt.

Cody looked at the sun's position in the sky. "Maybe another couple of hours, though if he's shooting blanks again today he could keep 'em digging by torchlight."

Roosevelt turned to Holliday. "We can't wait that long, just in case."

"Just in case *what*?" asked Cody.

"Just in case he doesn't get back by dark," said Holliday. "We're new to this place. We wouldn't know where to look for him."

"Then talk to him tomorrow."

"Today's better," said Roosevelt.

"Why do I get the feeling there's something you two ain't telling me?" said Cody.

"I don't know," answered Holliday. "You got any idea why he feels that way, Theodore?"

"Well, he's not telling you about dentistry and I'm not telling you about taxidermy, just for a start," said Roosevelt.

"All right, all right," said Cody. "Enough bullshit. If you want to see the Professor, we might as well go now, before I get so annoyed I blow the both of you away."

Cody led them to the stabling area—a crude lean-to with a bunch of water buckets and a long hitching post. A few minutes later they were saddled up and passing through the camp.

"Which way?" asked Roosevelt.

"They headed *that* way this morning," said Cody, pointing due north. "But even if they've moved, they'll be easy to find. They ain't the quietest bunch of men you've ever come across. And of course, any time they come to bedrock and start whacking away at it with their hammers, you can hear it at least a mile off."

"Then let's head north," said Roosevelt, moving his horse to the front of their short line as the trail began winding its way to higher ground.

Holliday began cursing his horse and briefly pulled him to a stop, much to Cody's amusement. He urged the animal to begin walking again once Cody had passed him, confident that the showman hadn't figured out that he'd been manipulated between them so they could better protect him should one of the dinosaurs suddenly appear.

But nothing appeared except some meadowlarks and a family of grey partridges, and they progressed slowly through the uneven landscape for the better part of two miles before they could hear a couple of men yelling to one another. Roosevelt angled his horse in the direction of the noise, and a moment later they came upon a rocky outcropping where Marsh was directing the work of two dozen men, while some others were digging about forty yards away.

Marsh noticed them and stepped away from the outcropping to approach them, and the second he did all work came to a halt.

"Mr. Roosevelt," he said by way of greeting. "Doc Holliday. I thought we'd seen the last of you. I'm delighted to see you back here, but you've come at an inopportune time. I'm afraid this site has nothing further to yield."

"I'm sorry to hear that," said Roosevelt.

"My only hope is that swine Cope is having the same luck where he's at."

"It was Cope we came here to talk about," said Holliday.

"Not before dinner," said Marsh with no hint of humor. "You'll ruin my digestion." He looked around at his men. "Nobody told you to stop working!"

"We'll keep hammering and digging, Professor," said one of them, "but I don't think there's anything here."

"You know that for a fact, do you?" demanded Marsh.

"No, but—"

"Then get to work!"

"Theodore," said Holliday softly, "the only way to get him to leave here, and especially to go work side-by-side with his favorite swine, is going to be at gunpoint."

"Perhaps," answered Roosevelt. "But let a politician try first."

"Be my guest."

Roosevelt edged his horse forward a few steps.

"So you're not having much luck here?"

"We've had better," replied Marsh.

"That's a shame," said Roosevelt. "You know we've just come from Cope's camp"—he purposely did not use the word *Professor*—"and given your acknowledged skills I would have thought . . ." He let the words hang.

"So the fool lucked out and found a fossil," said Marsh, his voice reeking with contempt.

"Actually, the fool found himself a whole dinosaur," replied Roosevelt.

Marsh stared at him furiously.

"A big one," continued Roosevelt. A pause. "Bigger than an allosaur." A longer pause. "*Alive*. Doc and I had to kill it."

Marsh staggered as if he'd received a heavy blow to the head. Then he stood up on a rock where everyone could see him.

"Pack your gear!" he cried as Roosevelt shot Holliday a triumphant grin. "We're breaking camp!"

21.

THE TRIP TO COPE'S CAMP took five uneventful hours. Marsh refused to stop and rest the horses, and they were all dripping with sweat when they arrived.

"We're here," announced Roosevelt, turning to Marsh, who was sitting atop his lead wagon. "I think you'd better let Doc and me go ahead and break the news."

"You do that," said Marsh. He turned to his men and raised his voice. "But just in case that bastard wants to keep this find all to himself, have your guns ready."

"We didn't bring you here to start a war," said Roosevelt, hoping that Marsh was so obsessed with his hatred for Cope that he wouldn't bother to wonder why they *did* bring him here.

"We won't fire the first shot," said Marsh. "But if there's any shooting, we'll by God fire the last." He turned back to his men. "Cody, get up here! I didn't hire you for your fancy buckskins! Get that gun out of its holster!"

"I sure am glad you're not looking to precipitate a gunfight," said Holliday sardonically.

"Says the notorious gunfighter!" snapped Marsh.

"Bill," said Holliday to Cody, "Cope knows you, doesn't he?"

Cody nodded his head. "Yes."

"Okay, hop on the wagon with me and come with us to meet him and explain our peaceful intentions."

"I don't know about that," said Cody.

"Oh, they're peaceful," said Roosevelt. He raised his voice and spoke to Marsh's men. "If there's any shooting, you men are going to be up against the Younger Brothers. Is he paying you enough to do that?"

Cody seemed about to mention that two of the three notorious Younger Brothers were dead, but Holliday caught his eye and shook his head almost imperceptibly. Suddenly Cody grinned and remained silent.

"That's good enough for me," said one of the men. "I'm quitting right now."

"You quit now and you aren't getting a penny!" snapped Marsh.

"You owe me for six weeks' work!" yelled the man. "They don't need the Youngers. Maybe I'll just shoot you myself.

"Stop!" said Roosevelt firmly. "There's not going to be any shooting! If you men keep your weapons holstered, you don't have to quit. And if you stay, and Professor Marsh doesn't pay you, I'll personally help you beat the money out of him. Is that fair enough?"

Marsh was apoplectic, but nobody else uttered a word.

"All right," said Holliday. "You wait here. We'll let Professor Cope know that he's got company, and since he's every bit as sweet and loveable as Professor Marsh, it'll probably take us a few minutes to explain to him that no one's going to shoot anybody. I expect you to stay right at this spot until we get back."

"Unless a dinosaur shows up," said another man. "I can't speak for my friends here, but the second that happens I'm going to run like hell."

"Yeah," said Cody. "I don't imagine you can reason with them."

"You can't outrun them either," said Roosevelt. "I've only seen the one dinosaur, and he was charging into the worksite at the time. But in general, almost every carnivore that's ever walked the earth is programmed to chase just about anything that's smaller than itself and runs away from it. It'll take all your courage, but you'll be much safer standing your ground than running away."

"It *sounds* good," said another of the men. "But saying it and doing it are two different things. Maybe I'll just jump off my horse and slap him on the backside. He'll take off like a bat out of hell. Let the dinosaur chase *him* and leave me alone."

"You could do worse," said Roosevelt, nodding his approval. "All right, Doc, Bill—let's go."

It took them about ten minutes to reach the clearing where Cope had pitched his camp. It had a new shack, doubtless built to accommodate the remains of the tyrannosaur.

"Howdy Doc, Theodore," said Younger, walking forward to greet them. Finally he begrudgingly added, "Hello, Bill."

"Hello, Cole," said Roosevelt. "We need to speak to the Professor."

Younger nodded and ushered them to the older shack, where Cope was cataloging the day's finds.

"Theodore and Doc!" he said with a smile. "Welcome back." He turned to Cody. "And the famous Buffalo Bill. I'm thrilled to see you've finally left that thieving swine."

"He loves you too," replied Cody with a smile, and Younger laughed aloud at that.

"To what do I owe the pleasure of this visit?" asked Cope.

"We've brought you some other visitors," said Holliday.

"Visitors?" said Cope, frowning. "If that bastard thinks he's going to share *my* find . . ."

"I hate to contradict you," said Holliday, "but that wasn't *your* find. You didn't go looking for it. Hell, if anything we were *its* find."

"It's *mine!*" bellowed Cope. "Any court in the land would see that!"

Holliday turned to Roosevelt. "Why don't I just kill them both? *That* ought to solve all our problems."

"I want you both out of my camp *now!*" yelled Cope. "Cole, run them out of here!"

Younger looked at Cope as if he was crazy, and kept his hands in plain sight.

"May I see your deed?" said Roosevelt.

Cope merely glared at him.

"Now, try to calm down enough to pay attention," said Holliday. "Because a lot of lives depend on it. Some of them are important lives, and some are yours and Marsh's, but what we're going to tell you is vital."

"That's *Professor* Marsh," said Cope.

Holliday blinked his eyes very rapidly. "I thought you hated his guts?"

"I hate the man, not the position."

"All right," said Holliday, "Professor Marsh. Now, have you got all the screaming out of your system?"

Cope glared at him and didn't answer.

"Then I want you to listen, and pay attention. Do you know where you and Marsh—Professor Marsh—are digging?"

"Wyoming," said Cope sullenly.

"That's true," interjected Roosevelt. "But you're also digging—desecrating, one might say—a sacred burial ground of the Comanche."

"What do you want of me—of *us*?" demanded Cope. "We have to dig where we think the fossils will be." He gestured to the piles of carefully stacked and marked bones. "And we were right. There's the proof of it."

"There's more proof than that," said Roosevelt.

Cope stared at him curiously.

"That tyrannosaur was further proof," concluded Roosevelt.

"What are you talking about?" demanded Cope.

"The reason we're here, Theodore and I," said Holliday, "is because Geronimo warned me that—"

"He's an Apache, goddamn it!" yelled Cope.

"He's a medicine man, and he told me that if you insisted on digging in their burial ground, their medicine men weren't going to risk any braves by attacking you." He paused and stared at the scientist. "They were going to resurrect some of these monsters and sic them on you."

"That's ridiculous!"

"Then how do *you* explain the creature we killed, a creature that you yourself assured me has been extinct for millions of years?" continued Holliday.

"I was wrong," said Cope. "Some clearly survived."

Holliday sighed deeply and turned to Roosevelt. "Can I kill him now, Theodore?"

Younger took a step forward, then decided that Holliday wasn't serious, and relaxed.

"It's awfully tempting," admitted Roosevelt. "Professor Cope, Professor Marsh and his crew are going to share your camp until we've resolved this problem. You can object all you want, but the fact of the matter is that due to the nature of Tom Edison's weapons and their need for a power source, we can't protect two locations at the same time."

"Let a carnosaur eat the son of a pig, and good riddance!" snapped Cope.

"Clearly the two of you come from different backgrounds," said Holliday with an amused smile. "He calls you a son of a bitch."

"I've unearthed twice as many species as he has!" yelled Cope. "I've written more than a thousand papers, and he's still short of two hundred. He should be working for me, not cursing and threatening me behind my back!"

"I'm sure he feels the same way about you," said Roosevelt.

"I can vouch for that," added Cody with an amused twinkle in his eye.

"Now, are you going to tell your men to behave peaceably when Professor Marsh's men join them?" said Roosevelt. "Or do I tell both groups that the first one who misbehaves gets to face Doc Holliday?"

Cope glared from Roosevelt to Holliday and back again.

"For how long?" he said at last.

"I don't know," replied Roosevelt. "But it can't be too long. Either we find a way to smoke a peace pipe with them, or we're going to be facing more monsters than Tom and Ned's weapons can handle."

"Well?" said Holliday after a moment's silence.

"I'm thinking," answered Cope.

"What's to think about?" demanded Cody. "You do as they say and you have at least a chance of living. Don't do it, and sure as hell you're some dinosaur's lunch in the next day or three."

"Sir," said Younger, speaking up for the first time, "I don't mean to be disrespectful, and I'm sure as hell not being disloyal, but I'd listen to them if I were you. I've *seen* that damned critter, and I sure as hell don't relish seeing a whole herd of them."

They all turned back to Cope, awaiting his decision.

"All right," he said at last.

"Good!" said Holliday and Cody simultaneously.

"One more thing," said Cope.

"What?" asked Holliday.

"I want that bastard to post his mealtimes and stick to them. I'll adjust my own schedule, but I don't want to see his loathsome face. It would ruin my digestion."

Cody agreed to get the schedule before Holliday could once again suggest killing him.

22.

NIGHT HAD FALLEN. There were two large fires, one at each end of the camp. Edison had spent most of the afternoon and evening picking Marsh's mind, learning what he could about the science of paleontology, and seemed somewhat disappointed that while his views differed in many particulars from Cope's, his conclusions were essentially the same. Holliday and Roosevelt had decided to split up so neither side would think they were being favored, and now Doc sat in the glow of the fire, wondering if he could get any of the men interested in a few hands of poker.

"I still can't imagine why the tyrannosaur came to *this* end of the burial ground," said Marsh. "If it was resurrected by the medicine men, as Holliday and Mr. Roosevelt claim, what made it think it could find its prey *here* rather than at my camp thirty miles east of here?"

"Just be glad he *did* come this way," remarked Holliday.

"Why?" demanded Marsh.

"There are only two weapons that could bring him down before he killed anyone, and they were both in this camp," answered Holliday.

"That's right," confirmed Edison. "We only made two."

"Can you make more?" asked Marsh.

"Not unless we go back East to our lab," said Buntline.

"I heard you had a laboratory in Tombstone, and another one someplace in Colorado. Denver, perhaps?"

"Leadville," Buntline corrected him. "But we don't have the materials we need in those locations. The best I could do is make you a suit of brass armor that even a dinosaur couldn't pierce or flatten, but you'd probably expire from heat stroke or asphyxiation before you ever came face-to-face with a dinosaur."

"There's only been one so far," added Edison.

"And why did it visit that back-stabbing villain?" demanded Marsh.

"Shall I assume you're speaking of Professor Cope?" asked Holliday with an amused smile.

"Who else?" growled Marsh.

"I hate to bring up a painful subject," continued Holliday, who clearly didn't hate it at all, "but what the hell set you two off against each other?"

"I had taken him under my wing, even gone out fossil-hunting with him," said Marsh, glaring balefully into the fire. "In 1870 I was preparing to publish about the finds I'd made in New Jersey and Maryland"—suddenly he was shouting—"when that ungrateful bastard beat me into print, writing about *my* discoveries, *my* theories!" It took him a full minute to regain control of himself. "Even then I was prepared to forgive him, but what happened next made him my mortal enemy for all eternity. He *stole* my discoveries in North Carolina and wrote them up as his own! He took full credit for *my* work! And now, wherever I go, he's there too, even here, a thousand miles from anywhere!"

Holliday had an almost irresistible urge to say, "But outside of that, what do you think of him?" and was barely able to contain himself.

"Where are you going to dig next?" asked Edison.

Marsh shrugged. "Colorado, probably."

"You know," said Edison, "if you left now, you could collect all the best specimens before Professor Cope decides to follow you . . . *if* Colorado is one of his destinations."

"It will be," said Marsh. "You can count on it!" He uttered an obscenity.

Holliday pulled out his flask, tried to take a swallow, discovered there were only a few drops left in it, arose, and walked to the bone hut where he'd discovered Cope's stash of liquor during his last stay in camp. He filled the flask, took a long swallow, decided he didn't want to listen to any more of Marsh's ranting, and walked to the fire at the other end of the camp.

"Come join us, Doc," said Younger. "Theodore's just been picking the Professor's mind about dinosaurs. Maybe you can bring the conversation back to something reasonable, like whiskey or women or gambling."

"You going to become a paleontologist when this little crisis is over, Theodore?" asked Holliday, seating himself on a tree stump.

Roosevelt shook his head. "I'm too many years behind our two geniuses here."

"*One* genius," Cope corrected him, tapping his own chest with a thumb, "and one relatively bright but exceptionally bitter man."

"What's he so bitter about?" asked Holliday.

"Losing," was Cope's curt answer.

Holliday took a swallow from his flask, then capped it and put it back in a pocket. "I heard his side of it. What's yours?"

"We were friends once," said Cope. "He was even my mentor for a few months. We went on digs together in the 60s, after the War Between the States. In 1869 I went on digs with him in New Jersey and

Maryland. He's a Darwinian. Believes in evolution, and survival of the fittest. I buy some of it, but look around you and tell me if anything on Earth—men, lions, elephants, *anything*—was capable of killing off the tyrannosaur we encountered. So we found different fossils, and interpreted them differently, and because I'm a faster and more competent thinker and writer than he is, I published first—and he never forgave me for that."

"Calm yourself," said Roosevelt.

Cope, his anger building, glared at him and continued without missing a beat. "He tried to blacken my name throughout the community. Even then I'd have forgiven him, but I went to a site in North Carolina that he'd already been to, found some unique fossils he'd totally overlooked, and published—and he accused me in print of stealing the fossils from him, that he'd gone home for a week or a month or whatever, but that the site was *his*. But my men will vouch that there was no fence around it, no 'Stay Away' signs, nothing to indicate that we couldn't dig there." Cope paused. "And that bastard has been defaming me, suing me, and sabotaging my work ever since."

"And of course you do the same things to him," noted Holliday.

"You fight fire with fire!" snapped Cope.

Holliday turned to Roosevelt. "You *do* fight fire with fire," he agreed. "But I don't think anyone will ever know who lit the first match."

"Say anything like that again and you'll no longer be welcome in my camp," said Cope.

Holliday smiled. "Once was enough."

Roosevelt began questioning Cope about dinosaurs again. Cope answered begrudgingly at first, then passionately, and just about the time Cope was explaining how he was able to tell from a jawbone or a femur what the entire creature had looked like, Holliday fell asleep.

He was awakened by a high-pitched hissing sound. At first he thought it was a bee buzzing around his face and tried to slap it away, but there was nothing there. Then he decided it was a rattlesnake, and he jumped to his feet, only to find that there were no snakes in sight.

The sun had just risen, and he blinked his eyes a few times, then looked around the campsite. Everyone at both ends had gone to sleep in their tents. Everyone but the shootist that no one dared bother or awaken, he thought ruefully.

He was about to go to his own tent for another couple of more hours of sleep when he heard the sound again, and this time he realized it was coming from just beyond the camp. He could see trees and bushes sway as whatever it was made its way toward the campsite.

He rushed to Edison and Buntline's tent, threw open the trunk as they opened their eyes and groggily demanded to know what he was doing, and pulled out the two weapons.

"Theodore!" he yelled as he passed Roosevelt's tent.

Roosevelt, his glasses off, stuck his head out of the tent. "What is it?" he mumbled.

"Catch!" said Holliday, tossing him a weapon that Roosevelt barely caught before it hit the ground.

A few of the men began emerging from their tents.

"Stay back!" cried Holliday. "There's something coming this way, something *big*!"

Cope, wearing only his nightshirt, was out of his tent instantly, running alongside Holliday, and from the other end of the camp the bearded, half-dressed Marsh was racing hell for leather to catch up with them.

"I'll get my rifle!" yelled Cody.

"Don't bother!" responded Roosevelt, out of the tent and catching up with Holliday. "We've got the weapons we need."

"Maybe so," said Younger, joining them. "But I think I'll come along anyway—and I'll be armed. You too, Bill!"

Holliday noticed that Younger was carrying his six-shooter in his hand.

"You're not going to stop it with *that*," he said. "Just shoot it in the eye. It's your only chance of hurting it."

Then they were in the trees surrounding the camp. They could smell the pungent odor of the animal, whatever it was, and the hissing grew louder—and closer.

Suddenly a huge head appeared between a pair of saplings, with two horns pointing forward from the top of its skull and what seemed like a high collar of bone surrounding it.

"Triceratops!" breathed Marsh, stepping forward in rapt fascination.

"Hold him back!" snapped Cope.

"So you don't hate him," noted Holliday as Roosevelt caught Marsh's arm in his vicelike grip.

"I was here right beside you," responded Cope. "I don't want that bastard claiming it's his just because he's ten feet closer to it when you kill it."

"My apology," said Holliday, shaking his head in bewilderment. "All right, does this thing eat people?"

"No," said Cope.

"Look at the size of its head!" said Roosevelt. "It takes up almost a third of its body!"

"I'd say this one weighs about eight tons," said Marsh.

"Ten," muttered Cope.

"Theodore?" said Holliday, never taking his eyes off the dinosaur. "What do you think?"

"We're not threatening it, and it's herbivorous," replied Roosevelt. "Maybe it'll turn around and go back where it came from."

"No!" cried Cope and Marsh simultaneously.

Cope found a small rock on the ground and threw it at the triceratops' nose. At the same instant, Marsh pulled one of Cody's pistols from its holster and fired point-blank at the creature.

The dinosaur's reaction was immediate and violent. Its hiss became indistinguishable from a roar, and it lowered its head so that its horns protruded ahead of it and charged.

The assembled men broke for cover, all except Holliday, Roosevelt, Younger, Cody, and the two scientists. Younger emptied his gun into it with no discernible effect, and the first two shots Holliday and Roosevelt fired seemed to have no effect either.

Holliday pressed the firing mechanism, kept it depressed, and trained his fire on the beast's left foreleg. Roosevelt decided there was far too much bone for a brain shot, and fired charge after charge into its chest, and still it kept coming.

It finally dropped to its knees when it was no more than twelve feet away, bleating furiously.

"This damned thing's used up," said Holliday, indicating his weapon.

Roosevelt trained his weapon on the triceratops' ear and fired. There was no effect. "This one too," he announced.

"Are you sure?" asked Cody.

"Bill, we killed something a lot bigger than this with these same weapons," said Holliday. "This guy just had more armor. We've used up our weapons' power."

"Someone give me a rifle," said Roosevelt, and Cody handed his own rifle over to him.

He walked up to the triceratops, ready to duck or run in an instant if it should find the strength to stand, but it merely glared at him. He walked around its muzzle, aimed the rifle in its ear, and fired—and the creature fell onto its side, jerked spasmodically, and then lay still.

"I've got to examine this!" cried Marsh, racing toward the enormous body. Cody blocked his way long enough to take back his rifle.

"After me, intruder!" yelled Cope, rushing up to the other side. "This is *my* camp, and that makes it *my* triceratops."

"Actually," said Roosevelt, "I fired the shot that killed it. That makes it mine. And I will allow both of you to examine my dinosaur as long as you behave yourselves." He turned his back on the two men and faced Holliday. "Doc," he said with a wink of his eye no one else could see, "if either of them causes any trouble, shoot him in the leg."

"It'll be a pleasure," said Holliday, smiling and returning the wink. "Where'll you be?"

"Might as well get some breakfast, and get these things re-charged," said Roosevelt, holding out his hand and taking Holliday's weapon. "The rest of you men, come on back to camp with me. You'll have all day to slice up the triceratops once we decide who gets what."

He turned on his heel and began walking back toward the campsite, accompanied by everyone but Cope, Marsh, Cody and Younger.

Cody approached Marsh. "I'm a goddamned showman, not a goddamned monster hunter," he said angrily. "Hunting for bones is one thing; hunting for *this* and anything like it is another." He turned to Younger. "I'm quitting this circus, Cole. Why don't you come on back to the show with me?"

"Thanks for the offer, but no, thanks," replied Younger.

Cody shrugged and began walking back to camp.

"I've had it with this craziness too," Younger confided to Holliday. "Come tomorrow I'm outta here."

"Then why didn't you take Cody up on his offer?" asked Holliday.

"Be a bit player in *Buffalo Bill's Wild West Show*?" said Younger contemptuously. "Not me. I'm hooking up with Frank James and starting my own show." He smiled. "We can always use a sharpshooter."

"I wish you good luck in finding one," said Holliday.

Younger was about to reply when they heard a very strange, very loud bellowing coming from the direction of a nearby river.

"God damn!" said Holliday. "Another one—and our weapons are empty. We'd better get back to camp and round up some rifles fast!"

"What about *them?*" asked Younger, indicating Cope and Marsh.

"You think you could make 'em leave?" asked Holliday. "Be my guest."

"You've got a point," agreed Younger.

But before they'd gone fifty yards Roosevelt, sitting atop his horse, galloped past them.

"What the hell does he think he's doing?" asked Younger.

"I don't know," replied Holliday. "But whatever it is, he's got a reason. He's always got a reason."

"If he's going to play at being bait, I hope whatever's out there is slower than his horse."

"I'll second that," said Holliday, starting to walk after him, followed by Younger.

"We're crazy, you know," said Younger. "Here we are on foot, with a pair of pistols to face something that dwarfs an elephant."

"I've got a knife, too," said Holliday with a smile.

Younger snorted a laugh. "Well, if it eats us right now, at least people can say we died grinning."

Suddenly they heard trees and bushes crashing, and thundering footsteps came to their ears—and then into the clearing burst a brontosaur, an immature one that weighed about thirty tons with a head that towered some eighteen feet above the ground.

Holliday aimed his pistol at it, though he knew it was an exercise in futility, and just before he pulled the trigger he noticed that the huge sauropod was leaning to its right.

"I'll be damned!" exclaimed Younger. "Look!"

And suddenly the brontosaur turned just enough that Holliday could see Roosevelt riding alongside it, and hanging on to the end of a lasso that he'd somehow thrown over the creature's head.

"Stand back, Doc!" he yelled. "I'm taking him to the river. Once he wades in he won't feel threatened and there'll be lots for him to eat!"

Holliday moved a few yards back to make sure he wouldn't be side-swiped by the brontosaur's enormous tail. A moment later Roosevelt and the creature were out of sight, and a moment after that he could hear the sound of a massive splash.

"Son of a gun!" exclaimed Younger. "What do you make of that, Doc?"

Holliday shook his head in wonderment.

"That damned cowboy never ceases to amaze me," he said. He sighed deeply. "Let's go grab some breakfast before the next one shows up."

23.

OTH FACTIONS HAD JUST FINISHED BREAKFAST. Holliday was sitting in the shade of a tree, his back to the trunk. He'd actually eaten some food rather than drinking his breakfast, and he wasn't sure how he felt. Different, to be sure. But better? He was still trying to make up his mind.

Roosevelt sat nearby, trading hunting stories with Cody, who hadn't left camp yet but reiterated every few minutes that he was now a free agent. Younger had broken his pistols and rifle apart and was cleaning them against the next time he had to face a dinosaur. Marsh was a few feet away, while Cope was still with the remains of the triceratops.

"I'm surprised you're back here," said Edison, wandering over from the other side of the campsite, which Holliday viewed as "Cope's side."

"I'll be going back later."

"The brontosaur, or whatever it was, may be gone by then," suggested Edison.

"It's my conviction that they spent most of their time in water. I've examined their femurs, and they simply aren't built for carrying seventy or eighty tons all day long. To say nothing of the muscle fatigue caused by lugging that weight around."

Edison frowned. "I understand your words, Professor, but I don't quite see what you're saying."

"I'm saying I don't have to rush back because I know where the creature will be," answered Marsh. "Standing in the river, where the water will help him handle that bulk. Also, our friend Theodore gave him quite a scare. He won't come out for hours because for all he knows Theodore is waiting for him."

"I didn't see him, of course," said Edison. "But you make him sound very predictable."

"This is *my* field, Mr. Edison," replied Marsh. "But even that charlatan Cope could have told you this. When you're eighty tons and buoyant, you find water that can accommodate your need for buoyancy."

"I hope you're right," said Edison.

"He'd damned well better be," said Younger, still polishing the firing mechanism of the rifle. "Believe me, Mr. Edison, you don't want that critter coming through camp here. He could probably kill forty men with a swipe of his tail and never even notice he'd done it."

Marsh walked over to Roosevelt. "Do you mind if I sit down next to you, sir?" he asked.

"Be my guest," replied Roosevelt.

"Thank you," said Marsh, carefully lowering himself to the ground. "That was some remarkable heroics you displayed this morning, sir."

"It was an interesting experience," replied Roosevelt.

"It was much more than that," said Marsh. "I would expect no less of a Harvard man."

"Coming from a Yale man, that's high praise indeed," said Roosevelt with a smile.

"We have more in common than you think," replied Marsh. "Especially in these surroundings."

"I don't think surroundings have much to do with the quality of a man's mind," answered Roosevelt, wondering where the conversation was heading.

"Ah, but no schools turn out better minds than Yale and Harvard!" said Marsh.

"Harvard and Yale, please, Professor," said Roosevelt with what was becoming a trademark grin. "Harvard and Yale."

"Harvard and Yale," conceded Marsh, which seemed to make Roosevelt even warier, for in his experience such a concession was unheard-of. "I'm glad that even in these surroundings we can converse like two civilized men."

"True," said Roosevelt, eyeing him suspiciously.

"In fact, you have so impressed me that I think I should be happy to have my principals fund a major endowment for Harvard."

"That's very generous of you," said Roosevelt.

"Ask him who you have to kill for it," said Holliday, who'd been listening from where he sat.

"Hold your tongue, murderer!" snapped Marsh, glaring at him. He turned back to Roosevelt. "How does this idea of an endowment sound to you, sir?"

"Dr. Holliday may lack a little something in tact and restraint," said Roosevelt, "but he does pose an interesting question. Is this endowment out of the goodness of your heart, or am I expected to do something for it?"

"All you have to do is support my claim to ownership of any dinosaur you kill or capture."

Roosevelt laughed aloud. "You have to work on your subtlety, my friend from Yale."

"You haven't heard the size of the endowment," said Marsh.

"I don't have to," answered Roosevelt. "The answer is no."

Marsh was silent for a moment. Then: "What is that scum paying you?"

"Not a thing."

Marsh frowned. "Then I don't understand."

"I know it's going to be difficult for the two leading paleontologists in the country to understand, but I'm not here to help either of you collect specimens. I'm here to save innocent people from a hideous fate that they did nothing to deserve, that may be visited upon them solely because you and Mr. Cope are desecrating a sacred burial ground."

"*Professor* Cope," said Marsh almost automatically.

"I'll call the two of you Professors when you stop acting like spoiled and petulant children and begin acting like mature, educated men."

Marsh was silent for a long minute, seemingly lost in thought. Roosevelt was sure he was about to apologize for his behavior. Finally he turned to Roosevelt and said, "Are you sure you won't consider my offer?"

"Mr. Marsh," said Roosevelt, "I don't use vile and obscene language, but you are tempting me almost beyond endurance!"

"I think Mr. Roosevelt has politely declined your offer," noted Holliday in amused tones.

"All right," said Marsh. "What would *you* want for the same thing?"

"Me?" said Holliday. "Eternal life. Failing that, twenty years of good health." A bitter smile crossed his face. "Do we have a deal?"

"Bah!" snorted Marsh. "You're almost as intolerable as that swine!"

"Roosevelt?" asked Holliday.

"No, the *other* swine!"

"You're in remarkably poor humor today, even for you," noted Holliday. "We did kill a triceratops, you know. You can spend all week measuring him and drawing him and cutting him into small, bite-sized pieces."

"You know," said Roosevelt, "we really have to get you and Mr. Cope out of here. The weapons Tom and Ned made for us might or might not kill one or two dinosaurs, but then they can't be used again for a day, and one or two herbivores like the triceratops or the brontosaur might unintentionally kill half the camp before anyone could do a thing about it."

"The land is empty," said Marsh adamantly. "I don't know where these few dinosaurs have come from, but there's nothing else out there."

"That's true right now," said Roosevelt. "But it may not be true this afternoon and it certainly won't be true tomorrow. We've *got* to move your men out."

"I'm not going anywhere, and neither is Professor Cope!" snarled Marsh angrily.

"You are, you know," said Holliday.

"You can't make me go!"

"Actually, we can and we will," said Roosevelt. "The longer you stay, the longer you put innocent men and women in danger."

"My men are all here voluntarily, and so are Professor Cope's!"

"I'm not talking about them," answered Roosevelt.

"We're staying!" insisted Marsh. "This is the opportunity of a lifetime!"

"That lifetime is of very limited duration," said Roosevelt.

"If you put us under guard we'll escape and come back," said Marsh angrily. "If you tie us up and carry us out on the wagons, we'll make our way back as soon as we're free. Even if you take us all the way back to the Eastern seaboard, we'll be back!"

"Why don't you just go to Colorado like a reasonable man?" said Holliday.

"Colorado's next," answered Marsh. "But Colorado doesn't have *live* dinosaurs and Wyoming does!"

"Colorado's got live men, and it won't be long before this part of Wyoming doesn't," said Holliday.

"Bah!" said Marsh. He got to his feet, walked to his tent, and disappeared inside it.

"That was some hullabaloo," said Younger, walking over and joining them. "Professor Marsh, he yells even louder than Professor Cope."

"He's going to yell a lot louder when we tie him up and toss him in the back of a wagon," said Holliday with a grin.

"So you're working for Professor Cope now?" asked Younger.

Roosevelt shook his head. "We're not working for any white man or any Comanche. Cope has to leave, too."

Younger frowned. "What the hell's going on?"

"Think about it, Cole," said Holliday. "You've seen what's walking around in these parts. Do you really want to stay?"

Younger considered the question for a moment, frowning. "When you put it that way, I guess we'd be crazy to stay, wouldn't we?" he said at last.

"I guess we would," agreed Holliday.

"OK," said Younger. "I'll go get Professor Cope, and we'll start packing up."

"May I make a suggestion?" said Roosevelt.

Younger turned to him. "Sure."

"Pack up *before* you tell him he's leaving. Every time you turn your back on him, he'll be off looking for dinosaurs." He paused. "Marsh, too," he added thoughtfully. "But if they have to come after us for their equipment, maybe we can actually get them the hell out of here."

"Yeah, I guess it makes sense when you put it that way," agreed Younger.

Suddenly an agonized scream came to their ears, followed by another in a difference voice just second later.

Roosevelt and Younger ran in the direction of the screams, followed by Holliday, who was in no condition to run.

When they arrived at the source, they saw that the side of Edison and Buntline's tent had been shredded. They burst in and found Edison propped up against a support pole, the left leg of his pants shredded and soaked in blood.

"Never mind me!" he rasped. "Help Ned!"

Buntline lay on the floor, a deep wound on his right side, blood spilling out.

"What the hell happened?" asked Younger as Roosevelt went to work on Buntline, who screamed in pain the instant Roosevelt touched him.

"Something small," grated Edison. "It just ripped the side of the tent and went after us before we knew it was there." He winced as Younger started applying a tourniquet around his calf. "It looked like . . . oh, hell, I don't know . . . a tiny tyrannosaur, but it moved much faster and was lightly built."

"Where is it now?" asked Holliday, who had just arrived. "Did you kill it?"

Edison shook his head. "The weapons are in the trunk, being charged. He was on us before we even knew he was there."

"This man's bleeding a lot," said Roosevelt grimly. "And there's no way we're going to be able to work on him under sterile conditions." He turned to Holliday. "Doc, find every bottle of whiskey they've got stashed here and bring 'em back. We'll use some on his wound and Tom's leg, and we'll pour the rest down Ned's gullet so he feels less pain."

"He's out cold," said Holliday, looking at Buntline. "Damn! He's a mess!"

"Being out cold is a blessing, but we've got a lot of work to do. Get the whiskey!"

Holliday nodded and headed off for Cope's cache of liquor, while the rest of the men gathered around the tent, looking in when they could, whispering among themselves.

Marsh forced his way past the men into the tent, took one look at Buntline, realized he was unconscious, and turned to Edison.

"What did it look like?" he said. "Mammal, reptile, or dinosaur?"

"It had to be a dinosaur," answered Edison, wincing as Younger cut his pants leg off at mid-thigh with a hunting knife. "Like I told Theodore, it looked like a baby tyrannosaur, or your drawing of an allosaur."

Marsh nodded. "One of the raptors," he said with certainty. "They come in all sizes." He turned to look at Buntline again. "Mr. Roosevelt, you're making a mess of this man's wounds. Let me do it. I've had some medical experience."

Roosevelt, his hands and sleeves covered with blood, gratefully straightened up and let Marsh kneel down next to Buntline, just as Holliday arrived with four bottles of whiskey.

"There's more," he said. "But this is all I could carry."

"It's a start, anyway," replied Roosevelt. He took a step out of the tent and faced the assembled men. "We've got a man in bad shape here," he said. "I'd like some of you to donate some clean shirts that we can use as swabs and bandages. If anyone's got any tape or any real bandages, bring them to the tent."

A few of the men left for their own tents to bring back the required goods or at least search for them. Roosevelt caught Holliday's eye and walked about thirty yards away, where they could speak in low tones without being overheard.

"There's no way we can move Ned for a week, even if he survives, and I don't even think Tom should move for another couple of days," he said. "We need another plan."

"I agree," said Holliday.

"And if we're stuck here a week, you know that we're going to see more dinosaurs, more than we can handle with Tom and Ned's weapons."

"Which means we're going to have to go find some of these creatures before they find us, and see if they can actually be killed by a shot fired from a rifle."

Roosevelt nodded. "We already know a six-gun's ineffective against the big ones, though from Tom's description it might have worked against the creature that attacked them. Anyway," he continued, "it's something we've *got* to find out. If we can kill one of the big ones, then we'll be able to position the men to guard the camp until Ned dies or is well enough to move. But if we *can't* kill something like a tyrannosaur or one of Marsh's allosaurs, then we have a serious decision to make."

"I know," replied Holliday. "Desert him, or stay here and die with him."

"The sooner we find out what our options are, the better," said Roosevelt. "Are you ready to go on a little hunt?"

"Yeah," said Holliday, walking to the stabling area with Roosevelt. "I'll borrow a rifle and some bullets, and I'm ready."

A moment later they were riding out of camp, side by side, when suddenly Holliday emitted a chuckle.

"What is it?" asked Roosevelt.

"Ever since I came out West I wondered what it would be like to face an enemy who didn't have a six-gun or a rifle. Well," said Holliday with a rueful smile, "I guess I'm about to find out."

24.

THEY WERE THREE MILES OUT OF CAMP, and hadn't seen anything but a few birds.

"I got a feeling this is going to be an exercise in futility," remarked Holliday as they passed through a small forest. "There's nothing alive in these trees except the occasional bird."

"That's a *good* sign, Doc," replied Roosevelt.

"Anything that means we don't have to face a dinosaur with a pair of rifles is a good sign," agreed Holliday.

Roosevelt shook his head. "You're misunderstanding me. It's a good sign because they know something big and dangerous is afoot. That's why they're all so quiet."

"Bigger and more dangerous than us?" asked Holliday grimly.

"Yes. Think about it, Doc. When you enter a forest, what's the first thing that happens?"

Holliday simply stared at him. "I give up. What *is* the first thing that happens?"

"All the birds start screeching, warning each other that there's a potentially dangerous intruder."

"They're quiet now, even though they see us," said Holliday. "What does that mean?"

"It means that something that can reach them is in the area," answered Roosevelt, "and they don't want to call attention to themselves."

"I don't buy it," said Holliday. "Some of these trees are eighty, maybe ninety feet tall. Even a full-grown brontosaur couldn't reach them, and you tell me he's a vegetarian anyway. The only way a tyrannosaur could reach one would be to climb the tree, and there's no way it could hold his weight."

"I'm just telling you what my training as a naturalist tells me, Doc."

"I've got a question," said Holliday, brushing some flying insects away from his face, "The brontosaur was a grass-eater or the equivalent, so why did they resurrect *him?*"

"The elephant's a herbivore too," said Roosevelt with a smile. "Have you any idea how much damage even one of them can do?"

"I know," said Holliday. "But if they're resurrecting them, surely they could choose all tyrannosaurs."

"Maybe not. Only our Apache friend would know for sure, and I haven't seen him since we signed the treaty."

Holliday nodded. "He's been scarce. I gather the second he lets his guard down, their spells will pull him part or chop him to pieces or whatever the hell one medicine man's spells do to another."

"You know," said Roosevelt with an amused smile, "Cody talks about putting you in his show, or Cole Younger, or Annie Oakley, but after spending a few days here I'm convinced the one he really wants is Geronimo."

"He'd draw a crowd, that's for sure," agreed Holliday. "Hell, he might do it one of these days. He's signed the treaty, and once we kill the dinosaurs or they kill us, he's got nothing else much to do." He frowned. "Why the hell did these madmen come all the way out here to dig? I know they've found dinosaurs back East. They both told me so."

"There are different ones out here," answered Roosevelt. "Bigger ones, I gather. And they're not digging up front lawns or public parks or valuable farmland to get to them." Suddenly he grinned. "Besides, you ought to be happier than anyone that they're digging out here."

Holliday frowned. "Why?"

"The way you tell it, you'd be dead by now if they hadn't started digging up the wrong turf."

"At least it'd be over now," replied Holliday. "Now I get to do it all over again, all for a year of lousy health and monsters from hell." He grimaced. "It was a poor bargain."

Suddenly Roosevelt held up a hand, indicating silence. Holliday concentrated, but couldn't hear anything. Roosevelt remained tense for another half minute, then relaxed.

"What was it?" asked Holliday.

"I thought I heard some—I don't know—some high-pitched whistling sound." Roosevelt frowned. "Not like any sound we've heard before."

"From what direction?"

Roosevelt shrugged. "I'm not sure. North, maybe northeast." He shrugged. "Maybe not." He pulled his rifle out of its sheath. "I think we'll carry these out in the open, just to be on the safe side."

Holliday decided there was nothing safe about carrying the extra weight while sitting atop his horse, and he simply let Roosevelt ride a few yards ahead of him, confident that he could withdraw his rifle in a hurry if he needed it. He wasn't sure that he *would* need it, or that it would be much use against any creature that could reach the birds on their perches at the tops of the trees that surrounded him.

As always, Roosevelt stopped his horse every few minutes to study a bird or draw a new flower or plant in his ever-present notebook. "Black bear sign," he said, pointing to some stool just off the trail.

Holliday couldn't see how it was different from grizzly stool, or even dog stool for that matter, but he was afraid if he asked, Roosevelt would spend twenty minutes explaining the difference, and he figured the sooner they found a dinosaur or decided there weren't any in the vicinity, the sooner he could get off his horse and relax. He pulled out his flask, and was just about to put it to his lips when Roosevelt suddenly whispered: "*There!*"

Holliday looked ahead and saw nothing. He turned right, then left, and still couldn't see anything.

"Where?" he whispered.

"*Up!*"

Roosevelt pointed to the sky, and suddenly Holliday was able to make out the biggest bird he'd ever seen—and as it glided closer he realized that it wasn't a bird at all.

"My God, it's *big!*" he said.

"It's a pteranodon!" said Roosevelt excitedly.

"A *what*?"

"A species of flying dinosaur. Marsh discovered it about ten years ago. I've seen the artists' renderings."

"Damned thing has a twenty-foot wingspan," said Holliday, still staring at it.

"Well, now we know why all the birds have been quiet," said Roosevelt, putting his rifle to his shoulder and lining up the pteranodon in his sights.

The creature opened its mouth and emitted a harsh whistling sound. Suddenly it dove behind a treetop, obscuring it from Roosevelt's vision before he could pull the trigger. But it appeared a few seconds later with a bird in its mouth, and as it did so Roosevelt fired his rifle.

The pteranodon released the bird, which was either dead or crippled, and the two plummeted to the ground about sixty yards away. Roosevelt rode up, dismounted, and in keeping with his philosophy, "paid the insurance" by pulling his pistol and firing a bullet into the dinosaur's head. There was no reaction, nor did he expect one.

"By God, this fellow is going to look great in the foyer at Sagamore Hill!" enthused Roosevelt.

"What the hell are you talking about?" said Holliday.

"I'm a taxidermist, Doc."

"That, too?"

"And I'm going to be the first man ever to stuff and mount a dinosaur. There's no way I could do it with any of the others we've seen, but this fellow is small enough to fit in a boxcar once we're done here."

"You're *really* going to take it home with you?"

"Absolutely. I wish we had a photographer with us. If I could get a photo of me with my foot on his neck and my rifle in my hands, I could have it in every newspaper east of the Mississippi—at least those that are advanced enough to run photographs."

A smile spread across Holliday's face. "You *are* running for office again, aren't you?"

"Probably," said Roosevelt. "And whether it's in a week or a decade, a photo like that wouldn't grow old." He paused, frowning. "I hate to call a halt to things, but I've got to get this baby back to camp. If we both leave it unguarded, I'm sure predators will rip it to shreds. I'll be happy to stay here and stand guard over it if you'll ride back to camp and come back with a team of horses and a wagon."

"*I'll* stay, Theodore," said Holliday promptly.

"You're sure?"

"It's an easy decision," said Holliday with a smile. "What would I rather do—ride that goddamned horse back to camp and then drive a wagon over this bumpy trail, or stay here and maybe come face-to-face with a hungry grizzly that's caught the scent of your trophy?"

Roosevelt shrugged. "Okay," he said, mounting his horse. "I'll be back as soon as I can."

"Not a problem," said Holliday. "Neither me or the dinosaur are going anywhere."

Roosevelt kicked his horse with his heels and it began cantering back along the trail. Holliday dismounted, tied his reins to a thin, low-hanging branch, and sat down with his back propped against a tree. Then remembering what he was about to do when Roosevelt had spotted the pteranodon, pulled out his flask, and took a swig.

"Damned good," he muttered, staring at the flask. "Or at least damned welcome."

He took another swallow, and then, as he was replacing it in his coat pocket, his horse screamed once, reared up, broke off the branch he had been tethered to, and raced off through the woods with the remains of the branch hanging from his reins, banging against his chest with every stride.

Holliday was on his feet instantly, his pistol in his hands, scanning the area. He saw some trees swaying about two hundred yards away, heard branches cracking as something moved through them, and heard the grunt of something large.

Very large.

He holstered his gun, then turned to reach for his rifle, but of course it was still with the horse.

"Shit!" he muttered.

He realized that the last place he wanted to be standing was out on the trail in plain sight of whatever it was, and he stepped back behind a tree.

And waited.

Now he could hear birds screeching their warnings, so he knew that it was something that couldn't reach as high as they were, but the knowledge didn't bring him any comfort.

He checked his pistol to make sure it was fully loaded. Maybe whatever it was would come at him with its mouth open, and there might be a vulnerability to a pistol shot placed somewhere in the back of its throat. If not, he'd put a bullet in each eye and at least make it a hell of a lot harder for whatever it was to find him.

He calmly and coolly considered his tiny handful of options, but he knew he was in deep trouble if it found him. He wished he had the rifle back, though he wasn't sure it would fare a lot better than a pistol. After all, they'd had Tom invent and Ned create those special weapons for a reason.

He heard branches cracking about sixty yards away, and the screaming of the birds intensified until it became deafening. He edged his head out from behind the tree, trying to see what was approaching, but it was still hidden by the trees.

Well, he thought, *maybe it's coming because it scents Theodore's dead bird-thing. Maybe it's just looking for a quick, easy meal.*

A moment later a tyrannosaur broke cover and, after testing the wind, walked over to where the pteranodon's corpse lay. It was leaning over, preparing to take a large bite—

—when Holliday sneezed.

Instantly the tyrannosaur straightened up. Slowly his head turned in Holliday's direction, and he took a tentative step toward him, then another—and then, as he finally saw the source of the sneeze, he opened his mouth and roared.

Holliday knew it was an act of futility, but he stepped back out onto the trail where he had a clearer view, held his gun out ahead of him, and prepared to sell his life as dearly as possible.

25.

THE TYRANNOSAUR FIXED ITS GAZE ON HOLLIDAY and took a single step forward. Holliday took aim and fired two quick shots at the creature's left eye. It screamed and began shaking its head vigorously, and he knew he'd hit his target even before the blood began gushing out of its eye socket.

It turned to better see him with its uninjured eye, and he fired off three more shots into it. It screamed again, even louder this time, seemed dizzy and disoriented, and began rubbing its head against the sturdy bole of a tree as blood streamed down its face and onto its body.

Suddenly it began thrashing its small forelegs wildly, and began swaying back and forth, and Holliday finally realized that at least one of his bullets had hit the brain through the only route a pistol shot *could* reach it.

The tyrannosaur fell onto its side, struggled to its feet, screaming and swaying. It suddenly stood still, sniffing the air, and just about the time Holliday was sure it had found his scent and pinpointed his location, it turned and bent over the corpse of the pteranodon, preparing to take a bite out of it—but before it could do so it fell heavily to the ground, and this time, despite its efforts, it could not get up again.

Holliday stood where he was, staring at the huge beast, for the better part of five minutes, amazed that he was still alive, and that he had killed such a monster with such a puny weapon.

Finally Roosevelt drove up in the wagon, took in the situation in a single glance, climbed down, walked over to examine the tyrannosaur, and saw one wing of the pteranodon sticking out from beneath it.

"So much for my trophy," said Roosevelt from where he sat on the wagon.

"So stuff and mount *him*," said Holliday, jerking a thumb in the tyrannosaur's direction.

Roosevelt smiled. "I have better things to do with the next thirty years of my life." He studied the creature's head. "You were lucky. The way his head is structured, I think the eye provides the only path to the brain for something with no more power than a pistol. Probably one or two bullets went all the way through to it."

"I *feel* lucky, I'll confess to that," replied Holliday.

"Well," said Roosevelt, pulling out his hunting knife and going to work, "let me at least take the wing back. Maybe I can do something with it."

He walked over to the wing and spent the next five minutes cutting it loose.

"I'll have to join you on the wagon," said Holliday, walking over and climbing up onto it.

"Where's your horse?"

"Probably miles away by now."

"Ah!" said Roosevelt with a grin. "So he's the smart one."

"You'll get no argument from me," replied Holliday. He withdrew his flask and drained the rest of its contents.

When they reached camp they found that Holliday's horse had preceded them, and Younger was getting ready to mount a search party. Holliday went off to refill his flask and returned as two men were unhitching the horses and Roosevelt was preparing to move the wing to his tent.

"I've made up my mind," announced Cody, walking up to them.

"That's good," said Roosevelt. "Everyone should always try to make up his mind. Now step aside, please."

"Damn it, Theodore! I'm leaving!"

"You don't have to leave," said Roosevelt. "Just step aside."

"I'm leaving this idiotic expedition, and I'd like you and Doc to come with me!"

"I don't have any skills that you can put on display," replied Roosevelt. "And to be honest, I don't have any interest in appearing in your show."

"Not *in* it," explained Cody. "But any guy who's run for office and won, especially in New York, should make a hell of a barker."

"Not interested."

"Okay," persisted Cody, "if not a barker, an advance man. You go to each city a day or two before the show gets there and talk it up, put up posters, things like that."

Roosevelt left the wing alone and turned to face him. "Bill, I like you, and I even like your Wild West show. I'd pay money to watch Annie Oakley do her trick shots. Now, it may be egomaniacal for me to say this, but I believe I have the capacity to do better things than hang an endless series of posters for you in one town after another."

"You're sure?" said Cody.

"Do I look undecided?"

"Well, I tried," said Cody. He turned to Holliday. "How about you, Doc?"

"I'm no trick-shot artist," said Holliday. "I just shoot people who are trying to shoot me."

"I can arrange that."

"*What?*" demanded Holliday and Roosevelt in unison.

"With blanks," said Cody with a grin. "Hell, we can even enact the Gunfight at the O.K. Corral every night."

"I've fought it once," replied Holliday. "That was enough."

"I could make you famous!"

"I've already got a little more fame that I can handle," said Holliday.

Cody sighed. "You two are a couple of hardheads. It's a shame I like you so much."

He turned and walked away. When he was just out of earshot, Holliday turned to Roosevelt. "He may like us, but he likes *Buffalo Bill's Wild West Show* better."

Roosevelt chuckled, then went back to moving the wing off the wagon, decided it was too awkward to carry, and placed it onto a cart that he could then take to his tent. Holliday began heading toward Edison's tent to see if he and Buntline were interested in seeing Roosevelt's grisly trophy when Cole Younger walked up to him.

"Cody try to buy you away?" he asked.

"He *tried*," acknowledged Holliday.

"You said no?"

"I said no."

"Good!" said Younger. "Because Frank James and I will pay you twice what he would have paid."

"You're really starting a show with Frank?" asked Holliday curiously.

"Yeah," said Younger. "Face it, Doc, the shootist's day is just about over. I suppose I could rob a bank or two, but it ain't as easy as the dime novels make it sound. I got shot up all to hell last time I tried, and it cost me and my brothers a lot of years in jail. No, I think a Wild West show is the answer. I mean, hell, you and me and Frank, we *are* the Wild West, or damned near all that's left of it anyway. Why don't you join us?"

"I don't think so."

"Hell, say 'Yes' and we'll even make you a partner!" said Younger.

"Cole," said Holliday, "that's a damned handsome offer, and under other circumstances I'd probably take it, but I'm afraid I've got to turn you down."

"You're sure?" urged Younger. "Why not cash in on your reputation? Believe me, it beats gambling for the rest of your life."

Holliday shook his head. *The problem*, he thought, *is that my life's of much shorter duration than you think.*

"Okay, I did my best," said Younger. He extended a hand. "No hard feelings."

"Between two members of a vanishing species?" said Holliday with a bittersweet smile. "None."

He continued making his way to Edison and Buntline's tent. Once there, he described the events of the day. Roosevelt joined them a moment later.

"That's a hell of a bird!" exclaimed Buntline, wincing in pain as he tried to sit up. "It must have an eighteen-foot wingspread."

"Twenty," offered Edison, moving his wounded limbs very carefully. "But look at the leather, Ned—and no trace of feathers, just the same kind of fuzz you find on a bat's wings. I wonder if it's a bird at all."

"It was once," said Roosevelt. "Millions of years ago." He paused. "Anyway, it flew, so I don't know what else you'd call it."

"Did it have teeth?" asked Edison.

"I don't know," admitted Roosevelt. "The head is buried under about seven tons of tyrannosaur."

"With the jaws it had, I don't know if they were necessary," added Holliday. "It grabbed a bird and just seemed to swallow him whole."

"But we don't know if birds were that small back when he was alive," noted Roosevelt.

"Too bad," said Edison. "It would have been interesting to examine him."

"Well, if you're so inclined, you can have someone cart you out there and examine something that tried to eat him for breakfast," said Holliday.

"I don't think *anybody* should go out there," said Roosevelt. "A body that big has got to attract scavengers . . . and around here, that means carnivores bigger than hippos and rhinos."

"When you put it that way, it sounds damned foolish to stay," said Buntline. "If we survive today's enormous carnivore, all that means is we have to face tomorrow's."

"What can we do?" said Edison. "You've met Cope and Marsh. You couldn't move either of them out of here if there were just fossils in the area. How are we going to convince them to leave when they can encounter real dinosaurs any time of the night or day?"

"Maybe we should just let the damned dinosaurs eat them, and then everyone can go home," said Holliday half-seriously.

Roosevelt shook his head. "You're a shootist, Doc, not a murderer."

"I'm adaptable," answered Holliday.

"Besides," continued Roosevelt, "we don't know that they look any tastier than the sixty or seventy men who are working for them and never bargained on having to face creatures out of their worst nightmares."

"So we just sit here until one of them develops either a conscience or, better still, an instinct for self-preservation?" asked Edison. "If that's the case, Ned and I had better go build a weapon for every man here."

"The problem is, most of the men probably won't be here any longer by the time you built the weapons and bring them back here," said Roosevelt.

Edison frowned. "I hadn't considered that," he admitted. "But it makes sense when you say it."

"Or I could just kill Cope and Marsh, and then everyone could go home," said Holliday.

"This is serious, Doc," said Roosevelt. "Stop your joking."

"Am I smiling?" replied Holliday.

26.

ODY HAD DEPARTED, taking two men with him, when Holliday awoke the next morning. He got up, looked around for his boots, finally realized that he had slept with them on, got to his feet, walked outside, and winced as he moved into the sunlight.

"I have *got* to start wearing a Stetson," he muttered to himself as he tried to shield his eyes from the sun.

When he'd adjusted to the brightness of the morning, he walked over to the remains of a campfire, realized he'd overslept breakfast again, and sat on a tree stump, waiting for everything to come into focus.

Buntline, on crutches, joined him a few minutes later.

"Good morning, Doc," he said.

Holliday winced. "Not so loud."

"I'm just speaking conversationally," replied Buntline. He raised his voice. "*This* is loud."

Holliday groaned. "I bet you think you're pretty funny."

"I have my moments," said Buntline with a smile.

"I'd tell you to draw, but you'd probably reach for a notebook and a pencil."

Buntline laughed. "So, how are you on this fine day?"

"Same as usual," replied Holliday. "Hung over."

"You know that the famous Buffalo Bill has deserted us?"

"He said he would. I may not like him all that much, but he's always been a man of his word," said Holliday. "Well," he added, "except when he's talking money."

"Maybe you should have gone with him," suggested Buntline. "He could have made you famous." He paused. "*More* famous, I mean."

"Most shootists would like *less* fame, not more," answered Holliday. "Half the men I've killed have been green kids out to make a reputation, kids I'd never seen before and that nobody will ever see again."

"I see what you mean," said Buntline. "When we get back East, I'm going to write a stage play about the West, and as a sign of friendship, your name will never be mentioned."

"Write about Billy the Kid," suggested Holliday. "Everywhere I go they're still singing songs about him."

"Maybe I'll do that," replied Buntline, wincing as he shifted his weight. "Or maybe Bill Hickok. Everyone's heard of Wild Bill."

Holliday snorted contemptuously. "One lucky shot from fifty yards away and he becomes the most famous shootist in the world!" Then he shrugged. "What the hell. Write about him. At least he doesn't have to worry about kids calling him out, unless they can call him up from hell."

"You didn't think much of him, I take it?"

"I don't think much of a lot of people," replied Holliday.

"I've noticed," said Buntline with a smile.

There was a sudden commotion at the far end of camp, and then Marsh and a dozen of his men appeared. Marsh dismounted and issued some orders. Holliday saw the men were all carrying things—bits and pieces of the tyrannosaur, he assumed—wrapped in cloth, and they carted them off to the tent that he was using to store his fossils.

Marsh saw Holliday and Buntline, and walked over to them.

"Good morning," said Holliday with no show of enthusiasm.

"It's almost noon," Marsh corrected him.

"Whatever."

"Do you know what that bastard did?"

"Which bastard are you talking about?" asked Holliday.

"There's only one, damn it!"

"Ah!" said Holliday. "You mean Mr. Edison."

"I don't like your sense of humor," said Marsh harshly.

"You've got a lot of company," said Holliday with no show of anger.

"That bastard left camp before sunrise so he could stake out a claim on the head all for himself," continued Marsh.

"Maybe you should call him out and shoot him," suggested Holliday pleasantly.

"It's just lucky I know what kind of backstabbing swine I'm dealing with," continued Marsh. A look of triumph crossed his bearded face. "I got there twenty minutes ahead of him!"

"No question about it," said Holliday. "You're an even better backstabbing swine than he is."

Marsh glared at him. "I don't think your presence is required here any longer, sir!" he snapped.

"Bullshit," said Holliday. "My presence and Roosevelt's is all that's kept you alive. But if you'd like to see the last of me, that can be arranged easily enough. Go dig in Colorado or Montana."

"When the greatest finds of all are right here?" demanded Marsh incredulously. "You must be mad!"

"Not yet," said Holliday. "But I'm getting there."

"Bah!" snorted Marsh. "You're hopeless!"

He turned on his heel and walked off to his fossil tent.

"Do you get the feeling that they turn every ounce of their intelligence onto their hobby and leave the rest of their lives to fend for themselves?" asked Holliday.

"I don't know that I'd call it a hobby," replied Buntline. "I think science is the word you're looking for."

"I've already found the word I'm looking for," said Holliday disgustedly. "It's *obsession*."

"May I point out as a friend and not a potential shootist that you're even more unpleasant than usual today?"

"Damn it, Ned," said Holliday irritably. "Yesterday I faced a tyrannosaur with a goddamned six-shooter. The only reason I'm here at all is to get you and Tom healthy and move these fools out of here before they're killed by dinosaurs." He spat on the ground. "Do you think it was worth the risk?"

"You were dying and now you're here," said Buntline. "Ask me an easy one instead."

"I'm *still* dying," said Holliday, coughing some blood into a handkerchief as if for emphasis. "I just wish there was anyone or anything around here worth dying *for*. Do I care what kills Cope or Marsh as long as it does it slowly and painfully? No. Do I care what happens to some Apache village I've never seen? No. So what the hell am I doing here?"

"Same as most of us," said Buntline, forcing a smile. "Trying to make it to tomorrow."

"True," said Holliday with a sigh. "I can remember days when I liked the odds better."

They fell silent for a moment. Then Buntline looked around. "Someone ought to be making lunch any minute now for those of us who stayed behind or returned to camp."

"Makes no difference," said Holliday. "I don't eat this early in the day." He took a sip from his flask and smiled. "It interferes with my digestion."

Buntline laughed just as Roosevelt drove a wagon carrying Edison into camp, lifted the inventor out of it, and helped him walk over to join Holliday and Buntline.

"That was a hell of an animal," remarked Edison.

"There were fifty or sixty men chopping it to bits this morning," said Holliday. "Is there anything left of it?"

Edison smiled. "About ninety-five percent of it. And I can tell you that you're lucky as hell to be alive."

"So says everyone who's not on this side of my lungs," replied Holliday.

"It was in the nature of an experiment," explained Roosevelt. "We won't leave camp without your weapons again." Suddenly he frowned. "I just wish he hadn't fallen on my pteranodon."

"There'll be more," said Holliday. Suddenly he smiled. "If you don't die from a snake or insect bite first."

"My friend the optimist," said Roosevelt with a smile.

"By the way, I don't suppose one of our scientists killed the other?" said Holliday.

"There were a couple of times I thought they would. Marsh wanted the right half—the tyrannosaur collapsed on his left side, if you'll recall. Cope decided making either side take the crushed half was unfair."

"That doesn't sound like him," said Holliday.

Roosevelt grinned again. "His solution was to take the front half and leave the back half for Marsh."

Holliday laughed aloud, which brought on another coughing seizure.

"Anyway," continued Roosevelt, "with Cody gone and Younger retiring from the security business, no one on either side was anxious to get into a gunfight over it, and for a minute there I thought Cope and Marsh would actually come to blows."

"So Theodore used the toe of his boot to trace out a boxing ring in the dirt, and invited Cope and Marsh to duke it out," said Edison with an amused grin. "After all, he came out here to referee one of John L.'s boxing matches, so he was the perfect choice to referee it."

"I suspect they each remembered they had urgent business back at camp," suggested Buntline.

Roosevelt shook his head. "Couldn't lose face in front of the men. Of course, neither of them wanted to lose any teeth either. Cope claimed he needed his hands for the fine work he had to do with his fossils, and he couldn't take a chance of breaking one of them on Marsh's jaw." Roosevelt chuckled at the memory. "Marsh claimed he was a coward, and did it so loud and for so long that Cope finally agreed.'"

"And?" asked Holliday. "I just saw Marsh, and he didn't seem any the worse for wear."

"He and Cope began arguing the rules," said Edison, still amused. "Marsh wanted a bigger ring. Cope wanted gloves. Marsh wanted bare knuckles. Cope wanted five-minute rounds, Marsh wanted three-minute rounds, Cope wanted to fight to first blood, Marsh wanted to fight to a knockout. After twenty minutes they realized they were wasting time, and that some of the men were playing cards, so they started yelling at them about getting back to work, and suddenly everyone forgot about the boxing match."

"I wish I'd been there," said Holliday. "I'd have booked bets on the fight and kept all the money when it didn't come off."

"Well, it's funny," admitted Roosevelt, "but it leaves us with the same problem we've had from the beginning. They have to leave, but they hate each other so much one won't leave if there's a chance the other can discover something new and valuable by staying behind."

"Well, as long as we're stuck here, at least you had a pleasant diversion," said Holliday.

"It's only pleasant in the retelling, Doc," said Roosevelt. "I like most of the men I know, but these two . . ." He shook his head. "I'd like to take 'em both on in the ring myself."

As the words left Roosevelt's mouth, Cope and his men entered the camp. Like Marsh, Cope began directing his men to put the morning's finds in the bone building, and when they had finished he posted two men armed with rifles on either side of the crude door.

"Trusting soul," remarked Holliday.

"Not without cause," said Edison. "I wouldn't put it past Marsh to try to sneak in there —him, or one of his men. After all, they've been stealing from and sabotaging each other for years."

"Well, it's a cluster of superlatives," said Holliday.

"What are you talking about, Doc?" asked Roosevelt.

"What we have here," explained Holliday, waving a hand at the camp. "The greatest shootist, the greatest scientist, and the greatest politician on the continent may all die trying to protect the two nastiest paleontologists from destroying each other and maybe the greatest medicine man as well."

"I'm not the greatest politician," said Roosevelt. Suddenly he grinned. "Yet."

"Seriously, what do you suggest, Doc?" said Edison. "It's pretty clear that we can't force them to leave, Ned and I are in no condition to travel anyway, and it's just as obvious that the Comanche have started resurrecting dinosaurs and won't stop until both parties stop desecrating their burial ground."

"I don't know," admitted Holliday. "Perhaps we—"

There was a shrill scream of terror from the stable area, followed a moment later by a dozen or more gunshots. Holliday and Roosevelt went off to see what was happening, and returned a few moments later.

"What was it?" asked Edison.

"Damned dinosaur killed one of the horses," growled Holliday.

"Huge one?"

Roosevelt shook his head. "No, he couldn't have weighed much more than four hundred pounds or so.

"Well, if they kill enough horses, that'll settle whether we're leaving or not," said Buntline.

"Goddamn it!" said Holliday grimly. "I'm getting mighty sick of paleontologists *and* dinosaurs! After all, a bargain's a bargain!"

"What are you talking about, Doc?" asked Roosevelt, frowning. "*What* bargain?"

"Geronimo made a deal with me," answered Holliday. "It was a shitty deal, but I agreed to it, and I haven't been keeping my end of the bargain." He stared off at the dead dinosaur in the stable area. "Enough is enough!"

27.

OLLIDAY GOT HIS HORSE and began riding out of camp in a northwesterly direction.

"I know you're watching me," he said in a conversational voice when he'd gone a little more than a mile. "If I'm heading in the wrong direction you'd damned well better tell me."

He felt an urge for a cigar, which puzzled him, as he hadn't smoked in years. He knew what the results would be: a worse coughing seizure than usual. He wrote it off to his body assuming he was going to his death and wanting one last smoke before then.

He thought he'd sing to keep himself company, then realized that he didn't know a single song. He reached for his flask, then decided against it. He wouldn't be able to fill it up again, and there was no sense using it up now when he was sure he'd need it later.

Suddenly he heard a large number of birds starting to chirp and squawk. At first he thought it was another dinosaur, but then he heard the sound of hoofbeats approaching, and a moment later Roosevelt pulled up alongside him.

"Did you really think you were going to do this without me?" demanded the Easterner with a smile.

"Do what?" asked Holliday.

"Whatever it is that you're off to do," said Roosevelt. He reached into a saddlebag and withdrew one of Edison's weapons. "Here. I thought you might need one of these."

"And you have the other, I assume?"

"Unless you want them both."

Holliday stared at his smiling companion. "You seem mighty chipper, especially given that you don't know where you're going."

"I'm just glad to be away from that madhouse," replied Roosevelt. "And while we're on the subject, just where *are* we going?'

"We're off to meet with Geronimo's Comanche counterpart," said Holliday. "He can't possibly be as unreasonable as those two idiots we left behind."

"That's for damned sure," said Roosevelt. He shook his head in puzzlement. "I wonder how the history books will treat them? In a way, they're the two greatest scientists America has produced except for Tom."

"If you consider digging in the dirt for bones an important science," said Holliday.

"It is, Doc," said Roosevelt.

"Bah!"

"You're an educated man, Doc," continued Roosevelt. "You *know* paleontology is important."

"What is so damned important about knowing monsters used to live here?" said Holliday.

"Something killed them all off and left no evidence," replied Roosevelt. "And it wasn't Man or any predator walking the earth today. Wouldn't you like to know what it was, so we can avoid the same thing happening to us?"

"It's not going to make much different to *my* life expectancy," said Holliday.

"Damn it, Doc."

"All right, all right, knowing it will make a difference," agreed Holliday. "But knowing how to cure consumption, to take an example I can speak to, will make a quicker and more meaningful difference to quite a few thousand people."

"Of course it will," said Roosevelt. "And the day someone cures it, or pneumonia, or purifying stagnant water, or a dozen other things, he or they will rank right up there, just behind Tom. But most of that work is being done in laboratories, in private, and we won't know about it until it's accomplished, whereas Cope and Marsh are publishing every find and every discovery they make."

"Only to prove that each is better than the other," noted Holliday.

"Be honest, Doc. Do you think either of them would have accomplished half as much if he didn't hate the other's guts and want to show him up as a fake or an incompetent?"

"No," admitted Holliday with a heavy sigh. "No, I suppose not." He frowned. "Which doesn't mean I wouldn't be happy to let 'em kill each other and to hell with paleontology."

Roosevelt laughed. "It's tempting."

Holliday allowed himself the luxury of a grin. "The thought of it is damned near as intoxicating as what I have in my flask." He paused. "The real shame of it is that if I can make any kind of deal with the Comanche, those two bastards will benefit from it. Unless you've got a better idea."

Roosevelt shook his head. "No, it's got to be done, if indeed we *can* make a deal. Otherwise we're going to be overrun by dinosaurs, and they're not going to stop once they've eaten our two paleontologists."

Roosevelt stared at Holliday. "How many men could have put a bullet in the eye, and hence the brain, of a raging tyrannosaur."

Holliday paused a moment in thought. "In my experience, maybe three: Clay Allison, Johnny Ringo, and me. And they say John Wesley Hardin was a crack shot with any kind of weapon, but I never saw it for myself."

"Then you see why we have to do what we can to get them to send these creatures back to whatever hell they've pulled them out of," continued Roosevelt.

They rode another few miles, and then Holliday pulled his horse to a stop.

"What is it, Doc?"

"I still don't know where I'm going." Suddenly he raised his voice and turned toward Apache territory a few hundred miles to the southwest. "*And I hope to hell someone is going to tell me before we waste too much more time!*"

"You really think he can hear you?" asked Roosevelt, dismounting.

"Maybe not with his ears, but yes," said Holliday. "He's already pulled my fat out of the fire once on this job or assignment or whatever the hell he wants to call it." He shrugged. "Of course, he told me he wouldn't do it again, but what the hell." He raised his voice again. "*If he wants this problem solved, he can at least point me in the right direction!*"

"Maybe we're going in the right direction," suggested Roosevelt. "Maybe that's why he hasn't stopped us."

Holliday smiled humorously. "That's too direct. His mind doesn't work that way."

"Well, climb down and give your horse a rest," said Roosevelt. As Holliday was dismounting, he added, "I forgot to pack any food."

Holliday looked up. "Sun's still in the eastern half of the sky," he replied. "Much too early to think of food. If you're hungry maybe an hour before twilight, we'll shoot something small and defenseless."

"You've already made me feel guilty about eating it," laughed Roosevelt.

"Okay, we'll shoot something small and defenseless for me. You can go shoot a dinosaur." Suddenly Holliday smiled. "Just be sure to clean up after yourself." He began hobbling his horse.

"I see you've learned your lesson," noted Roosevelt.

"Probably not, but which lesson are you referring to?"

"Tying your reins to a branch."

"True," admitted Holliday. "On the other hand, if I'd hobbled him he'd probably have been half a breakfast for the tyrannosaur. If I didn't hate horses so much I'd be quite proud of letting him escape." He stared at Roosevelt. "What are you grinning at?"

"I'm just imagining Kate Elder's reaction if you spoke like that about her favorite dog or cat."

"Funny you should mention it," replied Holliday, sitting down with his back against a broad tree trunk.

"I was right?"

"I have no idea if she liked them."

"Then I don't understand."

Holliday smiled. "There was a lot about Kate not to understand. Only animal I ever took a shine to was a dog that used to follow me home from the Oriental Saloon back in Tombstone—so she took one of my pistols when I was, shall we say, indisposed, and tried to kill it."

Roosevelt frowned. "Did she?"

Holliday shook his head. "She was a lousy shot. But I never saw the dog again."

"I grew up loving animals," said Roosevelt.

"Hasn't stopped you from stuffing and mounting enough of them," said Holliday.

"When I was young it was a way to make them seem alive again," replied Roosevelt. "After I got better at it, it became first a science and then at art."

"You've got an interesting notion of fun, Theodore."

"So do you."

Holliday shrugged. "Believe it or not, playing cards isn't much fun," answered Holliday. "But when you're a dentist, and all your patients go elsewhere when you keep coughing up blood all over them, you do what you can to make a living."

"Did you like dentistry?"

"I didn't work at it long enough to say," replied Holliday. "I think I'd have been a good one." He shrugged again. "But who knows?"

They sat in silence for a few minutes. Finally Roosevelt got up and started doing some stationary exercises.

"Don't you ever stop?" said Holliday.

"Got to keep fit," answered Roosevelt. "Usually I read at lunch, but I left my books in camp, and besides, we're not eating."

"You know," said Holliday, "we've never sat down and discussed books. Some of my pleasantest memories are of arguing the classics with Johnny Ringo. Well," he amended, "with what he'd become."

"What did he like?"

"Plato, Cicero, Thucydides," replied Holliday. "I could never figure out what he saw in *The Republic*."

"You didn't like it?"

"Liking it has nothing to do with it," answered Holliday. "The damned thing doesn't work. Too many philosopher kings, not enough street sweepers."

Roosevelt laughed. "I keep forgetting who I'm traveling with. We'll have to make up for lost time. Do you read much fiction?"

"Mostly just the dime novels, before I tear them up and curse the liars who write them."

"Well, then, let me tell you about a couple of Russians named Dostoyevsky and Tolstoy, and an English lady named Austen."

"I'm aware of them."

"But you haven't read them?"

Holliday shook his head. "Not yet." Then he remembered his circumstances and sighed heavily. "Not ever."

"Never say never," said Roosevelt, and launched into a rhapsodic discussion of the virtues of the three, and especially of Jane Austen.

Holliday listened intently. It occurred to him that Roosevelt could make almost anything interesting, that his boundless enthusiasm for whatever captured his interest—which sooner or later was almost everything—was infectious. Finally, after an hour, Roosevelt got to his feet.

"I'll be happy to keep talking," he said. "But it's mid-afternoon already. We might as well keep going."

"Going where?" asked Holliday with a smile.

Roosevelt came to a stop and frowned. "What do we do if he's not paying attention?"

"If he wants this thing concluded," said Holliday, suddenly raising his voice, "*he'd damned well better be paying attention.*"

Suddenly Roosevelt looked off in the distance. "Damn!" he said. "*Something* is paying attention!"

"Shit!" said Holliday. "Nothing tries to eat us for a few hours, and it's easy to forget what's walking around the damned countryside."

He walked to his horse and pulled Edison's weapon out of his saddlebag, while Roosevelt did the same with his own horse.

They could hear branches cracking and see bushes moving, and suddenly the screeching of birds became deafening, but they couldn't see what was approaching them, or even *if* it was approaching.

"What is it?" asked Holliday.

"Something big," answered Roosevelt. "And probably not a herbivore, or the birds are panicking for nothing." Suddenly he frowned. "Something's wrong."

"Besides the dinosaur?"

"The wind's blowing from him to us," said Roosevelt. "He couldn't have scented us or the horses. And we've been speaking very quietly."

"What are you saying, Theodore? That he was *sent* for us?"

"It's a possibility."

"Well," said Holliday, hefting his weapon, "he's got a surprise or two coming his way."

Roosevelt stared at where the sounds were emanating from, A moment later he blinked his eyes very rapidly. "Oh my God!" he muttered.

"What is it?"

"It looks like a tyrannosaur," said Roosevelt. "But it's twice as big as the giant you killed. There's something wrong here. No carnivore can be that big. He'd starve to death."

"What are you saying?" demanded Holliday.

"I don't think this thing ever walked the earth," answered Roosevelt.

The creature finally burst into the open. Holliday estimated his head to be twenty feet above the ground, possibly even higher, and his bulk seemed to almost match that of a brontosaur. Both men began firing their weapons, but the creature ignored them and kept approaching.

"Go for the eyes!" said Holliday, tossing Edison's weapon aside and drawing his pistol as Roosevelt ran to his horse and retrieved his rifle.

Holliday fired three quick shots to no effect. Roosevelt's could hear the *thunk!* as his rifle bullet slammed into an eye, but the creature didn't even blink or in any way acknowledge it had been hit.

And then, suddenly, a small man in a loincloth was standing between them and the creature.

Roosevelt stared intently at the man's back. "Geronimo?"

"Can't be," said Holliday. "Geronimo's a six-footer. This guy is maybe five feet on his tiptoes."

The monster was just two steps away now, and the small man raised his hand and started chanting in an unfamiliar tongue. The monster turned to him and opened its mouth wide as if to swallow him whole—

—and then two things happened simultaneously: the dinosaur froze in mid-movement, and the small man became visibly smaller. He uttered one more chant, and the creature suddenly crumbled and turned into a gray, powdery, shapeless dust that fell to the ground and covered it.

The man turned to face Holliday and Roosevelt.

"Damn!" exclaimed Holliday. "It *is* you! What the hell happened to you? You've got to be a foot shorter!"

"It has taken all of my powers and some of my essence to hold the Comanche medicine men at bay," answered Geronimo. "I lost even more just now as I defeated the creature created by the minds and will of the Comanche."

"I *knew* that thing could never have existed!" said Roosevelt.

"You are wrong, Roosevelt," said Geronimo. "It existed here and now." He turned to Holliday. "I told you the last time we met that I would not help you again."

"But you did, and we're grateful."

"And see what has become of me," said Geronimo. "What is left of me," he corrected.

"Why did you come, then?" asked Holliday.

"Because I have been observing, and the two madmen will never leave on their own. It is up to you two to treat with the Comanche, to have them call off their monsters. There is no other way."

"We were on our way to do just that, but we have nothing to offer them," said Roosevelt.

"And I don't think we can make Cope and Marsh stop digging here, short of killing them," added Holliday. "And while at this point I have no serious objection to killing them, the problem is that Cody's already gone back East, and he'll be taking tales of the dinosaur resurrections with him. There will be still more madmen anxious to come here."

"You will do what must be done," said Geronimo. "That is why I have chosen you."

"We'll do what we can," said Holliday. "But don't hold your breath. Now, where are we headed and who do we want to parlay with?"

Geronimo pointed to the north. "You will find them there."

"That could be a thousand square miles," said Roosevelt. "Can you be more exact?"

"You will go where I pointed, and you will find them, or they you."

"And who's the medicine man?"

"They have seven, but the most powerful, the one you must treat with, you will call Tall Bear."

"What does he look like, so we'll recognize him?" asked Holliday.

"You will know him," said Geronimo.

Holliday stared at him, then blinked. "You're fading away."

"I have saved you," said Geronimo, his voice becoming a hollow echo. "I can do no more."

"You can tell us—" began Holliday, but then Roosevelt reached out and held his arm.

"Forget it, Doc. He's gone."

"I know," said Holliday. "'That is why I have chosen you,'" he repeated sardonically. "As if there was anyone else left to choose."

"We're all he's got," agreed Roosevelt. "In terms of getting rid of the dinosaurs, we're all *anyone's* got."

Holliday walked over to the pile of dust that had been a humongous carnivore just a moment earlier, ran his foot through it, kicked some of it up in the air and watched it float back down to the ground. "This is the kind of dream I used to have when I'd drunk too much."

"I had a dream like that right before I went on my first date with a girl," answered Roosevelt.

"Oh, well, if the horses haven't fainted dead away, we might as well start going to . . . to wherever the hell we're going."

Both horses were heavily lathered, but hadn't broken free of their tethers and hobbles, and a moment later Holliday and Roosevelt were riding north.

"Shit!" snapped Holliday after another half hour. "Suddenly I'm seeing Comanche medicine men behind every bush."

"Well, it's better than seeing another dinosaur," answered Roosevelt.

They'd gone another five miles when Roosevelt looked up at the sky.

"It's going to be twilight in another half hour or so," he said. "Do you want to find some spot with water for the horses where we can bed down for the night?"

"No," answered Holliday. "I don't think we have to."

"Oh? Why not?"

Holliday nodded toward the foliage to the left of the trail. "We've got company."

28.

THEY CONTINUED TO RIDE NORTH. The Comanche—a dozen to their right, another dozen to their left—walked their horses in the same direction, never getting closer than twenty yards, never moving faster or slower than Holliday and Roosevelt.

"What do they want?" mused Roosevelt aloud.

"Nothing," replied Holliday. "They know where we're going. They're just making sure we're not the vanguard of a war party."

"It's making me nervous."

Holliday smiled. "That's another reason they do it."

"Oh, well," said Roosevelt, "at least we won't have to fight off any dinosaurs while they're with us."

"I don't know," said Holliday. "I have a feeling only the medicine men, maybe only Tall Bear, can control them."

"I agree. But Tall Bear won't put his own warriors at risk."

"Let's hope not," said Holliday.

They fell silent, and rode another two miles in silence, paced by the Comanche warriors. The ground became more level, the rocks disappeared and the trees thinned out, and finally they saw an Indian village in the distance.

They got to within a quarter mile of it, and then two of the warriors urged their horses forward and blocked the way.

Holliday and Roosevelt pulled their mounts to a halt.

"What now?" said Holliday. "As if I didn't know."

The warriors gestured for them to dismount and proceed on foot.

"I'll be too sore and too exhausted to talk once we get there," complained Holliday, painfully climbing down.

"Oh, come on, Doc," said Roosevelt, "you walk more than this every day."

"True," admitted Holliday. "But not all at once."

Half a dozen more warriors dismounted and walked silently alongside them.

There was a fire in the middle of the village, and a burly, middle-aged warrior sat before it, bedecked in many of the tokens of his tribe.

"He doesn't take chances, does he?" said Holliday with a smile.

"It's an old African custom too," said Roosevelt. "Put a double— well, not quite a *double*—out to greet your visitors in case they have any bad intentions. This fellow can't be much more than five feet six when he's standing up. There's no way he can go by the name of Tall Bear."

"Well, let's pretend we think he is, until they're satisfied we don't mean him any harm. If we ask for the *real* Tall Bear, they'll be sure we're here to kill him."

"I agree," said Roosevelt.

They were escorted to the seated Comanche, and then their guides stood back.

"You are Holliday, and you are Roosevelt," he said.

"That's right," said Holliday.

"And Geronimo has sent you here to kill me."

"No," said Roosevelt. "We're here to reason with you."

Holliday considered withdrawing his pistol and handing it, butt first, to the Comanche, but decided he'd probably be killed before it cleared his holster. "Have your men disarm us if you're worried."

"I am not worried," said a voice from behind them. "Nothing can kill Tall Bear."

They turned and found themselves facing a tall man, very close to seven feet in height, with a serious scar running from his right collar bone down across his chest to his left hip. His eyes were dark, his cheekbones high, his thick hair hanging down to his shoulders, his expression grim.

"Why have you come to my camp?" he said.

"We have come to bargain," said Holliday.

"I know of you, Holly-day," said Tall Bear. "You are a famous killer. Why should I think you have not come to kill me?"

"Three reasons," said Holliday. "First, if I had come to kill you, you'd be dead already; I'd have fired the second I knew you were Tall Bear. Second, I offered to let your men take my gun away. And third," he concluded, gesturing toward Roosevelt, "if I wanted to kill you, I wouldn't need help."

Tall Bear stared at him for a long moment, then slowly nodded his head. "Good answers, Holly-day." He turned to Roosevelt. "I know you too. You are the Roosevelt."

Roosevelt resisted the urge to correct him and explain that he was *a* Roosevelt. "Yes, I am," he answered.

"It is you who Goyathlay sought out, among all the White Eyes, to make a treaty with," continued Tall Bear. "He must think you are an honorable man."

"I try to be."

"So the killer and the honorable man have come to me together. Why?"

"I think you know why," said Holliday.

"You want no more nightmares from the past."

"That's right."

"But even *with* them, your men continue to desecrate our sacred ground," said Tall Bear.

"They're not *our* men," said Roosevelt.

"But you have lived and worked with them," said Tall Bear. "Do you think we are not aware of that?"

"I was sent here by Geronimo—by Goyathlay—to try to *stop* them," said Holliday. "Surely he's not keeping that a secret."

"And have you stopped them?" said Tall Bear. "The answer is no."

"No," admitted Holliday. "We haven't stopped them. And neither have your monsters."

"But mine *will*."

Holliday shook his head. "Not a chance. We can only stop them if we work together, and we can only work together if you will trust us."

"Why should I trust the killer, and the man who signed a treaty that allowed the White Eyes to invade my land?"

"Because you want them to stop desecrating your burial ground, and so far you haven't been able to," said Roosevelt. "And in your heart, you know we wouldn't be here if we didn't have something to offer."

"You think to buy the Comanche?" demanded Tall Bear, frowning.

"What we have to offer is a plan," said Roosevelt.

"Why should I listen?"

"You got anything better to do with your time?" said Holliday, and immediately wished he'd kept his mouth shut, certain that such a remark could cause both of their deaths.

Tall Bear stared at him again, even longer this time, and just when Holliday was certain he was going to order his warriors to run them through with their spears, he sighed heavily and said, "No, Holly-day. I have nothing better to do. Tell me what you came to tell me."

Holliday felt a sense of relief. His first instinct was to reach for his flask and take a swallow, but he realized that if he reached for *any*thing at all he was liable to be minus a hand two seconds later. So he settled for taking a deep breath, trying not to cough, failing, coughing some blood into his handkerchief, and speaking.

"You know the monsters that you have brought forth?" he began. "They are called dinosaurs by my people. And some of my people find them bewitching, and spend their whole lives studying them. The two expeditions—the two groups that are digging up the ground—are led by the two greatest lovers of these dinosaurs." He paused to make sure Tall Bear was assimilating what he said. "They have come from far to the east—a much greater distance than from here to Goyathlay's camp—to study these creatures."

"But they did not exist until after they began to tear up the sacred ground," said Tall Bear, frowning.

"They had no idea they would encounter live dinosaurs," Roosevelt put in. "Their studies told them that this is a very rich ground for fossils, which is to say, for the bones of long-dead dinosaurs."

"It is not a rich ground," said Tall Bear firmly. "We have tried to grow many things, but the ground is poor."

"It is poor on the surface," agreed Roosevelt, "but it is rich in the bones of dinosaurs, and that is what they have come here to find."

"And having found them, they will not go away until they have uncovered them all," added Holliday.

"Then my monsters will chase them away."

Holliday shook his head. "Your monsters will bring still more people who love dinosaurs. The thought of seeing living ones will bring them by the dozens, and will bring work crews by the hundreds."

"Then they shall all die," said Tall Bear.

"I killed the biggest of them with nothing more than this pistol I have at my side," said Holliday. "Look into my heart and tell me if you think I am lying."

"You speak the truth," replied Tall Bear promptly. "But you are Holly-day, born to kill with that. Others will not be as skilled."

"Then they'll hire men who *are* as skilled, or who will use better weapons. It doesn't matter. However many you kill, more will come, once they know what they will be able to see here."

"We shall see which will be the greater number, my creatures or your killers."

"They're not *my* killers," persisted Holliday. "And it won't make any difference who produces more in the end, because in the meantime they're going to be digging up your sacred ground every day. *That* is what we both want to stop, is it not?"

"I will ask the Roosevelt, for he is an honorable man," said Tall Bear. He turned to Roosevelt. "Does he speak the truth?"

Roosevelt nodded an affirmative. "About all things," he said. "But mainly, that we want to stop it."

Tall Bear turned back to Holliday. "You will speak, I will listen."

"All right," said Holliday, who wished Tall Bear would sit down and invite him and Roosevelt to do the same, rather than towering above them. "As long as these men think there are things to discover, either live dinosaurs above the ground or dead ones beneath it, they will remain where they are, and they will continue to dig in your sacred ground. You cannot frighten them away with your living nightmares, you can only attract more of them. That is the situation, the basic truth we must address."

"And how do you propose to address it?"

"I can't address it alone," replied Holliday. "We must do it together."

Tall Bear made no immediate reply as the firelight flickered off him, and Holliday saw a number of heads peeking out of their huts, staring at the two white men and the medicine man.

At last Tall Bear spoke: "I am still listening."

"What we have to do is make this area totally worthless to them. There must be no more dinosaurs walking the land. But that is just the first step. We have to convince them that there is nothing of interest here, or at least nothing remaining."

"And how will you do this?"

"Not *I*," replied Holliday. "*We.*"

"How will we do this?" said Tall Bear.

Holliday thought he might cough, took out his bloodied handkerchief, and held it to his mouth. Then the urge passed, he settled for merely clearing his throat. "I wasn't sure until we were attacked on the way here."

"You were not injured. Goyathlay saved you."

"I know. But it was what happened *after* he saved us that gave me the idea."

Tall Bear stared at him, but said nothing.

"He turned the dead dinosaur to dust," continued Holliday. "Not a bone, not a tooth, not a piece of skin remained. All dust."

"I know this," said Tall Bear.

Suddenly Roosevelt's eyes widened, to be followed by a huge grin. "The perfect solution!" he exclaimed.

"You are a great medicine man," continued Holliday, "or you could not have brought the nightmare creatures to life. Surely if Goyathlay could turn one to dust, so can you. The question," said Holliday, leaning forward, "is this: Is your medicine powerful enough to turn them *all* to dust? Not just those that are alive and walking the Earth, but also the few that Roosevelt and I have killed? And, every bit as important, the bones that they have dug up from your burial ground?"

Tall Bear looked from Holliday to Roosevelt, then back again.

"Yes, I can do this," he said. "But they will just tear up the sacred ground searching for more bones."

"Leave that to Roosevelt and me," said Holliday. "If you will do what I described, you will have no further trouble."

"Let me be sure I understand," said Tall Bear. "I must turn every living and every dead creature to dust, both those that have died recently and those that died many lifetimes ago. Is this correct?"

"Yes."

"And if I do this, they will leave and not return?"

Holliday nodded an affirmative. "Yes."

"So if I do this right now, they will vanish?"

"No," said Holliday. "You're not killing them. You're making the land worthless to them. Do this at noon tomorrow, and give Roosevelt and me until noon the next day."

"If this does not come to pass, I will turn the Roosevelt to dust," said Tall Bear.

"Just me?" said Roosevelt, frowning.

"Your friend is already dust," said Tall Bear. "Goyathlay has done for him what I did for the living nightmares."

"We have a bargain," said Holliday, trying not to dwell on what the Comanche had just said. "Roosevelt and I will begin riding back to the camp where these men are."

"I hope what you say comes to pass," said Tall Bear. "I will give you safe passage as you return to your camp—but if you lied to me, if they have not left by the time and day you promised, there will be an army of nightmares such as you cannot imagine."

29.

HOLLIDAY AND ROOSEVELT WERE IN NO HURRY to get back to camp before Tall Bear's magic went into effect, so they rode leisurely, stopping three or four times for welcome rests—welcome to Holliday, anyway—and slept out beneath the cloudless sky, secure in the knowledge that nothing from prehistory was going to bother them.

They timed their arrival for mid-afternoon, which gave Cope and Marsh plenty of time to realize that all the fossils they had collected during the past few weeks had turned to the same fine powder as the monster Geronimo had killed.

It also gave Cope and Marsh time to ride out to where the tyrannosaur and the pteranodon were, only to discover they too had become nothing but dust.

When Holliday and Roosevelt dismounted they were greeted by Edison and Buntline, the former with a makeshift cane, the latter on crutches.

"What the hell has happened?" asked Edison.

"A medicine man has kept his word," answered Holliday.

"And we've got maybe twenty hours, tops, to keep ours," added Roosevelt.

"Is there anything we can do to help?" offered Edison.

Holliday shook his head. "If I'm any judge of character, this should be the easiest thing of all."

"I agree," said Roosevelt. "But I think we'll keep your weapons another day, just to be on the safe side."

"It's the damnedest thing," observed Buntline. "At first Cope and Marsh were both screaming that it was sabotage, but then they realized it couldn't be, not when both of their collections of fossils were gone."

"And if there was any doubt, it vanished when they saw what had become of the tyrannosaur and the pteranodon," added Edison.

"So have they drawn battle lines anyway?" said Holliday. "It would make too much sense for them to combine forces to figure out what's happening."

Cole Younger rode up on horseback just then.

"Welcome back, Doc, Theodore. You'd have done better to stay away."

"So Tom and Ned have been telling us," answered Holliday.

"Just stopped by to say *adios*," continued Younger. "They're all crazy here. Next thing you know they'll be accusing *me*."

"Where are you off to?" asked Holliday.

"Like I told you," said Younger with a smile. "I'm gonna hunt up Frank James, and we're gonna give Bill Cody a run for his money."

"Good luck," said Roosevelt.

"Best luck I can have is making it back to civilization in one piece," laughed Younger. He spurred his horse, and was soon out of sight.

"So what do you have to do now?" asked Edison.

"Not a thing," said Holliday. "We'll go to work after dark."

They could hear Cope screaming and cursing at one end of the camp, and Marsh doing the same at the other. Each of them ate in solitary splendor as far from each other as they could get.

After dinner Holliday announced that since he and Roosevelt were reasonably fresh, they'd patrol the camp at night, just in case any Comanche or their creatures should return.

When they saw the kerosene lamp in Cope's tent go off, they walked by, seemingly lost in conversation.

"Yeah, it beats me too," said Holliday when they were within earshot. "I didn't realize there was such a limit on magic, that he could turn everything to dust here, but he can't make it reach to Colorado."

"Well, no sense telling them," replied Roosevelt. "They'll just go hell for leather to Colorado and run into those damned monsters there."

"Yeah, count me out," agreed Holliday. "I plan to live to a ripe old age without ever again seeing anything bigger or more dangerous than a horse."

They kept talking until they were out of range, and five minutes later they were carrying on the same "private" conversation alongside Marsh's tent, only this time the dinosaurs were roaming the hills and valleys of Utah.

The camp was a bustle of activity—well, two separate bustles—at sunrise, and by ten in the morning only Holliday, Roosevelt, Edison and Buntline remained.

"*Now* I guess we can give you these," said Roosevelt handing the two weapons back to Buntline.

"Are you going back East now, Theodore?" asked Edison.

Roosevelt nodded. "I've got a woman to marry, a house to finish, and"—he flashed the grin that would become famous—"I think I'll probably run for Mayor of New York."

"We're on the mend. If we may, we'll travel some of the way with you," said Edison.

"How about you, Doc?" asked Buntline.

Holliday shrugged. "I imagine I'll head on back to Leadville. Sooner or later I'm going to need that sanitarium again."

"Take care," said Roosevelt. "Perhaps we'll meet again."

I sure as hell doubt it, thought Holliday.

Epilogue

HE SPENT TEN MONTHS GAMBLING AND DRINKING. At one point he even moved back in with Kate Elder, but after a pair of knock-down drag-out fights in which he came off much the worse, he decided that he wanted the full year he'd been promised and moved out again.

Finally he wound up back in the sanitarium, in the very same room he had occupied a year ago. When it had been one day shy of a year, he opened his eyes and saw Geronimo, all six feet of him, standing at the foot of his bed.

"You look like you again," he said weakly.

"My argument with the Comanche is finished."

Holliday coughed, and blood trickled out of the corner of his mouth. "Thank you for the extra year."

Geronimo made no reply, but merely stared at him.

"So are you here to offer another bargain, or to say good-bye?" asked Holliday.

"Yes," said Geronimo.

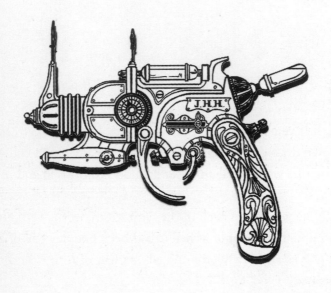

Appendix 1

THERE HAS BEEN QUITE A LOT WRITTEN about Doc Holliday, Theodore Roosevelt, Geronimo, William "Buffalo Bill" Cody, Cole Younger, and the so-called Wild West, as well as the infamous "Bone Wars" between Edward Drinker Cope and Othniel Charles Marsh. Surprisingly, a large amount takes place in an alternate reality in which (hard as this is to believe) the United States was not stopped at the Mississippi River until Theodore Roosevelt signed a treaty with Geronimo in 1884.

For those of you who are interested in this "alternate history," here is a bibliography of some of the more interesting books:

L. F. Abbott, *Impressions of Theodore Roosevelt*, Doubleday, Page (1919)

Alexander B. Adams, *Geronimo: A Biography*. Da Capo Press (1990)

C. E. Banks and R. A. Armstrong, *Theodore Roosevelt: A Typical American*, S. Stone (1901)

Stephen Melvil Barrett and Frederick W. Turner, *Geronimo: His Own Story*, Penguin (1996)

Bob Boze Bell, *The Illustrated Life and Times of Doc Holliday*, Tri Star-Boze (1995)

Glenn G. Boyer, *Who Was Big Nose Kate?* Glenn G. Boyer (1997)

H. W. Brands, *T. R.—The Last Romantic*, Basic Books (1997)

William M. Breakenridge, *Helldorado: Bringing the Law to the Mesquite*, Houghton Mifflin (1928)

Robert A. Carter, *Buffalo Bill Cody: The Man behind the Legend*, Wiley (2002)

E. Richard Churchill, *Doc Holliday, Bat Masterson, & Wyatt Earp: Their Colorado Careers*, Western Reflections (2001)

William F. Cody, *An Autobiography of Buffalo Bill*, Cosmopolitan Book (1924)

Edwin H. Colbert, *The Great Dinosaur Hunters and Their Discoveries*, Dover Press (1984)

Michael L. Collins, *That Damned Cowboy: Theodore Roosevelt and the American West, 1883–1898*, Peter Lang (1989)

Homer Croy, *Cole Younger: Last of the Great Outlaws*, Bison Books (1999)

O. Cushing, *The Teddysey*, Life Publishing (1907)

Paul Russell Cutright, *Theodore Roosevelt—The Making of a Conservationist*, University of Illinois Press (1985)

Jack DeMattos, *Masterson and Roosevelt*, Creative Publishing (1984)

Robert J. Desmond, *The Hot-Blooded Dinosaurs*, Dial Press (1976)

Mike Donovan, *The Roosevelt That I Know: Ten Years of Boxing with the President*, B. W. Dodge (1909)

G. W. Douglas, *The Many-Sided Roosevelt: An Anecdotal Biography*, Dodd, Mead (1907)

E. S. Ellis, *From the Ranch to the White House: Life of Theodore Roosevelt*, Hurst (1906)

T. T. Handford, *Theodore Roosevelt, the Pride of the Rough Riders*, M. A. Donohue (1897)

Albert Bushnell Hart and Herbert Ronald Ferleger, eds., *Theodore*

Roosevelt Cyclopedia, Theodore Roosevelt Association and Meckler Corporation (1989)

Mark Jaffe, *The Gilded Dinosaur: The Fossil War between E. D. Cope and O. C. Marsh*, Crown Publishers (2000)

Pat Jahns, *The Frontier World of Doc Holliday*, Hastings House (1957)

John Koblas, *The Great Cole Younger and Frank James Wild West Show*, North Star Press (2002)

John Koblas, *When the Heavens Fell: The Youngers in Stillwater Prison*, North Star Press (2002)

Uri Lanham, *The Bone Hunters*, Columbia University Press (1973)

Sylvia D. Lynch, *Aristocracy's Outlaw—The Doc Holliday Story*, Iris Press (1994)

Paula Mitchell Marks, *And Die in the West: The Story of the O.K. Corral Gunfight*, William Morrow (1989)

Edmond Morris, *The Rise of Theodore Roosevelt*, Coward, McCann, and Geoghegan (1979)

Edmond Morris, *Theodore Rex*, Random House (2001)

John Myers Myers, *Doc Holliday*, Little, Brown (1955)

Frederick Nolan, *The Lincoln County War, Revised Edition*, Sunstone Press (2009)

Robert Plate, *The Dinosaur Hunters*, David McCay (1964)

Adam J. Pollack, *John L. Sullivan: The Career of the First Gloved Heavyweight Champion*, McFarland (2006)

Fred E. Pond, *Life and Adventures of Ned Buntline*, Camdus Book Shop (1919)

Gary Roberts, *Doc Holliday: The Life and Legend*, John Wiley & Sons (2006)

Theodore Roosevelt, *An Autobiography*, MacMillan (1913)

Theodore Roosevelt, *Hunting Trips of a Ranchman*, Putnam's (1885)

Theodore Roosevelt, *Ranch Life and the Hunting-Trail*, Century (1888)

Theodore Roosevelt, *The Rough Riders*, Scribner's (1899)

Theodore Roosevelt, *The Strenuous Life*, Century (1900)

Theodore Roosevelt, *The Winning of the West*, 4 vols., Putnam's (1888–1894)

Elizabeth Noble Shor, *The Fossil Feud*, Exposition Press (1974)

David A. E. Spalding, *Dinosaur Hunters*, Prima Publishing (1993)

Karen Holliday Tanner, *Doc Holliday—A Family Portrait*, University of Oklahoma Press (1998)

Paul Trachman, *The Old West: The Gunfighters*, Time-Life Books (1974)

Ben T. Traywick, *John Henry: The Doc Holliday Story*, Red Marie's (1996)

Ben T. Traywick, *Tombstone's Deadliest Gun: John Henry Holliday*, Red Marie's (1984)

David Rains Wallace, *The Bonehunters' Revenge*, Houghton Mifflin (1999)

Helen Cody Wetmore, *Buffalo Bill: The Last Great Scout*, Alexander Books (2013)

R. L. Wildon, *Theodore Roosevelt—Outdoorsman*, Trophy Room Books (1994)

Cole Younger, *The Story of Cole Younger, by Himself*, Borealis Books (2000)

Appendix 2

In that "alternate history" in which the United States extended all the way to the Pacific, there are also a number of films made about the principals in this book, and a number of very popular actors portrayed them. Here's a list of them:

Some Movie Doc Hollidays:

Victor Mature
Kirk Douglas
Jason Robards Jr.
Cesar Romero
Stacey Keach
Dennis Quaid
Val Kilmer
Walter Huston
Arthur Kennedy

Randy Quaid (TV)
Douglas Fowley (TV)
Gerald Mohr (TV)

SOME STAGE AND MOVIE THEODORE ROOSEVELTS:

Brian Keith
Tom Berenger
Karl Swenson
Robin Williams
Frank Albertson (TV)
Peter Breck (TV)
James Whitmore (Broadway)
Len Cariou (Broadway musical)

SOME MOVIE THOMAS ALVA EDISONS:

Spencer Tracy
Mickey Rooney

SOME MOVIE NED BUNTLINES:

Lloyd Corrigan
Thomas Mitchell

SOME MOVIE GERONIMOS:

Chuck Conners
Wes Studi
Jay Silverheels (four times)
Monte Blue

SOME MOVIE COLE YOUNGERS:

Wayne Morris
Alan Hale Jr.
Frank Lovejoy
Cliff Robertson
David Carradine
Randy Travis

SOME STAGE AND MOVIE BUFFALO BILL CODYS:

William O'Neal (Broadway musical)
Art Lund (Broadway musical)
Ron Holgate (Broadway musical)
George Hearn (Broadway musical)
Louis Calhern
Joel McCrea
Paul Newman

A MOVIE EDWARD DRINKER COPE:

Steve Carell

A MOVIE OTHNIEL CHARLES MARSH:

The late James Gandolfini was to have portrayed Marsh; no replacement has been announced as of press time.

Appendix 3

THIS IS A "WHO'S WHO" of the book's participants in that fictional alternate reality where the United States extended to the West Coast.

Doc Holliday

He was born John Henry Holliday in 1851, and grew up in Georgia. His mother died of tuberculosis when he was fourteen, and that is almost certainly where he contracted the disease. He was college educated, with a minor in the classics, and became a licensed dentist. Because of his disease, he went out West to drier climates. The disease cost him most of his clientele, so he supplemented his dental income by gambling, and he defended his winnings in the untamed cities of the West by becoming a gunslinger as well.

He saved Wyatt Earp when the latter was surrounded by gunmen in Dodge City, and the two became close friends. Somewhere along the way he met and had a stormy on-and-off relationship with Big Nose Kate Elder. He was involved in the Gunfight at the O.K. Corral, and is generally considered to have delivered the fatal shots to both Tom and Frank McLaury. He rode with Wyatt Earp on the latter's vendetta against the Cowboys after the shootings of Virgil and Morgan Earp, then moved to Colorado. He died, in bed, of tuberculosis, in 1887. His last words were: "Well, I'll be damned—this is funny." No accurate records were kept in the case of most shootists; depending on which historians you believe, Doc killed anywhere from two to twenty-seven men.

THEODORE ROOSEVELT

Theodore Roosevelt was born in New York City in 1858. A sickly child, suffering from extreme asthma, he worked at strengthening his body through exercise and swimming, and by the time he attended Harvard he was fit enough to become the college's lightweight boxing champion. Even prior to that he was a devoted naturalist, and was acknowledged—even as a teen—as one of America's leading ornithologists and taxidermists.

His *The Naval War of 1812* was (and is) considered the definitive book on that battle. Shortly thereafter he developed an interest in politics and became the youngest-ever minority leader of the New York State Assembly. His wife and mother died eight hours apart in the same house in 1884, and he quit politics, headed out to the Dakota Badlands, and bought two ranches. He signed a contract to write the four-volume *The Winning of the West*, became a lawman, and caught and captured three armed killers during "the Winter of the Blue Snow."

Coming back East, he married again, served as police commissioner of New York City, later was secretary of the navy, assembled the

Rough Riders and took San Juan Hill during the Spanish-American War, became governor of New York, was elected vice president in 1900, and became president less than a year later with the assassination of President McKinley.

As president, Roosevelt fought the trusts, created the National Park System, won the Nobel Peace Prize, and turned the United States into a world power. When he left office in 1908 he embarked on a year-long African safari. He ran for President in 1912, was wounded by a would-be assassin, lost, and spent a year exploring and mapping the River of Doubt (later renamed the Rio Teodoro) for the Brazilian government. He was a strong advocate for our entry into World War I, and it was assumed the presidency was his for the asking in 1920, but he died a year before the election.

During his life, he wrote more than twenty books—many of them still in print—and over 150,000 letters.

THOMAS ALVA EDISON

Born in Milan, Ohio, in 1847, Edison is considered the greatest inventor of his era. He is responsible for the electric light, the motion picture, the carbon telephone transmitter, the fluoroscope, and a host of other inventions. He died in 1931.

NED BUNTLINE

Buntline was born Edward Z. C. Judson in 1813, and gained fame as a publisher, editor, writer (especially of dime novels about the West), and for commissioning Colt's Manufacturing Company to create the

Buntline Special. He tried to bring Wild Bill Hickok back East, failed, and then discovered Buffalo Bill Cody, who *did* come East and perform in a play that Buntline wrote.

GERONIMO

Born Goyathlay in 1829, he was a Chiricahua Apache medicine man who fought against both the Americans and the Mexicans who tried to grab Apache territory. He was never a chief, but he *was* a military leader, and a very successful one. He finally surrendered in 1886, and was incarcerated—but by 1904 he had become such a celebrity that he actually appeared at the World's Fair, and in 1905 he proudly rode in Theodore Roosevelt's inaugural parade in Washington, DC. He died in 1909 at the age of eighty.

EDWARD DRINKER COPE

Cope was a child prodigy who developed an interest in paleontology as a young man. Originally a friend of Othniel Charles Marsh, the two soon became bitter rivals, belittling each other in print, sabotaging each other's discoveries, racing to get their own finds into print first, even trying to get laws passed against one another. When the dust had cleared, Cope had produced more than 1,400 scientific papers— still a record—and discovered and named more than 1,000 vertebrate species. The "Bone Wars," as his rivalry with Marsh came to be known, bankrupted him and he died in poverty in 1897 at the age of fifty-seven, living in a single room, his cot surrounded by fossils he had not yet sold or given away.

OTHNIEL CHARLES MARSH

A graduate of Yale, thanks to the generosity of his uncle, George Peabody, Marsh developed an interest in paleontology and soon became involved in a lifelong feud with Edward Drinker Cope, a feud that has become known as the "Bone Wars." Marsh discovered eighty species of dinosaur, as well as early horses, flying reptiles, and ancient toothed birds. Much of his work was funded by Yale and its Peabody Museum, where many of his finds remain. He died in 1899 at the age of sixty-eight with $186 in the bank, the remains of a million-dollar fortune.

COLE YOUNGER

Originally one of the famed Quantrill's Raiders after the Civil War. By 1868 he and his brothers Jim, John, and Bob became notorious bandits. John was killed in a shootout with the Pinkertons, but Cole, Jim, and Bob thrived until September of 1876, when they led the notorious Northfield, Minnesota, raid; all three were badly wounded, captured, and sentenced to life imprisonment. Bob died of his wounds, Jim and Cole were released in 1901, Jim committed suicide, and Cole joined Frank James in the Cole Younger and Frank James Wild West Company in 1903. He died in 1916 at the age of seventy-two.

WILLIAM "BUFFALO BILL" CODY

Cody earned his name: he personally killed more than 4,200 buffalo. He also earned a Medal of Honor for "gallantry in action" during his military service. In between the hunting and the military, he was also a

Pony Express rider. He began his Wild West show in 1872; toured the country and later Europe with it (including a command performance for Queen Victoria); and made stars out of Annie Oakley, Frank Butler, Calamity Jane, and others. He combined with Pawnee Bill's show, becoming the *Two Bills Wild West Show* in 1908. He died at the age of seventy.

JOHN L. SULLIVAN

When sports fans refer to "the Great John L.," this is the man they're talking about. He was boxing's last bare-knuckle champion and its first gloved champion, winning his title in 1882 and holding until "Gentleman Jim" Corbett defeated him in 1892. He retired with a record of thirty-six wins, one loss, and two draws, and he died at the age of fifty-nine.

APPENDIX 4

THIS IS WYATT EARP'S DESCRIPTION and recollection of Doc Holliday, in his own words:

By the time I met him at Fort Griffin, Doc Holliday had run up quite a record as a killer, even for Texas. In Dallas, his incessant coughing kept away whatever professional custom he might have enjoyed and, as he had to eat, he took to gambling. He was lucky, skillful, and fearless. There were no tricks to his new trade that he did not learn and in more than one boom-camp game I have seen him bet ten thousand dollars on the turn of a card.

Doc quickly saw that six-gun skill was essential to his new business, and set out to master the fine points of draw-and-shoot as cold-bloodedly as he did everything. He practiced with a Colt for hours at a time, until he knew that he could get one into action as effectively as any man he might meet. His right to this opinion was justified by Doc's achievements. The only man of his type whom I ever regarded as anywhere near his equal on the draw was Buckskin Frank Leslie of Tombstone. But Leslie lacked Doc's fatalistic courage, a courage induced, I suppose, by the nature of Holliday's disease and the realization that he hadn't long to live, anyway. That fatalism, coupled with his marvelous speed and accuracy, gave Holliday the edge over any out-and-out killer I ever knew.

Doc's first fight in the West ended a row over a Dallas card-game. He shot and killed a topnotch gunman, and as Doc was comparatively a stranger where his victim had many friends, Doc had to emigrate. He went to Jacksborough, at the edge of the Fort Richardson military reservation, where he tangled with three or four more gunmen successfully, but eventually killed a soldier and again had to take it on the run. Next, he tried the Colorado camps, where he knocked off several pretty bad men in gun-fights. In Denver, Doc encountered an ordinance against gun-toting, so he carried a knife, slung on a cord around his neck. Bud Ryan, a gambler, tried to run one over on Doc in a card game, and when Doc objected, Ryan went for a gun he carried in a concealed holster. Doc beat him into action with his knife, and cut him horribly.

Doc gambled in the Colorado and Wyoming camps until the fall of '77, and fought his way out of so many arguments that, by the time he hit Fort Griffin, he had built up a thoroughly deserved reputation as a man who would shoot to kill on the slightest provocation. That reputation may have had some bearing on the fact that when I first met him, he had not yet found anyone in Fort Griffin to provide him with a battle.

It was in Shanssey's saloon, I think, that Doc Holliday first met Kate Elder, a dancehall girl better known as "Big-Nosed Kate." Doc lived with Kate, off and on, over a period of years. She saved his life on one occasion, and when memory of this was uppermost Doc would refer to Kate as Mrs. Holliday. Their relationship had its temperamental ups and downs, however, and when Kate was writhing under Doc's scorn she'd get drunk as well as furious and make Doc more trouble than any shooting-scrape.

Perhaps Doc's outstanding peculiarity was the enormous amount of whiskey he could punish. Two and three quarts of liquor a day was not unusual for him, yet I never saw him stagger with intoxication. At times, when his tuberculosis was worse than ordinary, or he was under a long-continued physical strain, it would take a pint of whiskey to get him going in the morning, and more than once at the end of a long ride I've seen him swallow a tumbler of neat liquor without batting an eye and fifteen minutes later take a second tumbler of straight whiskey which had no more outward effect on him than the first one. Liquor never seemed to fog him in the slightest, and he was more inclined to fight when getting along on a slim ration than when he was drinking plenty, and was more comfortable, physically.

With all of Doc's shortcomings and his undeniably poor disposition, I found him a loyal friend and good company. At the time of his death, I tried to set down the qualities about him which had impressed me. The newspapers dressed up my ideas considerably and had me calling Doc Holliday "a mad, merry scamp with heart of gold and nerves of steel." Those were not my words, nor did they convey my meaning. Doc was mad, well enough, but he was seldom merry. His humor ran in a sardonic vein, and as far as the world in general was concerned, there was nothing in his soul but iron. Under ordinary circumstances he might be irritable to the point of shakiness; only in a game or when a fight impended was there anything steely about his nerves.

To sum up Doc Holliday's character as I did at the time of his death: he was a dentist whom necessity had made into a gambler; a gentleman whom disease had made a frontier vagabond; a philosopher whom life had made a caustic wit; a long, lean, ash-blond fellow nearly dead with consumption and at the same time the most skilled gambler and the nerviest, speediest, deadliest man with a six-gun I ever knew.

~⚬~

And here's Doc as seen through the eyes of one his many biographers, Sylvia D. Lynch:

Doc was a very complicated man who lived an intense and prismatic life, and who seemed to exist on sheer will and determination. And when John Holliday committed himself to something or someone, he apparently held on with a death grip that nothing could pry loose. He was one of those people who seemed to have an unusual penchant for drawing extraordinarily back luck in some of his endeavors, while at the same time enjoying the benefits of extraordinarily good luck in others. He was a walking paradox who never shied away from encounters which had the toughest odds, and he kept his poker-faced attitude toward the world as he moved within his self-made cosmos. Those who knew him, those who saw him work his craft day after day, have testified that when he became involved in one of those awkward moments for which he was so well known, that it was most often wise counsel to leave him to fend for himself, so fend for himself he did, and very well at that.

And even though so many of his more memorable circumstances revolved around relationships with others, he seemed to be the one who rarely asked anything from those with whom he associated. He had an uncanny knack for being at the wrong places at the wrong times, and on many of those occasions, when the bad timing wasn't present in the nature of the situation, he seemed to delight in creating his own extenuating circumstances. Some say he thrived on whiskey, some say he thrived at the gaming table. Others say he drew his persistent strength from the deadly confidence with which he drew the nickel-plated weapons from underneath his coat in a split second's warning, much to the final regret of many of those who stood at the opposite end of his gun barrel.

There may be a good case for the argument that he thrived on boldly "bucking the tiger," on pushing his luck just as far as he could possibly shove it, whether it be in a card game, in his personal relationships, or in his private battle with the disease that was slowly consuming his body while he was making a name for himself in the West. There may also be truth in the theory that he carried with him an irreversible death wish for almost half his life span, and that his brash, confident manner was nothing more than the manifestation of his lack of assurance of being around the next day— the cruel uncertainty of having nothing to lose.

APPENDIX 5

So why would anyone spend so much time, as I have done, writing science fiction stories and novels about Theodore Roosevelt?

Well, they have a lot in common, science fiction and Roosevelt. Both of them deal with ideas. Both of them are entertaining. And most of all, both of them are bigger than Reality.

You think not?

Let's take a look at Roosevelt's life.

Roosevelt was born in New York City in 1858. As a boy he suffered from a debilitating case of asthma. Rather than give in to it, he began swimming and exercising every day—and like every pulp hero you ever read about, he built himself up to where he was able to make the Harvard boxing team.

But he'd been making a name for himself before he went to Harvard. Even the Gray Lensman and Doc Savage weren't exclusively brawn, and neither was Roosevelt. An avid naturalist to the day of his death, he was already considered one of America's leading ornithologists and taxidermists while still a teenager. Nor was his interest limited to nature. While at Harvard he wrote what was considered the definitive treatise on naval warfare, *The Naval War of 1812*.

He graduated Phi Beta Kappa and *summa cum laude*, married Alice Hathaway, went to law school, found it boring, and discovered politics. When Theodore Roosevelt developed a new interest, he never did so in a halfhearted way—so at twenty-four he became the youngest man ever elected to the New York State Assembly, and was made minority leader a year later.

He might have remained in the state assembly, but on February 14, 1884, not long after his twenty-fifth birthday, his beloved Alice and his mother died in the same house, only hours apart. He felt the need to get away, and he went west to become a rancher (and, being Theodore Roosevelt, one ranch couldn't possibly contain him, so he bought two).

Not content to simply be a rancher, a sportsman, and a politician, like hundreds of pulp and science fiction heroes he became a lawman as well, and, unarmed, hunted down and captured three armed killers in the Dakota Badlands during the fearsome blizzard that was known as "the Winter of the Blue Snow." Could Hawk Carse or Lije Baley have done any better?

He began building Sagamore Hill, the estate he made famous in Oyster Bay, New York, married childhood sweetheart Edith Carew, and started a second family. (Alice had died giving birth to his daughter, also named Alice. Edith promptly began producing sons—Kermit, Theodore Jr., Archie, and Quentin, as well as another daughter, Ethel.) In his spare time, he wrote a number of well-received books. Then, running short of money, he signed a contract to write a four-volume series, *The Winning of the West*. The first two volumes became immediate bestsellers. He was also an avid correspondent, and it's estimated that he wrote more than 150,000 letters during his lifetime—and what science fiction writer, I ask you, is not an avid correspondent?

He was now past thirty years of age, and he decided it was time to stop loafing and really get to work—so he took the job of police commissioner of the wildly corrupt City of New York . . . and to the amazement of even his staunchest supporters, he cleaned the place up, just like heroes from The Shadow to Lincoln Powell had done. He became famous for his "midnight rambles" to make sure his officers were at their posts, and he was the first commissioner to insist that the entire police force take regular target practice.

He made things so uncomfortable for the rich and powerful (and corrupt) of New York that he was kicked upstairs and made assistant secretary of the navy in Washington. When the Spanish-American War broke out, he resigned his office, enlisted in the army, was given the rank of colonel, and assembled the most famous and romantic outfit ever to fight for the United States—the fabled Rough Riders, consisting of cowboys, Indians, professional athletes, and anyone else who impressed him—and what classic space operas don't have a crew of romantic misfits just like that? They went to Cuba, where Roosevelt himself led the charge up San Juan Hill in the face of machine-gun fire, and he came home the most famous man in the country.

Less than three months later he was elected governor of New York, a week after his fortieth birthday. His new duties didn't hinder his other interests, and he kept turning out books and studying wildlife.

Two years later they kicked him upstairs again, finding the one job where his reformer's zeal couldn't bother anyone: he was nominated for the vice presidency of the United States, and was elected soon afterward.

Ten months later President William McKinley was assassinated, and Roosevelt became the youngest-ever president of the United States, where he served for seven years.

What did he do as president?

Not much, by Rooseveltian standards. Enough for five presidents, by anyone else's standards. Consider:

He created the National Park System.

He broke the back of the trusts that had run the economy (and the nation) for their own benefit.

He created the Panama Canal.

He sent the navy on a trip around the world. When they left, America was a second-rate little country in the eyes of the world. By the time they returned, we were a world power.

He became the first president ever to win the Nobel Peace Prize when he put an end to the Russo-Japanese war.

He mediated a dispute between Germany and France over Morocco, preserving Morocco's independence.

To make sure that the trusts didn't reclaim their power after he was out of office, he created the Departments of Commerce and Labor.

When he left office in 1909 with a list of accomplishments equal in magnitude to any galactic president in science fiction, he immediately packed his bags (and his rifles) and went on the first major safari ever put together, spending eleven months gathering specimens for the American and Smithsonian Museums. He wrote up his experiences as *African Game Trails*, still considered one of the half dozen most important books on the subject ever published. Clearly he had a lot in common with science fictional hunters, from Gerry Carlyle to Nicobar Lane.

When he returned to America, he concluded that his hand-chosen successor, President William Howard Taft, was doing a lousy job of running the country, so he decided to run for the presidency again in 1912. Though far and away the most popular man in the Republican Party, he was denied the nomination through a number of procedural moves. Most men would have licked their wounds and waited for 1916. Not Roosevelt. He formed the Progressive Party, known informally as the "Bull Moose Party," and ran in 1912. It's thought that he was winning when a would-be assassin shot him in the chest while he was being driven to give a speech in Milwaukee. He refused all medical aid until he had delivered the speech (which ran ninety minutes!), then allowed himself to be taken to a hospital. The bullet would never be removed, and by the time Roosevelt was back on the campaign trail, Woodrow Wilson had built an insurmountable lead. Roosevelt finished second, as President Taft ran a humiliating third, able to win only eight electoral votes.

So *now* did he relax?

Fat chance. This is Theodore Roosevelt we're talking about. The Brazilian government asked him to explore a tributary of the Amazon known as the River of Doubt. He hadn't slowed down since he was a baby, he was in his fifties, he was walking around with a bullet in his chest, all logic said he'd earned a quiet retirement—so of course he said yes.

This trip didn't go as well as the safari. He came down with fever, he almost lost his leg, and indeed at one point he urged his party to leave him behind to die and to go ahead without him. They didn't, of course, and eventually he was well enough to continue the expedition and finish mapping the river, which was renamed the Rio Teodoro in his honor. (I don't really need to compare him to the hundreds of explorers who inhabit the worlds of science fiction, do I?)

He came home, wrote yet another bestseller—*Through the Brazilian Wilderness*—then wrote another book on African animals, as well as more books on politics . . . but his health never fully recovered. He campaigned vigorously for our entry into World War I, and it was generally thought that the presidency was his for the asking in 1920, but he died in his sleep on January 6, 1919, at the age of sixty—having crammed about seventeen lifetimes into those six decades.

He was so fascinating, so talented in so many fields, so much bigger than Life, that I decided (and I hope you agree) that he belonged in the one field that could accommodate a man with those virtues—science fiction, where he could finally find some challenges that were truly worthy of his talents.

APPENDIX 6

DID THIS NOVEL EXAGGERATE THE COPE-MARSH FEUD? Try this, from R. W. Howard's *The Dawnseekers,* on for size:

"Cope spent hours each day on a hilltop spying on the Marsh dig. This encouraged Marsh's crew to assemble a skull from the jawbones, teeth, eye sockets and horns of a dozen species. They buried Old-what-you-may-call-it just before Cope showed up for his daily spell at the telescope. When he did arrive, they put on an elaborate pantomime of arduous shoveling and great excitement. Cope sneaked over that dusk, dug up What-you-may-call-it and wrote a paper about its significance."

Cope's response?

He began dynamiting his own digging sites when he was done, so that no one from Marsh's camp could possibly find some treasure he'd overlooked.

Marsh's response to that?

He used his political connections to get the Department of the Interior to demand that Cope turn over all his finds to them.

Cope's response?

He went to the press, pointing out every mistake and misstatement Marsh had ever made.

Marsh's response?

The same.

End result?

Each man started with a huge fortune, and each man bankrupted the other.

But when the dust had cleared, these two men had advanced American paleontology a couple of centuries.

APPENDIX 7

Doc Holliday Museum
209 North Thirteenth Street
Griffin, GA 30223

Theodore Roosevelt Memorial
American Museum of Natural History
Central Park West at Seventy-Ninth Street
New York, NY 10024

Buffalo Bill Museum
199 North Front Street
Le Claire, IA 52753

Thomas Edison Center at Menlo Park
37 Christie Street
Edison, NJ 08820

Othniel Charles Marsh collection
Peabody Museum of Natural History
170 Whitney Avenue
New Haven, CT 06520

Edward Drinker Cope collection
Academy of Natural Sciences at Drexel University
1900 Benjamin Franklin Parkway
Philadelphia, PA 19103

The Buntline Special is on display at:
The Autry Museum
4700 Western Heritage Way
Los Angeles, CA 90027

APPENDIX 8

THERE IS A GAME—*The Game of Ruthless Paleontology*—based on Marsh and Cope's rivalry, created by James Cambias and Diane Kelly, and produced by Zygote Games.

APPENDIX 9

ALMOST ALL THE GREAT SHOOTISTS AND ADVENTURERS of that era have been immortalized in song, but here's a link to a song I'll bet you didn't know about:

"Bone Wars, Marsh and Cope (to the tune of 'Two Black Cadillacs' by Carrie Underwood)," YouTube video, 5:12, posted by "Zack Neher," April 21, 2013, http://www.youtube.com/watch?v=iA3fhPs1aKk

ABOUT THE AUTHOR

Mike Resnick has won five Hugos (from a record thirty-six nominations), plus a Nebula Award and other major awards in the United States, France, Spain, Poland, Croatia, Catalonia, and Japan, and has been short-listed in England, Italy, and Australia. He is, according to *Locus*, the all-time leading award winner, living or dead, for short science fiction. Mike is the author of seventy-four novels, twenty-five collections, over two hundred sixty short stories, and three screenplays; he has edited forty-one anthologies. He is currently the editor of The Stellar Guild book series and *Galaxy's Edge* magazine. He was the Guest of Honor at the 2012 World Science Fiction Convention.